I0584185

# FACES & LIES

# FACES & LIES

*by*

Margaret Podmore Emery

Your Author Journey Begins Here

Copyright © 2021, Margaret Podmore Emery

All rights reserved. Printed in the U.S.A.

No part of this publication may be reproduced or transmitted in any form or by any means, electronic or mechanical, including photocopy, recording or any information storage and retrieval system now known or to be invented, without permission in writing from the publisher, except by a reviewer who wishes to quote brief passages in connection with a review written for inclusion in a magazine, newspaper or broadcast.

**Quantity Purchases:**
Companies, professional groups, clubs, and other organizations may qualify for special terms when ordering quantities of this title.
For information, email info@ebooks2go.net,
or call (847) 598-1150 ext. 4141.
www.ebooks2go.net

Published in the United States by eBooks2go, Inc. 1827 Walden Office Square, Suite 260, Schaumburg, IL 60173

ISBN: 978-1-5457-5465-8

Library of Congress Cataloging in Publication

With gratitude to Lois Gene Sanford

Who made a shy ugly duckling feel special

# CONTENTS

# CHAPTER ONE

*March 1998 is going, going, almost gone. I just can't wait till April Fools' Day to step up my game, because this is all getting to be so much fun!*

Yawning, Devin Marques paused in front of a dresser on display at a store in the Connecticut Post Mall. She'd had three hours of sleep since returning early that morning from a week-long horse show in Virginia, and wished she were still sitting at the kitchen table in her bathrobe, enjoying a cup of coffee with the newspaper.

Mondays following the shows were always filled with chores and errands. By five the next morning, like every other Tuesday morning during the ten-month competitive season, Devin would have Hightower Farm's truck packed, the horses loaded, and be on the road again for the next show.

*The exciting life of the professional horsewoman.* She slipped her car keys into her purse. Yawning again, she ran her fingertips along the top of the dresser. *Where are we going this week?*

As she inspected the chest of drawers, she squinted at her likeness in its attached mirror. "There must be a law somewhere in the building code," she mumbled, making a face at the unflattering image. "Store lighting has to make you look dead or at least deathly ill or they rip it out and–"

A motion in an upper corner of the mirror's reflection caught her eye, light flashing off the lenses of someone's glasses, under a thatch of blond hair.

Could it be the person she'd seen watching her house?

She spun around to look, but found a saleswoman waiting there instead, smiling expectantly. A saleswoman with short black hair, and no glasses.

"Was someone beside you a second ago?" Devin demanded. She looked beyond the clerk as a cleaning person trundled a mop and bucket past the store's entrance to the mall.

"A gentleman asked the time, my dear. I saw you admiring this lovely piece. Is there anything–why, I know you!" The woman threw up her hands. "My daughter watches all those horse-jumping shows on television! You're Devin Marcus–Markees–"

"It's pronounced 'Marks.'" She shrugged, pretending to smile. "*Everybody* has trouble with it."

"Well, my daughter will be so jealous when I tell her I saw you in person, and you're so beautiful, with those green eyes and such lovely long auburn curls!" She reached out a hand, stopping a fraction of an inch from Devin's hair.

Devin shrank back from the outstretched hand, glancing all around to see if the glasses-wearer was anywhere nearby. She wanted to be on her way, but she remembered how she felt after attending a concert where the star was collecting money for his "pet cause," but didn't even look at her face as he took money from her and limply shook her hand. "Do you think your daughter would like an autograph?"

As the saleswoman gushed, "Oh, she'd love that!" Devin opened her purse.

"I think I have a piece of paper here." She opened a small notebook and scribbled "Keep your head in the ring and your

2

eye on the judge" and her name. As she held out the paper, she maintained her pleasing-the-public smile. "This is my standard advice for a young rider. I gotta run."

A smile lit up the saleswoman's face. "Oh, thank you so much! This just makes my day." She glanced from the paper to Devin's face. "I won't keep you. Thanks again!"

Devin hurried away, hoping her heart would stop racing. There were too many items on her shopping list to allow herself to worry about something all her friends insisted was her imagination. The reflection in the mirror, the hair and glasses? Just another shopper, a passer-by. A gentleman asking the time, as the clerk had said. *Calm down.*

She paged through her notebook to her errand list. The item at the top: *lace-trimmed white blouses at The Limited.*

Twenty minutes later, as Devin flipped through a rack of frilly white tops, a tall clerk with a short, asymmetrical blonde hairdo covering one eye bumped into her. Devin gasped and dropped her purse. Keys, pens and change spilled underneath the display rack.

"Oh, ma'am! I'm so sorry!" the clerk exclaimed as she dove to scoop up the small leather bag and its contents.

"It's all right." Devin tried to maintain a pleasant face as she straightened a hanger on the chrome display stand. "My mind just seems to be somewhere else today." She dumped everything back into her purse and hurried from the store.

There! In the Electronics Boutique across the mall! Was that him, beside an advertising poster for *Titanic*—how many Oscars did Ria say it had won a couple months ago? Devin shook her head. Ria had seen the movie six times before the Oscars, and couldn't understand why Devin hadn't.

She craned her head to see around a group of women with baby strollers ambling along the broad walkway between the stores. When they had passed, the only person she could see among the racks and displays in the electronics shop was the large black man who owned and ran it.

She squeezed her eyes shut and leaned her forehead against the window. *Please, God, make it stop.*


The next item on her list: *Wedding present Cam and Jen. Whoever they are.* She looked from face to passing face as she hurried to the card shop where she knew she'd find the cut crystal picture frame her great-aunt Aggie Hall, her grandmother's sister, had decided upon for the wedding gift. The dear little lady had been delighted to be invited to the Memorial Day wedding in Nantucket of her best friend's hairdresser's grandniece or nephew, "or something like that," Aunt Aggie had explained with a flip of her hand. Her face would glow when she recounted the marvelous details, and she'd probably bring Devin a slice of wedding cake.

For Devin, an afternoon of drinks and small talk had little appeal when compared to riding back into the ring before a cheering audience to collect a blue ribbon, trophy and check. She occasionally regretted sacrificing social events to ride at the top level on the jumping circuit. Not often enough, however, to walk away from standing at the in-gate, watching the ring crew build the fences and obstacles, seeing the crowd of spectators grow and feeling electricity fill the air.

She savored the excitement of bringing each horse to the ring, feeling its energy as they waited for the gate to open. As Apollo pawed or Shaman bucked and reared, she would lick her lips in anticipation and her heart would begin to pound.

*Aunt Aggie will be so excited when she hears I'm going to the Hampton Classic.* The late-summer Bridgehampton event, part of a week-long equine competition, was a backdrop for *the* social extravaganza of the year. Devin's highly successful riding record so far this year would probably make Aunt Aggie welcome in some of the invitation-only tents. Her aunt would love the catered buffets, serving people fussing over her, the ring-side tables, the people-watching. A galaxy of stars from sports and various entertainment fields always attended this show, to compete or be seen.

The clerk slid the gaily-wrapped box across the counter. "Would you like a shopping bag? Or do you need a card?"

The perky questions brought Devin back from her daydream. Did Aunt Aggie need a wedding card? Picking out a couple to choose from wouldn't hurt.

The circular card rack beside Devin suddenly spun wildly, throwing cards in every direction. A tall man with scraggly blond hair reached out a gloved hand and swept Aunt Aggie's gift off the counter as he roughly elbowed past. She tried to identify the retreating back as he hustled away. Was he the one she'd seen on the park bench, watching her house? She felt light-headed, her pulse pounding in her ears.

She retrieved her aunt's gift and gave it a cursory shake to assure herself it hadn't broken. She *had* to have a cigarette, and, once outside the closest exit, she wasted no time lighting up. "I know, I know, Ria," she mumbled between drags. "I'm supposed to be quitting."

In her mind's eye, she could see her roommate, Ria St. Amont, scowling and pursing her lips, her brown eyes even darker than usual against her honey-brown skin, as she went into her standard lecture, given any time she saw Devin reaching for her lighter and cigarette pack.

Devin thought she had been doing well, even going two or three days without a single smoke, even though since

5

February, she or Ria had regularly noticed someone sitting on the park bench across the street from the cottage they shared, apparently watching their home. And there were phone calls that came several times a night when she was home, phone calls where no one talked, then hung up. Phone calls in the middle of the night at the motels in Tampa, Palm Springs, North Carolina and Virginia, where the spring shows had been.

And today, someone was following her.

*WHY WHY WHY?* echoed through her mind. *Go home.*

She knew there was no point in going to one of the security guards to complain about the man, no matter how frightened she was. What had the Florian police told her and Ria so many times?

*"We can't stop him from sitting on a public bench looking in the direction of your house, or shopping in the same place you are. That doesn't break any law. We can suggest he move on, but if no actual threat is made, we can't do anything."*

Place, time, what happened, that's what the cops had told her to write down, whenever the stalker appeared. She crushed out the cigarette. Exhaling sharply, she pulled out her notebook and scrawled wobbly words across the lines. As she reread her notes, she sighed.

*Like this is going to make them believe me.*

Devin squared her shoulders and yanked open the door. If she could maintain total concentration in the show ring and ignore anything beyond the fence for the fleeting seconds she had to complete a jump course—keep her head in the ring, as she had written for the saleswoman's daughter—she could finish a few chores in a shopping mall without some slob spooking her.

A tiny shop near the food court had quilts on sale, and one she'd seen there would be a perfect Christmas gift for Ria's mom. She tossed her head, a sweep of auburn curls swirling around her shoulders. She sighed again.

*It's the last week of March, and I'm Christmas shopping.*

After choosing a plate of brightly-colored stir-fried vegetables for lunch, Devin juggled her tray, her purse and the bags containing the large, bulky quilt and Aunt Aggie's picture frame as she picked her way around strollers, bundles and other shoppers. She saw one empty table near the railing, overlooking the mall. Several young mothers with their babies and small children sat at two nearby tables, chatting and laughing.

She felt a pang of jealousy for their companionship. It faded when one of the tots spilled his milk and two women yelled at him and cursed as they mopped up the mess.

*They probably envy my solitude.*

After a few mouthfuls of vegetables, Devin looked away from the neighboring table to the crowd of people streaming out of the glass-encased elevator car nearby. The blond man stood near the elevator shaft, hands in his jacket pockets, beside a tall potted tree. He seemed to be staring at her.

Tall and unkempt, his hair was greasy-looking and he wore mirrored sunglasses. She looked down at her lunch, then back to the elevator. He had disappeared.

No longer hungry, she picked up her things and dumped the rest of her lunch into the trash.

*That's it! I'm done here! Groceries for tomorrow, then home.*

Juggling her bags as she hurried to the escalator, Devin pulled out her notebook again and scribbled a couple of lines about the incident.

As she stepped off the escalator, the stranger appeared again, half-smiling as he sauntered around the corner of a jewelry kiosk a few feet away. She stumbled against a trash barrel, then sank onto a slatted wood bench. The man drifted into the CD store nearby.

*The police can't do anything.* The phrase rang in her ears as she hurried out the double exit doors to the nearest phone. She looked across the parking lot as she fumbled the required coins into the slot and willed her numb fingers to hit the right buttons. As the phone rang and rang, she turned to watch a rowdy group of teenagers jostling through the exit. The scruffy man waited between the doors, off to one side, facing her way.

Finally the ringing ended and the voice-mail message offered mailbox choices. She tapped the "1" and Ria's message chirped, "I'm not picking up right now. Leave a message."

After a series of beeps, Devin wailed, "Somebody's following me around the mall, Ria. He's everywhere I go!"

Devin saw the stranger again, in the cookie aisle in the supermarket across the road from the mall. She ran her shopping cart into the display rack as she grabbed at a box she had knocked down. *How did he know I'd be here?*

She threw her groceries onto the belt at checkout, asking herself the question that never had an answer: *Who is he, and why is he doing this to me?*

The slowest checker in the world rang up the food order. At the end of the counter, Devin grabbed the cans and boxes as quickly as they passed the scanner and stuffed them into grocery bags. When she lifted the bags to place them into her cart, they split and she had to repack everything. As she worked, she glanced all around, looking for the unkempt man.

"Ma'am? Fifty-nine ninety-five?" The clerk punctuated her impatient request with a snap of her gum.

As Devin handed over the required amount, she looked out the window into the parking lot. The man stood in the fire lane, just beyond the window. He smiled and gave her a snappy salute.

*Why's he wearing gloves?*

She flung the rest of her grocery bags into the shopping cart, trying to ignore him. Twenty feet to the automatic exit door, turn left, walk normally, breathe normally. As the door swished closed behind her, tires squealed and a small red car rocketed onto the highway from the supermarket parking lot.

The broad expanse of pavement was empty except for a store employee rounding up carts, an older couple putting their groceries into their van, a mother strapping a toddler into a child safety seat in the back of a station wagon, and Devin's car.

*Where did he go? How does he disappear so fast?*

She approached her car warily. Was that paper flapping under the windshield wiper a note? No. Deli coupons. She packed her groceries into the trunk as quickly as she could. Once in the driver's seat, her hands shook so much she dropped the keys onto the floor. She locked the door, smoked one cigarette, then another.

As she crumpled the empty pack, she slowly backed the car away from the line of shopping carts left in front of it. Would that man suddenly appear in her rearview mirror? She shifted into first gear and roared around the carts, executing a turn any NASCAR driver would envy.

At the end of the parking lot, she reached behind the passenger seat and felt around for the handgun hidden there under a blanket. Her fingers curled around the butt.

9

As she pulled the gun from its hiding place, she steered the car out onto the highway.

Devin glanced down at the Beretta in her lap.

When she saw a piece of paper wrapped around the gun barrel, secured with a rubber band, she slammed on the brakes. The bright red car fishtailed to a stop in the middle of the road. She ripped the rubber band off and unrolled the paper. Spelled out in letters cut from a newspaper was, "I see the moon, the moon sees me. I see you, but you NEVER see me."

With no thought of speeding tickets, she raced home, weaving through traffic on the turnpike. Relieved to see Ria's gray Honda parked in front of their cottage, Devin unloaded her car in one trip, so laden with bags and bundles she struggled to free two fingers to turn the knob on the storm door.

She coaxed it open with first the toes of one foot, then an elbow. Dangling from the knob of the front door, strung like chili peppers, were the blood-soaked bodies of three little kittens, a gray-striped, a tortoiseshell, and a yellow tabby. A puddle of blood oozed over the edge of the doorsill below.

"Ria!" Devin shouted, thumping an elbow against the door as she tried to get a key into the lock. When she finally wrestled it open, she dumped her armload of bags onto the hall floor. "Ria, we're calling the police!" She flung down her purse as she reached for the cordless telephone in the living room. "You should see what's on the front door!"

Ria came from the kitchen, then waited by the kitchen door, offering no help, slowly folding her arms across her chest. "I already saw what's on the front door." She nodded toward two suitcases in the foyer. "I'm going home."

The phone dropped from Devin's hand, shattering on the slate floor. "What do you mean?"

Ria walked over to the maple dining-room table. She placed her fingertips on the polished tabletop, displaying beautiful hands with long manicured nails. She stared at Devin for a few moments, licked her lips and inhaled, a short raspy wheeze, before responding.

"You think I'm involved in what's been going on lately. You wrote down all that's happened–the phone calls, the guy watching the house, the car parked across the street, the times we thought someone was in the house. I saw my name right near the top of the list of people you suspect."

"What?" Devin slumped into a chair at the opposite end of the table. "What list? I don't know what you're talking about." She cocked her head to one side, puzzled. "You're the only person I think I can trust."

"You think?" Ria screeched. "You think?" She raced around the table, slapped her palms down on the polished top and leaned over Devin. "You lived with my family for four years while you were at MIT. You're like a daughter to my parents. Last fall, Momma only let me take a job here in Florian because I was going to live with you. We've been like sisters, and now you tell me you 'think' you can trust me?" She turned away, then whirled around. "How dare you?"

"Wait a minute." Devin slowly stood up. "I get calls at the motels where I stay when I'm on the road, and somebody followed me at the mall today, every place I went like he had my list." Devin struggled to keep from crying. "I don't blame you for being afraid and wanting to go home. And maybe I understand why you don't like me saying 'I think I can trust you,' but what makes me afraid is knowing that everything got worse after you moved in with me last fall."

Ria scowled. "But you 'think' I'm not involved. Well, thank you very much."

"The day after we had the locks changed and picked a new security code, someone walked in the front door like the alarm system wasn't even there." Devin tried to keep her voice calm. "We've changed the unlisted phone number four times, but we still get weird calls. It has to be somebody one of us knows."

"I don't know why you suspect me."

"And I don't know anything about some list I supposedly made that says I do."

Ria thrust a sheet of lined yellow paper into Devin's hand. "If that isn't your handwriting, whose is it?"

As Devin read the page covered with scribbled notes, Ria continued, "When I first saw that, I wondered whether the suspects were in order of perceived guilt or as you thought of them. If it's the latter, I wasn't surprised to see Mark's name before mine."

Devin looked up from the paper. "I didn't do this, Ria. I–I–" Her mouth hung open as she shook her head. "No. These may be things that happened and people I know, but I didn't write this list."

"Well, whatever. I can't stay here anymore." She stepped around Devin, into the foyer, and jerked open the front door. This was the last straw." She stepped back for Devin to take a look.

Not even a speck of blood was on the white door where the bodies of the kittens had hung, and the doorsill had been wiped clean. They stared at one another. "We both saw them. They were just there," Devin whispered.

Ria slammed the door, giving Devin a sidelong glance before dropping her eyes to the paper Devin held.

Devin took in the look. "When did you find it, and where?"

Ria paused a moment before replying. As she spoke, she inspected her nails. "Thursday, because the cleaning lady had been in." She gave a slight nod of her head. "That was on your nightstand."

Devin glanced from Ria's face to the paper and back, shaking her head. "I don't know how to make you believe me, Ria." She raised her arms and let them flop back to her sides.

"Where'd it come from then? It looks like your writing. What am I supposed to think? People walk into our house like they live here, steal our stuff. Dead cats on the front door, sick people leaving sick messages on my voice mail–" Ria's lips trembled and she pressed a shaking hand against them.

"What messages?"

"Somebody keeps telling me what you really do with your stallions when you're spending all those hours in the barn out at your farm." A shudder shook her entire body.

"Ewwww." Taking a backwards step, Devin stared at Ria for a long moment. "Did you recognize the voice?"

"No, but I always check the Caller ID. All the calls are from Cambridge." Ria's voice had a smug, triumphant tone to it. "You ought to have Mark arrested."

"Ria, Mark's not the only person we know who lives in Cambridge. Your family, your relatives, live in Cambridge. MIT and Harvard are just two of the universities in Cambridge. There are at least six others." She picked up a bag of groceries and went into the kitchen. "Why do you insist it's Mark?"

Ria followed her. "Why not? Why do you insist it isn't?"

Devin set the grocery bag on the kitchen island, then the paper, aligning its edge with the counter edge with exaggerated care. "I can't believe–"

"No, you *refuse* to believe. You've loved Mark Frasier since forever. He's tall, blond, gorgeous and perfect. And he lives in Cambridge, where all the phone calls are coming from. Tell me, what am I supposed to think?"

Devin retrieved the rest of her groceries from the hall. "You don't know Mark." She placed a gallon jug of milk on the top shelf of the refrigerator. "Messages like that–something that gross–it's not anything Mark would say."

"You are so in love with that face and that body you don't see anything else."

Devin slammed the refrigerator door. "You saw him–what, twice? How he looks–that's all you know about him, Ria. You never talked to him or got to know him. Don't tell me what he's all about, because you haven't a clue."

"Huh. He dumped you after he finally got you into bed. That told me all I ever wanted to know about him."

"There's so much–"

Ria slapped a hand on the counter. "No. Men don't treat my girlfriends that way. And what about his suicide attempts?"

"That was years ago, Ria, a couple years after I met him. He was maybe fourteen. His father had told him he didn't love him and didn't want him, and his grandparents had abused him. There were siblings – it must have been hard to watch them being loved when he wasn't."

Ria clicked her tongue. "An answer for everything. Why do you care about him?"

The ticking of the clock echoed in the silent kitchen for nearly a minute before Devin responded. "We were friends. Mark understood how it felt to be unwanted." She carefully placed one box of granola bars on another before continuing. "Something you didn't know anything about."

They stared at one another.

Ria rolled her eyes and lifted one eyebrow. "People change, and love is blind." She retrieved the kitchen phone and glanced at the keypad, then Devin. "I think Daddy told you there isn't a man out there worth dying for."

Ria put the receiver to her ear, frowned, punched a button and listened again. She looked up at Devin. "There's no dial tone."

# CHAPTER TWO

Ria handed the phone to Devin. As Devin pushed the buttons but heard nothing on the dead phone, Ria whispered, her voice wavering, "I made two calls since you left your message. I know this phone was working an hour ago."

The charging base was in a small rolltop desk in a corner of the kitchen. Devin pulled out the desk chair and tugged on the phone cable and power cord. Both had been unplugged.

"Don't touch the plugs! There might be fingerprints!" Ria ran to the stairs. "I'll use the phone in the office!"

Two police cars arrived soon after Ria's call. Devin opened the front door to two policemen; two others were directed to inspect the outside of the house and the yard.

"You think someone might still be in the house?" The Florian policeman wore a nametag inscribed McChesney. He was short and slightly overweight, with clear blue eyes and thinning reddish hair. The odor of cigars hung around him like too much cologne.

"Do you have a basement?" Ria and Devin shook their heads. He opened the powder room door and looked in the closets under the staircase. He motioned to the other man, who went upstairs. "We'll get someone over here to check for fingerprints. Can you show me the telephone you say was unplugged?"

As Devin led the policeman to the kitchen, Ria shook her head as she mumbled, "I was here! I never heard anything."

"Where were you?" McChesney stopped and looked from Ria to Devin.

"Upstairs." Pause. "Taking a shower, doing my nails. I guess my music was pretty loud." She shrugged. "I used the phone an hour ago–I called my dad after Devin called." She gave Devin a sidelong glance. "Then I called my boss and quit my job, because I'm going home."

The cop nodded and made some notes, as the other policeman came downstairs, reporting he had found nothing. "Well, then, why don't you talk to this young lady, "indicating Ria, glancing at his notebook, "Miss St. Amont said she was here in the house." He turned toward Devin. "And I'll chat with Miss Marques, who I believe had someone following her at the mall today."

McChesney hadn't finished speaking before Ria asked, "Can we go outside?" and hurried to the foyer before the other policeman could respond. As she opened the door, she threw over her shoulder, "Don't forget to tell him about the kittens, Devin."

Devin retrieved the yellow paper Ria had showed her. "Here. Don't forget this. You found it."

Devin watched Ria walk toward the street with the policeman. McChesney cleared his throat. "You need to tell me something about kittens?"

She grimaced, screwing up her face and shuddering. "They were from my farm, just babies so little their eyes had just opened."

"And your farm is where?"

"Hightower Farm. It's about five miles from here, on Walker Road." She glanced from McChesney's face to Ria, who had taken a seat on the park bench across the street from the cottage. "That's where he sits."

"Who?"

"The person who watches the house." Devin kept her eyes on Ria.

"Do you mind if we use the table?" Officer McChesney reached past her to close the door.

Devin motioned to the dining room, directing the policeman to a chair at the end as she took a seat on his left.

"Okay, you said the farm is five miles from here. Has anything strange happened there?" McChesney glanced over his notes. "No, lets go back to the kittens. What happened to these kittens?"

"When I came home, they were hung on the door. Ria also saw them. Then they disappeared."

"Did you see these kittens before or after you found the phone unplugged?"

"Before. Ria said she saw them before I got home, and they were there when I came in from running errands."

The policeman nodded as he wrote. "The man who was following you today-have you seen him before?"

"I'm sure he's the one who's been watching the house."

"Any idea who it might be?"

"Ria insists it's Mark Frasier, a former friend of mine."

"'Former friend.'" He raised an eyebrow. "Who do you think it is?"

Devin fidgeted in her chair. "I don't know, but the person I saw today wasn't Mark. He wasn't tall enough." Pause. "I mean, he had scraggy blond hair and wore mirrored sunglasses, maybe trying to look like Mark, but it wasn't him."

"I'll come back to this former friend. Can you describe the person you saw today-eye color? Weight? Maybe he limped?" The policeman waited for more details, pen poised above his notebook.

"He was wearing gloves."

"Gloves?"

"Yeah. And he wore mirrored sunglasses. He was big. Not obese, but big. Maybe two-sixty, two-seventy. Grubby-looking. Dirty blond hair, bad haircut. He kind of ambled along when he walked." She studied the table. "I tried not to look at him."

"What about this Mark Frasier? Where's he?"

Devin sighed. "Harvard. According to a mutual friend, he teaches several classes and is studying for an additional master's degree beyond his MBA. I haven't had any contact with him since I left Cambridge eighteen months ago, after graduating from MIT. We had been friends for a long time. I don't know what happened, but we didn't part under the best of circumstances."

McChesney asked, "And you have no reason to believe he'd bother you?"

She shook her head. "I just figured I was part of an unpleasant past he was trying to leave behind."

"Unpleasant?"

Devin didn't immediately answer. She looked McChesney in the eye. "I–it's the ugly stuff you see on TV and don't want to know happens in real life, much less to someone you know."

McChesney nodded. "I'll need his last known address and telephone number." He paused. "You have no reason to think he'd be trying to get your attention?"

Devin gave her head a slight shake. "None whatsoever. And I doubt any address I give isn't current. And I never had his phone number."

"Is there anything else you can tell me about the person following you today?"

"He always seemed to know where I was going, like he had a copy of my shopping list." She waited for a response, but the cop said nothing. "I have a registered Beretta semi-automatic in my car. Ria's dad gave it to me for protection when the phone calls started last fall. I—"

McChesney interrupted. "Phone calls?"

Devin leaped to her feet. "Don't you guys have to keep records or make reports or something? Ria and I have called the police I don't know how many times in the last eight months, about nuisance phone calls, about someone being in the house—and three times you guys laughed at us and told us to quit bothering you."

"Miss Marques, I was never here before. I saw only two complaints on record before I came here tonight."

"No, we've called and called! Stuff has been stolen, our house was vandalized—"

The policeman carefully laid his pen across his notebook. "Miss Marques, I don't know what happened to your other complaints. There were only two on file when I checked before coming here tonight. One was on a broken window on the back door, and the other was vandalism done to Miss St. Amont's car."

"Am I wasting my time talking to you now?"

The policeman leaned back in his chair and seemed to be studying the tabletop. After a few moments, he smiled and extended his right hand. "Hi. My name's Stan. Can I call you Devin?"

She stared at him warily as she reached for his hand.

The policeman smiled again. "Bear with me, indulge me by telling the story one more time. Somebody's been watching your house, and there have been phone calls. A man followed you around today. You have evidence that someone was in the house today, and someone put some dead cats on your front door. Let's go back to the guy at the mall. And the gun in your car."

Devin took a deep breath. "The man was every place I had to go at the mall. Every single store, just like he had my list. He even went up to the food court on the third level when I had lunch. Then he was in the grocery store across the street from the mall while I was picking up things for my trip tomorrow. When I was checking out, he was outside, in front of the store, watching me. He waved at me, then he just disappeared. After I saw him there, I pulled the gun out from where I keep it in the car. Even though I always keep my car locked, somehow somebody had put a note on the gun." She went to the kitchen and brought back the paper. "Would you be able to get fingerprints from it?"

The officer shook his head. "I have to be honest with you, Miss Marques. Devin. This is the real world, not *Law and Order*. If this person hasn't been fingerprinted for any reason–been arrested, for instance, applied for a passport, or been in the military or worked for the government in any capacity–fingerprints on that piece of paper won't help. I know that's not what you wanted to hear. We can dust it. Maybe we'll get lucky."

He read the cut-and-paste message. "Does this mean anything to you–'I see the moon, the moon sees me—" He stopped reading and looked up. Devin was shaking her head.

"Okay. What can you tell me about the person you say watches the house?"

"We keep seeing a beat-up brown Toyota station wagon. It doesn't have plates on it, and most of the chrome trim is gone around the headlights. I think part of the grille is missing too."

"Any bumper stickers? Or are the bumpers missing as well?"

Devin had to smile at Stan's attempt at humor. "It does have bumpers." She paused, picturing the car in her head. "And one wheel cover. Driver's side, rear. That tire is a whitewall."

"One whitewall. That's different."

Two more uniformed men, carrying briefcases and equipment, entered the foyer.

McChesney got up. "I see the crime team finally arrived." He spoke to them briefly, in a low voice, and returned to the table as they opened their equipment and began their work.

"How long has this person been sitting across the street, watching the house, or following you?"

Devin watched a man carefully dusting the front door with what looked like an oversized makeup brush. "Today was the first time I was aware of anyone following me." She glanced at McChesney then turned her eyes back to the door. "We started seeing him on the walk along the retaining wall around the end of February or early this month. At first, we thought he was watching the work crews fixing the storm damage along the beach, but he was still there after they had finished and left." She looked from McChesney's notepad to his blue eyes. "As far as his description—" She hunched her shoulders and shook her head. "Tall, big, shaggy blond hair. Just like the person today."

"What about the phone calls? When did they start?"

"A year ago? Last Easter? I'm not exactly sure. I didn't think anything of it at first–how many colleges are in the area, y'know? The phone would ring, I'd answer and hear background noise, but whoever was there didn't say anything. Then I'd hear the phone disconnect. After Ria moved in last September, if she answered, the caller would apologize for a wrong number and hang up."

"How often did you and Ria get those calls?"

"If Ria's here, there's maybe one call a night. If I'm alone, the phone keeps ringing and ringing, and I let the automated voice mail answer. But they just call back. We subscribed to Caller ID as soon as it was available to see if we could find out who the caller was."

"Have you kept a record of the phone numbers?"

"That's why Ria insists it's Mark–most of the calls originate from the Cambridge area, specifically on and around the Harvard campus."

"May I see that list?"

"Of course." She went to the desk in the kitchen and opened one drawer, then another, note pads, pencils and pens flying during her futile search. "It's gone! It's gone! It's gone!"

McChesney stood in the door. "Maybe Miss St. Amont moved it. Why don't you just get a drink of water, take a deep breath, and sit back down."

Devin returned to the table. "They even called the motels where I was staying on the road."

"Where has that been?"

"Last fall, Harrisburg, Pennsylvania, New York City near Madison Square Garden, Washington, DC. Tampa and Palm Springs earlier this year. Last month, I was in North Carolina, and, last week, Virginia. Calls every night. Sometimes four or five calls a night. I didn't want to turn off the phone in my room or have the desk hold the calls in case my groom had a problem at the barn."

"Have you changed your phone numbers?"

"Huh!" Devin waved a hand. "Four times! It's been a nightmare! I have an unlisted phone number. Once when I changed it, my groom lost the number and couldn't get it from information, but the weirdo did."

"Your groom." The policeman nodded as he scribbled in his notebook. "What about him?"

"Her. Wendy Hilliard." She gave her head a hard shake. "She's devoted to my horses."

"Does she have a key to your house?"

"No, and we don't have any hidden outside."

"Who else might, aside from you and your roommate?"

"The cleaning lady, Talia Andrews–she lives in West Haven, in the Gianotti School Apartments–she has a key to the front door. Ian used to–"

One of Stan's eyebrows shot up. "Who's Ian?"

"Ian Marques. My cousin." She gave her head another shake. "We're not really related. His father and my stepfather are brothers." As McChesney set down his pen and folded his arms, she explained, "I have your typical screwed up childhood: my father died; my mother remarried. My mother died; my stepfather couldn't be bothered with me. So he sent me to live with his brother's family, who didn't want me either. But I was heir to a huge estate, and came with a large maintenance check for whomever cared for me. Thus, I have cousins who aren't really cousins." She paused, shrugged, then continued, "Ian used to

24

be a partner in Hightower Farm, but we had a falling-out last summer and he insisted on being bought out."

McChesney leaned forward. "Do you care to share the nature of this falling out?"

Ria and the other policeman came in before Devin responded.

McChesney motioned to his counterpart. "Can you give us a few more minutes? We're almost done here."

After they took seats in the living room, he looked back at Devin.

"Mostly, Ian can't stand Wendy."

Devin paused; before she continued, McChesney asked, "Do you know why?"

"I'm not sure. She was a homeless high-school dropout at the time, just kind of drifting around. Child of a white prostitute and one of her black- "She cleared her throat – "patrons." She glanced at the cop. "Since she started working for Hightower, she's gotten her GED and just took college entrance exams." Pausing, staring at the table top, Devin folded her arms in front of her. "As for Ian, he didn't like the shows I was choosing to ride in and thought I should be competing in a different event. We had a riding stable leasing space in the barn but he hassled them so much the owner, Susan Holt, didn't renew the lease in the fall. At least two other organizations wanted to lease space for riding schools, but he basically told them to forget it. When he asked me to buy him out, I didn't hesitate."

"Would that failed business relationship make him inclined to harass you?"

"I don't want to think so."

"Do you suspect your roommate?"

"She thinks I do."

"Do you?"

"No."

Officer McChesney looked back through his notes. "I wrote here that you said things have been stolen. I get the impression persons unknown have entered your home more than once."

"It doesn't matter how often we change the security code. Or the locks. They walk in like they live here."

The cop nodded. "Can you tell me what's missing?"

"The dumbest stuff. Shoes, panties, a blouse, a photograph, a music box. A box of wrapping paper. With the exception of Ria's coat, nothing of any real value." She shrugged. "Now a damned piece of paper with phone numbers on it."

"Tell me about Ria's coat."

"Denim and leather, with a quilted silk lining. A designer original. We both wore it."

"It just disappeared?"

"Ria said she might have left it at the gym, or maybe I left it at the barn, but anyone at either place would know whose it was."

Ria appeared in the doorway. "Are you done? I wanta go."

McChesney closed his notebook. "You said other policemen have responded to your calls. Did any of them tell you to keep a log of any time anything happens, even if it's just one of those phone calls?"

"Date, time, what happened. I feel like I'm writing in it all the time."

"Keep it in a safe place." He stood up, placed a hand on the table and leaned toward Devin. "A box of wrapping paper? Who'd steal that?"

"That's what I said!" Ria replied. "The cleaning lady probably threw it out."

Devin shook her head. "You had to know where it was, and Talia would never have found it."

"What was so special about it?" McChesney inquired.

"She's a sentimental slob," Ria sniped, waving her hands dramatically. "Mark always wrapped her presents in beautiful silver paper tied with gold ribbon. She saved every scrap. When that damned box of paper and ribbon went missing, you would have thought the house had been ransacked. If you're done with me, I'm going upstairs to finish my packing." Ria headed toward the staircase.

McChesney arched an eyebrow. "I'm done. They—" he indicated the crime crew—" should be out of here shortly. Keep that log. Keep the doors locked. Apparently we're dealing with someone who knows the law, and his rights. We can't arrest him for sitting on a public bench on a public beach, even if he IS watching your house."

When Devin let out a sharp little "Why?" he held up his hand.

"Apparently you've heard this before." As she nodded, he continued, "We can't do anything but tell him to move along if he's following you around in public. Unfortunately, even if you *feel* threatened, we can't do anything until he actually approaches you and threatens you. We'll check these papers and see if we have any fingerprints on file to match anything that might be on them, or any we may find here in your house."

After the policemen left, Devin found Ria throwing the last of her things into an overnight bag and a gym bag laid open on her bed. "I'd ask you to go with me if you weren't leaving for a horse show tomorrow morning," Ria said softly. "I wish you wouldn't stay here anymore."

"I'll be at the show all week. I'll be fine."

"What if he's there?"

"If it's Mark you're worried about, in all the years I've known him, I haven't seen him at a horse show yet."

Ria made a face and rolled her eyes. "Look, I'm sorry. There are times I wish I'd met the person you knew." She gave a little smile. "He sure could pick out gifts to make you happy. Like that collage of your father's medals and pictures and the rubbing of his name on the Viet Nam memorial wall. And the music box with the carousel horse that looks like Chief. And the car parts when you were building your Thunderbird." She raised carefully tweezed brows. "What a guy."

"I never knew for sure Mark was the Parts Fairy." That had been their name for the phantom who had left fenders, bumpers, doors and a hood, piece by piece, in the St. Amont carport, until the car was finished.

"Well, everyone else insisted they didn't do it. I always thought it was Mark." Ria closed the lid of one bag and fastened its latches as Devin refolded a sweater tossed into the other.

"So he's not such a terrible, worthless scuzzball totally lacking in redeeming qualities after all, hmmm?" With exaggerated care, Devin tucked the sweater into a corner of the gym bag and zipped it closed as she waited for Ria to look at her.

"He's out of your life, Devin. I just wish you'd find somebody else." Ria picked up the overnight bag and glanced around the bedroom, now empty except for the bed, a chair and a dresser. "I'll arrange to get everything else later." She slung the gym bag over her shoulder and walked to the stairs.

Devin followed her to her car, in silence, one of Ria's bags in each hand.

As Ria heaved the bulging suitcases into the trunk of her Honda, Devin asked, "Do you really have to go tonight?"

Ria nodded. "Yes. Daddy insisted. You know how he is." Her smile faded, and her voice grew cold. "And then there's that list of suspects you have me on, right near the top." She vigorously slammed the trunk lid to punctuate her comment.

"Ria—"

She looked at Devin, unsmiling. "I heard what you said to the cop about not knowing who might have keys to the house." She extended a hand, open palm out, displaying two keys. "Here. You don't have to worry about mine anymore." She slid behind the steering wheel and lowered the window halfway. "Call me when you trust me again."

"Wait a minute. I have something you need to take to your dad." Devin went to her car and retrieved the Beretta. She removed the clip, closed the gun and handed both to Ria. "Tell him about the note I found on it. Now that they know about it, I'm afraid I'll open my eyes some time and find the barrel on the bridge of my nose."

Handling the gun and clip with a finger and thumb, Ria slid them under the passenger's seat. "I guess I understand why you feel that way, and I'm sure Daddy will, too."

Devin stood in the middle of the road, watching Ria's car until it turned the corner at the end of the next block and disappeared. She paused at the end of the walk, studying her house, whispering, "Will I be safe here one more night?" She weighed two options: changing the security code again, making sure all the windows were locked and pushing furniture in front of the doors before she went to bed, or staying at a motel. She didn't think either option would result in a good night's sleep.

When she stepped up onto the concrete slab that formed a tiny front porch, she saw a large brown envelope tucked behind a flower pot. Scrawled across the front was, "I took this off that old brown car you've seen parked in front of your house. Your neighbor."

Devin pulled out a bent, rusted Connecticut license plate, its registration stickers scraped off. FCT 897. The last place she had seen it was on a blue Pontiac Trans Am, and exotic Firebird splashed across its hood, the car Mark had owned when she left for her last semester at MIT.

# CHAPTER THREE

*Ria kept her bedroom door locked at night, but you never did. So many times I stood over you, watching you sleep. You cry in your sleep, mumble to yourself, unintelligible words. You didn't leave me the phone number for where you were staying this week. You thought you could hide from me. We are sisters, you and I. You should feel my breath on your face, hear my heartbeat. And you will. You will.*

5:00. The red LED numbers stood out in the dark room. Devin sat straight up in bed, wondering what had startled her awake. Saturday morning, and she was *somewhere* for a horse show. No phone calls in the middle of the night for four nights. She plopped back onto the pillows, remembering that Ria had moved back to Cambridge, taking with her the need to leave a note with an emergency contact number by the phone in the kitchen.

*Where am I?* Devin closed her eyes a moment. A small guest room at a polo club two hours from home. Only one class today, in the evening, an easy day after a morning class and an evening class each of the past two days.

Shower. Dress. Go to the barn, where Wendy would report on each of the three horses in her care. She would be leaving shortly after Devin arrived, taking her first day off since being hired the previous summer. She'd be talking in her excited rapid-fire manner, giggling her squeaky little-girl giggle, anticipating attending a friend's wedding.

Yawning and rubbing her eyes, Devin headed for the bathroom. *A hot shower has to be the one of the best parts of a day.* The hot spray poured over her head and she closed her eyes as she shampooed her hair. She let the water pelt her shoulders before leaning back to rinse her hair. Moments later, she turned off the shower, certain she had heard a knock on the door and someone calling her name. Swathed in towels, dripping, she reached the door as the person on the other side knocked and called her name again, then identified himself as one of the polo club stewards.

She peered through the peephole, turned the deadbolt and opened the chained door a crack.

"Sorry to bother you. We just had a call for you, and the person was pretty insistent we deliver the message right away." He slipped a folded piece of paper through the slender opening.

Devin opened the page and read aloud, "There's no place you can hide from me." Craning her head to see his eyes through the slightly open door, she asked, "You took the call?"

He nodded. "That's all that was said, then the person hung up."

Devin shivered. "You said a person–"

"I'm not sure if it was a man or a woman. I know you said yesterday your groom wouldn't be here today, and I heard you talking about some of the other stuff that's been happening to you. We'll make sure someone's keeping an eye on you and your horses today. And they're being moved to the main barn right now."

"Thanks." She closed and locked the door and slumped against the wall, staring at the ceiling. "Who am I supposed to be hiding from?" she demanded of the rows of acoustic tiles.

By the time Devin had dressed and found her stalls in the polo club's main barn, Wendy was busily organizing things there.

"Oh, Miss D, I can't go tonight!" little five-foot-nothing Wendy stated, tugging up the sleeves of the University of Massachusetts sweatshirt she rarely took off.

"You've planned this day for so long—you're getting your hair done, you're getting your nails done—this is your day, sweetie, and you deserve it."

"There's just too much to do here."

Devin took a blanket from Wendy's hands. "I saw that fancy little cobalt blue dress and those sexy little silver sandals with their three-inch heels—no UMass sweatshirt tonight, sweetie!"

Wendy looked down at her favorite garment and frowned. "But what about–"

Devin put her arm around Wendy's shoulders and marched her to the stall door. "I have all day to take care of this. Someone from the polo club will be here watching the horses, and I already made arrangements for an attendant for Chief during tonight's class."

Wendy looked up, her light brown eyes open wide. She touched Devin's arm. "What about you?"

"I'll be right here tomorrow morning, impatiently waiting to hear all the details from your big night out. Deal?"

Wendy nodded, her kinky blonde hair swirling around her head.

"Okay. That gentleman over there is walking you to your car." She gave Wendy a little squeeze. "Have a wonderful time tonight!"

Around noon, Devin found herself thinking, "Wendy should be admiring her french manicure right about now." Then she heard Ria, asking for "the Hightower horses," and in a louder voice exclaim, "Don't you even tell me I can't go in there. Where is she? Is she all right?"

Devin popped her head out of the stall and looked around for her friend. She ran to Ria and flung her arms around her. "I can't believe you're here!"

"Daddy gave me a talking-to about friends and watching each other's back." She stepped back. "We need lunch, girl. Those food tents out there are just callin' our names!"

As they settled at a table in front of one of the food tents, Ria asked, "Was that guy here this morning?" When Devin shook her head, Ria continued, "Don't you wish the police at home took this as seriously as the people here do?"

"Remember what we were told about private property and the rules being different?"

"Oh, yeah, that private property thing." Ria waved a hand, as if to shoo a pesky bug. "But don't you feel a little safer?"

"It's creepy, Ria. All I want to know is who it is and why. What did I do?" She pushed pieces of fruit around the Styrofoam serving bowl. "It's like whoever is doing this knows how important tonight's class is to me."

"Why?"

"Chief has to do well tonight because he has to be in the class tomorrow."

"Aren't your other two horses already in? Shaman and Apollo."

Devin nodded, surprised Ria recalled the horses' names.

"Aren't two enough?"

"It's a point of pride. Ian says I can't manage without him, that I need him to tell me what to do. I've done just fine all week without him. All Chief has to do is qualify for the jump-off tonight, and then, even though he's still considered an Intermediate horse, he's in his first Grand Prix event."

Ria shook her head. "I thought Intermediate was a rider level, and you rode whatever horse you wanted."

Devin laughed. "Oh, no, that's way too simple!" She slowly lowered her plastic fork as she watched Ria. "What?"

"Do you know how long it's been since I heard you laugh? We used to get so silly we'd almost wet our pants laughing. Now all we do is scream at each other. Whatever's going on around you has got to stop. I want my friend back, not this scared little person who picks at her food and jumps at every noise."

Tears welled in Devin's eyes. "Wendy and I took turns staying with the horses, two nights each. The phone in the guest room never rang, no matter which of us was there. This morning, somebody called the steward's office and left a message for me. The person who took the message isn't sure if it was a man or woman." She dabbed her eyes. "Whoever it was could be at the next table. And I have to carry on, business as usual."

"Where's Wendy today?"

"A wedding. The girl who tutored her for her SATs." She smiled. "She's so excited about it."

"From what you've told me about her life, there wasn't much partying to look forward to."

Devin nodded. "She's come a long way, getting a GED and taking SAT tests all in the same year. Homeless last year, college next year." She looked around the tent. "And Ian treats her like a piece of trash."

"Ian's got his own problems, mostly caused by that mega-ego of his and that snooty babe Jesse he's seeing."

Devin glanced at her watch. "I'm supposed to be observing a class to figure out why a child who's supposedly her instructor's star pupil can't win a ribbon." She picked up her half-eaten fruit salad. "Don't worry. I'm taking it with me. Gotta check on the guys, and then we'll go to the ring."

"So what sort of class is this we're going to watch?" Ria asked as they approached the grandstand and ring area.

"It's a hunter seat equitation class. Hunter seat is the type of saddle anyone who jumps uses. There are about thirty entries in the class; they'll ride at a walk, trot and canter in both directions around the ring. The judge will eliminate anyone whose form isn't proper enough. Those left, usually about ten people, will take their horses over a few jumps."

"Do you get told why you were dismissed early?"

"That's what your instructor or coach is for. This girl's parents have come to me because they don't like what the string of coaches she's had have been telling her."

"Which is?"

"You told me once that you quit coming to shows because I ignored you when I was getting ready for a class and when I was in the ring."

Ria nodded in agreement. "Yeah, so?"

"Remember last month when we were watching the NCAA Basketball finals–"

Ria shrugged. "Yeah. First weekend you were home in ages. Kentucky was playing Utah. Nobody thought Kentucky would get that far much less win with a new coach."

"Remember how all the players were talking about being in the zone?"

Ria rolled her eyes. "It was so boring! In the zone. In the zone. One player commented that he heard nothing but his teammates, the ref and the other team. And the crowd was on its feet, screaming. That's all they talked about." She glanced at Devin. "What do riders call it?"

"Keeping your head in the ring. Concentrating on your ride and nothing else. And this little girl pays way too much attention to what the audience is doing." Devin pointed to a fenced area where young riders and their mounts milled around. "That's the warm-up ring. The riders will get last-minute instructions from their coaches; the attendants do the last little bit of spiffing up their horse and rider–combing out their tails, wiping off any mud or dirt from the ring on their tack, boots, the horse before they go into the ring. Since it's a jumping class, there are some jumps set up. There's a person called a ring steward who tells the riders what order they're riding, or when it's time to be ready for their event. There's another one in the show ring, in addition to the judge."

The horse-rider teams were queued up behind the gate to the main ring when a garbled voice came over the public address system, calling the class. The gate opened and the horses surged in.

Devin ignored a little girl's trilling voice, "Hi, Devin! Over here!" as she and Ria strolled around the perimeter of the show ring.

"That's Kaitlin. Obviously, she hasn't learned yet," Devin mused, studying her foam-encased fruit salad and popping a piece of pineapple into her mouth.

"How long does learning that concentration take?"

Devin turned to Ria, chewing, swallowing. "It all depends on how hungry you are to win."

"And how much you have to prove?"

Devin smiled, nodding. "That too."

They watched the class in silence as the riders circled the ring. One, two, three, four horses were pointed out, and the riders came to the center. The ring steward barked, "Stop!" and, in a disorderly array, all the competitors finally halted their mounts. Three more horses were pointed out, and the ring steward told those seven riders they were dismissed. The ring gate opened, and they filed out.

Ria adjusted her sunglasses. "So they're done? Isn't that kind of cruel?"

"That's how it is. You enter shows to prove whether you're as good as you think you are." She glanced at the riders remaining in the ring. "Good. Kaitlin survived the first cut."

"You sure changed the subject fast when I commented about Ian."

As Ria spoke, the child rode past and said, "Hi, Devin!"

In the next instant, Kaitlin was called to the center of the ring.

Devin shook her head. "Who Ian dates is his business." She watched Kaitlin glance her way, then ride to the center of the ring. "And I got tired of being told every decision I made about shows and classes was wrong."

"Jesse's *so* not his type though. I've heard him complain more than once about all the cold showers he's had to take."

Devin shrugged, watching the class entries circle the ring. "Allegedly, she's saving herself for marriage, and even made him reserve two rooms when they went to Aruba last fall and Vail in January." She looked over at Ria. "He wants to marry her."

"Oh, really?"

"So he told me, more than once."

"What do you know about her?"

"Not my problem, so long as she's not in my face or my space."

"She always looks so perfect and put together. Where does she work?"

Devin shook her head. "I don't think Ian knows. Supposedly she's taking some college courses and works two part-time jobs, so he doesn't see her often." She glanced at her empty bowl and then looked Ria in the eye. "Now you get to see what a bitch I am, telling people with more money than God why their only angel child doesn't win. Four people I consider good instructors have said she has talent, but they can't make her see what she has to do to win."

"You sound like you've done this before."

"I'll hear that I wasn't paying any attention to Kaitlin, I was eating, I was talking to you. And I will ask what side of the fence I was on, and–"

"Who'll do that, the parents or the girl?"

"Probably the parents. Kaitlin will be crying alligator tears. None of them should have been looking at me at all, only what was going on in the ring."

"Even the parents?"

"In my opinion, they should only be watching their pride and joy. You'll see."

"You *have* done this before."

"Too many times. Some of them go from instructor to instructor to instructor and never get it." Devin threw the empty food container in a trash barrel as she and Ria walked toward the warm-up ring fence, where the child, still on her horse, her instructor and parents waited.

They were at least twenty feet from the warm-up ring when Kaitlin's mother exploded, "I am not paying you to chit-chat with your girlfriend and eat your lunch while my child is humiliated in front of a crowd!"

Ignoring the mother's outburst, Devin looked at the child, who had fat tears rolling down her cheeks. "How many different instructors have you had, Kaitlin?"

"F-f-our," she stuttered, between sniffles.

"How many of them have told you to pay attention to the judge, not Mommy or the birds overhead or your favorite aunt up in the stands, or anything outside the fence, just the judge?"

Before the child could reply, Kaitlin's father demanded, "And what does that have to do with whether she wins or not?"

"Everything." There was a cold edge on her voice. Devin noticed the riding instructor nodding his head. "Kaitlin was dismissed as soon as she spoke to me. It's all about discipline." Devin's tone softened when she spoke to the little girl. "You're a good rider. You have a good horse. You have to listen to these instructions you don't want to hear, and it's *hard*. But nobody outside the ring can give you a ribbon, only the judge. That man or woman and your horse, that's all you can pay attention to when you're in the ring."

Devin didn't wait for further comment. As she turned to walk away, Kaitlin's father snapped, "Wait just a minute!"

"No. You asked my opinion about why your daughter doesn't bring home ribbons. I've talked to all of Kaitlin's instructors, and they claimed they all told her the same thing I just did. Either she learns the discipline, or she keeps getting dismissed in the middle of the class. That's how it is."

Ria and Devin had walked halfway around the perimeter of the warm-up ring when Ria put her hand on Devin's arm. "That woman just said she was *paying* you to do what you just did."

Devin shrugged. "They offered."

"Isn't it sort of obscene to take money for that?"

Devin squinted as she gazed out across the show ring. "Parents ask for my honest opinion of their children's talent and problems. They say they'll pay anything for their little precious to be able to win ribbons. I tell them up front that I may not say anything they want to hear. And if I actually do get paid–and frequently I don't–that money is donated to a therapeutic riding program for handicapped people. It's something I'd love to see happening at Hightower."

"I remember you arguing with Ian about it. Isn't that one of the things he derailed just before the two of you had that big argument?"

"One of several."

Ria took a few steps and stopped again. "You really don't like talking about the problems you've had with him, do you?"

Devin took several moments to answer. "Your dad always told us to trust our gut, and I didn't with him. I kept being told 'oh, he's family' so I should keep him on as a partner. I don't know if I can undo some of the damage he did to the Hightower name."

"Does that girlfriend have anything to do with it? Aside from you not wanting her around you?"

Devin paused to consider Ria's question. "There's something about her I don't like, and I can't pin it down." Again she shrugged. "She's his problem; just keep her away from me."

Ria shook her finger at Devin. "Just before I left the other day, didn't you say you haven't seen Mark at a show yet?" As Devin nodded, Ria planted a hand on one hip. "Tell me, Missy, with all this concentration you do when you compete, is it possible that he's been there and you didn't see him?"

As they picked their way around a knot of people, Devin made a face. "Of course it's possible. He knows all about the zone thing, competitor that he is. Basketball, jai-alai, racquetball, rowing." She brushed against someone and mumbled a perfunctory 'excuse me'. "If he didn't make himself very obvious by standing along the fence between the warm-up ring and the main ring, I wouldn't see him."

"I don't get how you do that—see nothing beyond the fence."

"Like I told Kaitlin, it's what you do to win."

Ria shook her head. "What's it like? I've heard you talk about walking the ring, and how the things that hold up the poles on the jumps are placed determines how easily they come down, and how the person who designs the jumps puts them up so they'll trick the horse."

Devin had to think a moment to figure out what Ria was talking about. "Oh, how the course is laid out—it's a series of problems the horse and rider have to solve. How many strides between jumps, how tight a turn they can make so the horse can clear the fence. How the cups that hold up the jump rails are turned, or are they the flat ones. That's all stuff the riders look at when they walk the course before a class. Why don't you come in with me when I do it tonight?"

"Won't that mess up your concentration?"

"I'll suffer, just this once." Devin smiled. "And I'll love it."

"Don't you look all fine and professional up there," Ria remarked after Devin settled herself in Mystic Chief's saddle, adjusted her stirrup irons and reins, and pulled the saddle girth one notch tighter.

Devin pulled on her gloves, fussed with her shirt collar, nudged the competitor number tied around her waist, smoothed a corner of Chief's saddle blanket. Then she smiled at Ria.

Ria sighed. "I think I'm bothering you."

"Riders are really superstitious. We all have our little routines we do before we go into the practice ring, then again when we go in to ride. You just saw one of mine." A tractor rumbled past, towing a trailer full of potted plants. "They're starting to build the jumps out in the ring. Why don't you watch them while I warm Chief up? You'll hear them announce when the course is completed and open to the riders."

"Are you sure you want me in there with you?"

Devin stroked Chief's jet-black neck. "There's a first time for everything. Maybe you'll catch the excitement I feel when I'm out there."

Ria rolled her eyes. "I don't know about that."

"Wait where I showed you. I'll meet you there."

Walk, trot, controlled canter. Turns to the left and right. Walk, trot, controlled canter the opposite way of the ring. Every rider concentrated on his or her mount while going through a similar warm-up routine. Does everything feel right? Is the horse doing exactly what I'm telling him or her to do? Is the response time after a command right? Is he tossing his head or bucking more than usual?

Devin was aware of the growing crowd around the warm-up ring only because the array of colors in her peripheral vision increased, as did the hum of conversation. The only face she clearly saw was Chief's appointed attendant for the evening, a young Mexican.

He motioned toward the row of three jumps set up across the middle of the ring. Devin nodded. Yes, Chief was ready to jump.

The young stallion cleared the fences in perfect style. As Chief cantered away from the jumps, Devin heard a garbled public address message she knew was "The course is ready for the riders' inspection."

She lightly slapped the side of Chief's neck, and he tossed his head in reply. "Okay, son, it's almost time. Be nice for your attendant."

He threw a cooler, a light blanket, across Chief's hindquarters.

Dismounting, Devin pulled the braided reins over Chief's head and handed them to the young man. "Keep him moving, please," she instructed in Spanish. When he pursed his lips, she quickly added, "I'm sorry. I know you've done this before—"

"Ma'am, yes, ma'am," he replied, in English. He nodded, smiling, and reached for the reins. "Chief will be fine."

Devin met Ria at the appointed spot by the in gate. As they entered the ring with several other riders, Ria remarked, "Chief looked so beautiful jumping those fences."

"He's 'on' tonight. He feels really good." Devin motioned toward the other end of the ring. "The course starts up there. Each jump is numbered. We were given the course layout earlier—you saw it. I know it didn't make much sense to you."

"It's a different language!" Ria shook her head. "Oxers. Triples. Verticals. Liverpools. What's the hardest?"

"It depends on which horse I'm on, the footing and the weather. I have the best of everything tonight. Perfect weather, good footing, and a horse that loves to jump and hates to hit the rails. Or lose. Okay, here's where we start. See, there's the marker over there. Some rings have an electric eye we have to pass to start the clock."

"Clock?"

"It's a timed event. We have seventy-seven seconds to run this course. If we knock down one rail or a whole fence, it's four faults. If we come to a fence and Chief refuses to jump, that's four faults. If he refuses a second time, it's six. Three times and we're disqualified. If we take a jump out of order, we're disqualified. If one of us falls, we're disqualified."

"Has that happened to you recently?"

"Not in a long time, and I don't plan on changing that tonight." Devin glanced at the marker again, motioned for Ria to walk with her, and started walking and counting. When she reached the first fence, she explained, "It's four of my strides for every one Chief takes. From the marker to here, he'll take twelve strides before he jumps. That's what I'll be counting after each jump." She wiggled a pole on the jump, a plain vertical jump with red-and-white striped poles. "This jump will be easy because the cups are turned up and the rail won't roll out unless it's hit really hard."

Ria glanced around. "These jumps look huge! How high are they?"

"These range from five feet to five-seven. It depends on the show and course designer, and variables like the footing and size of the ring. The spread jumps, like that one over there with the three fence elements at different heights, aren't as high, to compensate for the horse having to make the extra effort to get across it. That's not the same as a triple-jump combination. We'll get to one of those in a minute."

They walked to the other side of the jump and Devin glanced at Ria before stepping off to count. "Ready? Start counting. Test at the next fence!"

When the duo reached the next fence, a simulation of a curved-top gate in a white picket fence, Devin asked Ria, "How many strides will Chief have to take to clear this fence?"

"Four?"

"Very good! Before you know it, you'll be out here doing this with me all the time!"

They continued on, taking strides and counting, to the other end of the ring, where a plain vertical jump had been erected. The three lower rails in the jump were red and white, and the top rail was all white. After a quick look at the obstacle, Devin stated, "This is the problem jump. Every course has one. This one will come down most often tonight."

Ria reached out as if she was going to touch one of the poles, but stopped. "I can see that the cup things that hold it are flat, maybe even curved the wrong way."

"Yep! That, and the top rail is white, so the horses will have trouble seeing it against the ring's white fence."

"Can you tell if this course is going to be hard or easy?"

Devin looked around the ring. "It's going to be hard for several reasons." She pointed at the next fence and began taking long strides, with Ria trying to keep up. "The course designer didn't place a lot of foliage around the obstacles, so, again, the horses will have trouble seeing the rails. We'll start in daylight, but we'll go into the jumpoff ring under lights, so everything will appear different to the horses."

Ria let out a little whistle. "How long does it take to learn all the tricks?"

"You don't."

"Because the tricks change with every course?"

"And every horse."

They were close to the gate where they had originally entered the ring. Ria stopped. "I'm going to leave now so you can do your ring thing and you can concentrate."

Devin looked surprised. "You don't have to. We're almost done."

"Are you sure?"

"Definitely. I won't start ignoring you until I'm back in the warm-up ring. Chief goes fifth in the order, and I won't say anything to anyone—except possibly the attendant—until Chief's done with his first round."

The fence Devin had predicted would be the course's main problem had fallen four times when she and Chief entered for his turn at the jumps. As she rode past, Ria called out, "You go, girl!"

The evening was different in several ways. The main one was the security guard prowling around the area between the warm-up ring and the main ring. Ria had joined her at a time when she was accustomed to solitary preparation and thoughts. And Devin was sure she had seen Mark on the far side of the warm-up ring, leaning on the top rail of the fence.

# CHAPTER FOUR

*You didn't even see me when you said "Excuse me." All that talk about concentration and not seeing anything but what's in the ring being how you win. I bet you didn't even see us on the other side of the ring, Mark and I. Of course not! You were too busy showing off to that nigger friend of yours. I should be the one doing things with you, not her. I don't even exist to you. But that's all about to change.*

*Why, when I'm already distracted, did Mark have to show up tonight?* Maybe Ria had been right. Maybe Mark had been there all those years and Devin just hadn't seen him.

Taking one deep breath after another, she rode up the center of the ring, trying to clear her mind of every random thought except the clock and the fourteen difficult obstacles Chief had to clear to qualify for the Grand Prix event on Sunday.

She looked at the triple jump combination on her left. Three tall, spare vertical jumps, top rails set on flat cups. One stride between jumps. Think about the strides, the jumps, nothing else.

*There's the starting marker. We're as ready as we're going to get.*

Devin turned Chief in a small circle, then urged him into a slow canter. *Nine…ten…eleven…twelve…big jump! Good! Clean! Two…three…four… curved gate on deep cups Up! Up! Damn! Hard rub.*

A wake-up call. Devin glanced back. The whole "gate" rocked back and forth in the cups. *Three…four…whoa whoa…big jump! Good. Clean.* She took a quick look at the scoreboard. No faults. The gate had stayed up.

The problem jump was next, and, to this point, she had been a little more careful, riding a little slower than she should have been on the long, complicated course. *Three…four…c'mon, son, really big jump! Clear!*

Chief flipped his ears.

The crowd must be cheering. *Let's give them a clean round. Triple jump combination next. Pick up the pace. Can't have time faults. Up! One up! One up! No rails down. Liverpool next. No water in it, just blue tarp. Go go go! Whoa back! Wide! Don't step on the tape! Turn turn tight turn this is the triple oxer not high but wide…four…five up YES! Still clean! Five to go. Two jump combination three…four…five…UP! Good! Two…three… Wide! Good! Tight turn make up time three…four…I know that brown rail is hard to see. Oh, clean! Good! Green fence two… three…four…yes! Still clean! Last one, son! Go go! We're close on time! Three…four…Up! Yes! There's the finish marker! We did it!*

She glanced at the scoreboard and slapped Chief's neck, letting out a sigh of relief when she saw a zero, representing no faults, under the time, 76.35. "We did it, son!" Just barely. She pulled him to the side of the ring to allow the next competitor in, and he shied and tossed his head. Devin stroked his neck. "You did good, kid."

As Devin anticipated, the attendant was waiting at the entrance to the warm-up ring, ready to throw the cooler across Chief's hindquarters. She waved him away as the excited young horse side-stepped and fought to pull the reins looser in her hands. "He's a little wound. I'm going to walk him out."

Walk. Right. Chief did anything *but* walk. Maybe the cheering crowd had overexcited him. Maybe something he saw had spooked him. Devin would have liked to dismount and lead Chief to a quiet empty area to walk him and talk to him, but she couldn't leave the warm-up ring without being disqualified from the class. Maybe she'd stuff his ears with cotton for the jump-off.

She aimed the horse toward the far end of the ring where few horses were being exercised, trying to pull him down to a trot. He whipped his long tail and tossed his head with almost every step, yanking at the reins.

"You must really think you're hot stuff there, kiddo, making such a big deal of getting the first clean round," she told Chief.

He flipped his ears, shook his head and threw in a buck for good measure.

He didn't usually behave this way after a class, Devin recalled. Maybe it's because Wendy isn't here. But she suspected her own unease contributed to his.

Halfway around the ring, the tail-swishing had stopped; he was quieting down. He had his head up and his chin tucked, and she knew how classically regal he looked, trotting along the fence. Ian had been bugging her to try three-day eventing, but she never had a good jumping horse that would settle down for the complex dressage routine. Maybe Chief would be that horse.

*Get Ian out of your head.* She sat back into the saddle, the signal for the horse to walk. He promptly skittered sideways halfway to the center of the ring, yanking his head this way and that with each step. Devin pulled him into tighter and tighter circles until he had to walk, and, finally, come to a stop. He stood there, swishing his tail, as she stroked his neck.

"What *is* your problem? There are twenty more chances you won't be in that class tomorrow if you don't settle down." She watched the long black ears flip back and forth as the horse took in her voice and the other sounds around them.

Chief turned his head back and slobbered on her boot.

The audience around the show ring erupted. Another clean round. Chief snapped to attention at the noise and resumed side-stepping.

Chief's attendant approached cautiously. "Ma'am, is he all right? Can I do something?"

Devin dismounted. "Hold him tight. I'm going to resaddle him. Maybe there's a wrinkle in the pad bothering him." As she pulled the tack off, one of the warm-up ring stewards approached.

"He seems a little excited tonight," the woman observed. "He wasn't that way the other night."

"No, it isn't like him," Devin agreed.

"That was an excellent ride out there."

Devin carefully placed the saddle pad on Chief's back, taking extra care to smooth it down. "I hope he settles down enough to do it again."

"You only have to place tonight."

She tugged the girth tight. "Most of the rest of the field has more experience than he does, and he hasn't been under lights a lot. But thanks for the encouragement." Devin turned to the attendant. "I'll take that cooler now, please."

She and the ring steward crossed the ring, followed by the attendant, who was chattering away at the horse he was leading.

"Is everything all right? Is there anything else we can do?" the woman offered.

Devin laughed, an unamused, brittle noise. "Everyone's trying to help, and I appreciate that, but everything's different tonight, from my groom not being here to the guards who ARE here because of me. And *why* they're here has me rattled."

The steward nodded. "I spoke to your friend. You have a lot to be worried about. Everyone's doing what we can within reason, and consideration to the other competitors, to keep your horses safe."

Five horses would compete in the jumpoff. Some course designers liked to have as many competitors as there were ribbons awarded, but tonight's designer preferred five. And Chief would be first.

Devin ran through the jumpoff course in her mind one more time before entering the ring. Eight obstacles, spaced far apart across the ring. Long run to the first vertical, tight turn back to the double. Tighter turn back to the third vertical and the fourth, a tall blue and white vertical. Three strides to the fifth, a wide-set double with brown rails. The sixth was that "problem" vertical from the first round. Long gallop to the seventh, a green triple oxer, eight strides to the last jump, the Liverpool. In forty-eight seconds or less, preferably with no faults.

"Okay, son, we can do this," she told Chief as soon as she heard the announcement the ring was ready for the final competition. She knew he could take down every fence and be qualified for the next day's event since he was among the top five in tonight's class. Devin turned him toward the chute between the two rings. "Let's give 'em something to talk about."

Ria reached out a hand, palm out, as she rode past. Devin slapped it, a high five. "Get 'em!"

The floodlights over the show ring made it much brighter than the warm-up ring. Devin had planned to hold Chief to a slow trot across the ring so he could become accustomed to the different light. Chief, however, broke into a canter two steps into the ring and headed straight for the starting marker.

"I guess I'm along for the ride, then, son," she told him. "Don't forget what the jump order is."

They passed the timer and she turned back towards the first jump at the opposite end of the ring. Chief's ears remained pitched forward as he crossed the ring's sand and clay floor in huge strides. *Five…six…seven…eight… nine… ten…eleven… twelve…huge jump, lots of air…turn turn turn tight turn four… five…six…big jump…turn turn turn back to those planks you don't like… three…four…five…oh lots of air good for you! Last big turn, then you get to run three…four…up! This one isn't that big…two…three…you didn't like this one before…clear yes! Good good! Four…five…six…up up up! That white one again… go go go big one coming…go…six…seven…eight…really big! Good! Now go go go go! Back a little…last one clear so far whoa…up up…don't step on the tape…one…two…three… timer…you did it!*

She didn't have to look at the scoreboard to know Chief had a clean round, but the time surprised her, 34.98 seconds. Three of the four horses to follow could beat that, but could they also leave up the fences? She slapped Chief's neck. "Great job! Look at that time!"

He tossed his head.

"Yeah, I hear them cheering for you. You deserve it."

The next horse and rider entered the ring as Devin and Chief approached the gate. A thin cheer went up from a section of the grandstand. She knew that team was the hometown favorite, but not likely to match Chief's time.

They went back to the warm-up ring to wait and find out what color ribbon Chief would wear the next time he left the show ring.

Ria stood at the ring entrance. "That was beautiful! You were flying!" she exclaimed as a cooler was thrown over Chief's hindquarters.

"Walk him, please, away from the other horses," Devin directed as she dismounted. She turned to Ria, her back to the show ring. "I can't watch the other riders."

"Are you all right?"

"This is the hard part, the reason riders hate to go first. Even after that ride, we might be no better than fifth place."

A groan went up from the crowd.

"Sounds like at least fourth place," Ria corrected. "But you're in that class tomorrow for sure."

"He could have won twelfth place and qualified, but making the jumpoff is better."

A horse and rider team left the warm-up ring, and the second entry returned a few moments later.

"Still can't watch?" Ria asked.

Devin shook her head as her eyes followed her horse around the ring.

"Mark's here tonight," Ria stated in a matter-of-fact tone.

"I thought I saw him."

"He came over and introduced his friends and asked how you were doing."

Devin glanced at Ria then looked back at her horse. "And what did you tell him?"

"I told him to check out the security guards because they're for you."

"What did he say to that?"

"That's when the tractors and equipment and everything to set up for the jumpoff started to clear out. He told me to wish you luck, and they left before you came up to ride."

The crowd groaned again.

"Sounds like third place now," Ria added, smiling.

Devin returned a thin smile. Her heart pounded in her chest. She watched another horse and rider head for the chute to the show ring gate. "That's the one who can beat Chief's time and leave up fences," she remarked. "These fractions of minutes take forever when you're waiting." She forced herself to keep her eyes on Chief as she listened to the cheering audience. Another rider headed toward the show ring, as the competitor in the ring completed another clean round.

"Thirty-five-four, you're still in the lead," the warm-up ring steward called over to Devin. "One to go."

Devin motioned to Chief's attendant as the gate opened to the final jumpoff team. The pair leaving the ring trotted past as Devin threw the reins over Chief's head and pulled the stirrup irons down.

The last horse took down the first fence.

"You won!" Ria exclaimed, her words barely audible over the groan from the audience.

A huge grin on her face, Devin hugged Ria. "And you thought you'd distract me. You'll have to be here all the time now!"

6:30 a.m. Devin glanced at her watch as she measured feed for Shaman, Apollo and Mystic Chief. *Wendy should be here any minute. I hope she had a good time, and it was all she'd hoped it would be.* She nested the buckets one inside the other and closed the bin.

The club steward who had knocked on her guest room door the previous morning stepped into the open stall door.

Devin juggled the buckets, startled to see him. "No more mystery callers, I hope," she remarked.

"Your groom called to say she's having car trouble, and she'll be here as soon as possible."

As soon as possible. By 10:30, after morning workouts and vet checks on the horses, Wendy hadn't arrived or called with an update. Devin was cleaning and sorting tack when Ria breezed in.

"What's wrong?"

"Wendy's not here yet. They said she called at 6:30 with car trouble, and I haven't heard–"

Ria interrupted. "That's not at all like the Wendy I've heard about."

Devin shook her head. "I called the house where she rents a room. The lady there said she looked absolutely darling when she left for the wedding yesterday. She came in, all smiles, at eleven last night, chattering away about what a good time she had. And she was out the door at six like always, headed for the farm this morning. There's no answer at Wendy's boyfriend's place, the barn or at Ian's."

"Where's he?"

"He supposedly was helping somebody move, and his parents are away on vacation. And Wendy's boyfriend might be at church. He always gave her grief about having to work on Sunday."

"And you're worried."

Devin fussed with a bridle.

Ria persisted. "What if she doesn't show up?"

"This isn't like Wendy." Devin draped the bridle over a saddle. "I'm sure there's a good reason–"

"What about this afternoon–who's helping you?"

Devin placed an entry number card on each of three sets of tack. "The attendant from last night is standing by."

"And I'm here."

Devin took a minute to absorb Ria's offer. "Ria, it's a wonderful thing you're offering to do, but you don't know the horses and they don't know you."

"How hard is it to hand you blankets and walk a horse and all?"

"Ria, I don't want you to get hurt. You saw Chief last night. He was probably all wired because I'm a wreck. That times three– and he's the most predictable of the three. Are you sure?"

A moment passed before Ria answered. "I heard you tell that policeman the other night you didn't think I was part of what's been happening to you. Do you or don't you?"

"I don't lie to cops, Ria."

"Well, don't you want to know someone you trust is there with those horses you value more than anything?"

One of the polo club's stable hands stuck her head in the stall door. "We had a call from your farm. Wendy left about twenty minutes ago, but she might be stuck in traffic because there's a big accident on the east-bound side of the turnpike."

"Okay," the women responded in unison. "Thank you."

"What has to be done between now and that class, Devin?"

Devin looked around the supply stall. "I won't need the feed and some of this equipment anymore today, so I was going to load some of it so I won't have to do it later."

"I thought I saw your truck when I was driving in."

Devin nodded. "Right in the front row."

Ria twitched an eyebrow. "Good place for it. Everybody can see it."

"Let's go get the hand truck so we don't have to lug this stuff." They walked to the barn door, crossed a driveway and an emerald green swath of lawn to the van parking lot. "The stuff's heavy. You ready?"

"We'll make a lot of trips, get our exercise in for the day. Then we'll get some lunch."

Devin stopped. "Are you sure? I mean–"

Ria admired her nails. "You mean, I might ruin my manicure or break a nail. You mean, I've never so much as offered to touch one of your horses or their stuff. If that's what you mean, well, that was before all this weird stuff started. Let's do it." She gestured in the direction of the show's concession area. "The sooner we're done, the sooner we have lunch. And there's not a tent over there that doesn't have to-die-for food."

They loaded two of the three tack trunks, a feed bin and remains of hay and straw bales. Devin locked all the compartments and glanced around the parking area.

"Is something wrong?" Ria sounded worried.

Devin glanced at her, nodding her head. "The third food tent over there has Mediterranean food, and I swear I just heard Baklava calling our names. I'll stop at the office and see if they heard anything more from Wendy, then we can eat."

"On with the show," Devin remarked as she pulled on her second tall black riding boot. She turned her attention to Ria, who seemed to be inspecting Devin's riding coat for lint or tears. "As of right now, I have to quit wondering where Wendy is and start thinking about the ring layout and how I'll ride each horse over it. If you have any questions, ask the attendant–he speaks English–or the ring steward. I'll point the steward out once we get to the warm-up ring. Riding order is according to points standing, so Chief goes first and Shaman and Pal–Apollo—are back-to-back. I was able to trade to have warm-up time for each of them. Shaman has to go earlier in the order than he likes. Sometimes I think he can count!" She looked at Ria. "I think I'm babbling."

Ria nodded and smiled.

Devin checked her watch. "It's game time. I need to put numbers on the horses' saddle blankets, and they'll be ready, and I'm as ready as I'm going to be today. Any last questions?"

Ria shook her head.

"Let's do this."

Forty-five minutes later, Devin rode out of the show ring on Shaman, the second of her three entries to qualify for the jumpoff round. A state patrolman stood beside Ria at the entrance to the warm-up ring.

The warm-up ring steward caught Shaman's reins. "Given the circumstances, you won't be disqualified if you walk over there for a little privacy."

Devin dismounted and approached Ria and the trooper. Devin pointed into the warmup ring. "I think we'll get more privacy there than outside."

They walked about twenty feet into the ring. The trooper cleared his throat. "The polo club president is a friend, and he called this morning when it seemed like more than car trouble was keeping your groom from getting here." He glanced at the loose clay at his feet. "About twenty minutes ago, we found a stolen SUV abandoned in a ditch not far from here. It was on its roof and the windshield was smashed. A license plate from Wendy Hilliard's Escort was on it."

# CHAPTER FIVE

*Enjoy yesterday's big win. Maybe you'll win again today. But your world is about to come crashing down. Literally.*

Devin should have been warming up Apollo for his round at the jumps, but she couldn't move. "You found a stolen car with her car's license plate on it."

"That's right, ma'am."

"She wasn't in it."

"No, ma'am. The vehicle had been abandoned."

The ring steward touched Devin's arm. "Debbie says she'll trade places with you, but Apollo will be disqualified if you aren't ready after her ride."

Devin nodded. "I think I'm almost done here." She turned back to the trooper. "I don't know what I'm supposed to say except find her."

He nodded. "We'll do what we can. We'll keep you posted."

He turned and took two steps before Devin said, "Wait!"

She put up a hand to stop the attendant approaching with Apollo. "Was there a bad accident on the east-bound side of the turnpike this morning, some time between ten and eleven?"

The patrolman shook his head. "None I'm aware of. Why?"

"Someone allegedly called the club office somewhere in that time frame to say Wendy might be stuck in traffic there due to an accident."

He shook his head again. "Today's been the only good day we've had on the turnpike this week." He glanced toward Apollo. "Good luck."

As he exited the ring, Devin walked toward her horse. She exhaled and repeated like a mantra, "Task at hand task at hand task at hand."

"Nothing is wrong, Miss Lady?" the attendant asked as he boosted her up onto the tall stallion.

"Nothing that can be fixed right now. I need to get Apollo ready for his turn."

As Devin rode toward the show ring, shaken and distracted, she was thankful elegant, predictable, dapple-grey Apollo was the horse under her. Crowd noise didn't bother him; he actually preferred cheering, clapping audiences. Daylight, artificial light, pouring rain, muddy footing—none of those mattered. Just turn him toward the jumps and give him enough rein. "I hope you remember the jump order, Pal, because I'm not sure I do," she remarked as they entered the ring.

She took a deep breath and exhaled loudly.

Apollo flipped his ears and swished his tail, and she signaled him to break into a trot. "Okay, Pal, the kid's time was sixty-one-even, and Sammy's time was fifty-eight-three. What time sounds good to you this round?" She nudged him into a canter. As they passed the timer, she lined Apollo up for the first jump. "Let's do it, Pal. This round's for Wendy."

For fifty-eight seconds, Devin's world was outlined by Apollo's grey ears. As colors and noises swirled around her, all she saw were the obstacles ahead, heard nothing but the thud of his hooves. After they passed the timer to stop the clock, Apollo tossed his head and bucked, his celebration after a clean round.

Devin was fairly certain she had held her breath the entire time.

As the last horse and rider came in, she quickly scanned the faces around the in-gate. No new uniforms, only the security personnel who had been there before. Ria waited at the entrance of the ready ring, holding Apollo's cooler.

"Mom and Dad are here, and plan to go for supper after your class is done. They want you to come with us, but I told them you probably wouldn't leave the horses."

"Three more rides, Ria, then I need to get home and see about Wendy." She dismounted and ran the left stirrup iron up on its leather.

Ria gave her head a slight shake. "I don't know how you do it."

Devin shrugged, reached for the cooler Ria held, and threw it over Apollo's hindquarters. She handed the attendant the reins, ducked to Apollo's right side and raised the other stirrup, and the horse was led away.

Ria patted the horse as he moved past her. "I know. It's how you win."

Devin pinched her lips together. "Today, it's how I let whoever it is know they aren't getting to me."

"Do you think they're here?"

Devin glanced beyond the white fence around the ring, seeing nothing but a kaleidoscope of colors. "I'm sure of it."

Chief stumbled coming off a jump. Shaman slipped as they took a tight turn. Apollo had a hard rub at the last jump and the pole rocked dangerously until they had passed the timer's electronic eye to stop the clock. Devin shook her head as the collective moan rose up from the crowd when the pole dropped. She turned back to look at the board; the "0" designating no faults remained lit.

She looked away, then back to the board, sure she'd see the "0" change to a "4."

Then the crowd roared. Apollo had won! Even with the other mishaps, Shaman placed second, and Chief came in third. Devin was wiping tears from her face as she rode in to collect their ribbons. *I wish Wendy had been here to see her boys win.*

Security personnel lined the walkway as the three horses were led back to the barn. Devin paced nervously from stall to stall, watching over the polo club grooms readying the three horses for transport back to the farm, and packing up the rest of their tack, assorted gear and feed. She declined an offer from a club steward for someone else to bring her truck up to the barn.

"It's just across the driveway. I need some air."

Walking ahead of her flashlight-toting escort, she looked up from picking through her key ring as she reached the driver's door. She cocked her head to one side, and stared at the truck's back end. She didn't recall parking in such a deep rut to make it sit so low. She reached for the flashlight and trained its light on the tires.

"Oh, God!"

Both of the dual back tires on the driver's side were flat. Kneeling beside the big wheels, she touched the strands of steel belting where a big hole had been hacked into each tire.

Her heart pounded as she walked around to the passenger side, holding her breath until she saw those tires were intact. As Devin came around the front of the truck, she noticed the hood wasn't latched. She reached out to touch it but jerked her hand back.

She pointed to the club employee who'd escorted her. "You stay here."

Dodging moving vehicles and other people, she sprinted to the clubhouse. At the door she yelled, "Somebody call the police! My truck's been vandalized!"

Two hours later, night had completely settled in as Devin left the polo grounds for home. Hunching her shoulders, she shivered and nudged the heater lever up a little. She wished she had some driving gloves. All the thoughts she'd struggled to keep at bay came to sit with her in the darkened truck cab. The phone call Saturday morning, Wendy's absence, the deception regarding the turnpike accident. Wendy's license plate on the wrecked stolen car. The vandalism to her truck. She patted her pockets, dug in her purse and emptied the truck's glove compartment looking for cigarettes. Sighing, she recalled her vow that the last cigarette she'd smoked yesterday was to be her last.

She kept checking the rearview mirrors, relaxing a little when she realized there was no sign of a vehicle deliberately following the silver and blue truck. They lumbered past acres of farmland and small towns shut down until the next morning. Stars filled the blue-black sky. She tried to pick out the Big Dipper and North Star but became distracted by a pink haze at treetop level. Northwest, somewhere between Florian and Orange. Maybe a college group celebrating the weekend with a bonfire.

Devin turned off the main road, relieved to be only a few miles from her farm. She shuddered. The pink haze was much too big for a campus bonfire, and, without a doubt, from a large fire, very close to her farm.

*Please let it be at one of the homes in the new development across the road from Aunt Aggie's house!*

But she knew the light in the sky was too far to the right to be one of her aunt's neighbors. She slowed the truck, not ready to go around the next bend in the road, not ready to confirm the fear knotting her stomach.

She tried to concentrate on the road, the guard rail around the shoulder, the reflectors marking the turn. But her eyes flew back to the break between the trees, where, in daylight, she could see the cupola atop the roof of farm's big stone barn. That cupola, topped with its horse and hound weathervane, was a first glimpse of home, a marker for the last two miles.

Tonight, flames raked the sky. "NO NO NO!" Her eyes filled with tears, and she could barely breathe. Devin stopped the truck, covered her face with her hands and wept.

The bleating of a small car's horn roused her from her misery as it rocketed around the truck, heading toward the farm. One more bend in the road, and the flaming hulk of the big barn stood behind the silhouettes cast by a thin stand of trees. Cars abandoned by curious spectators created a maddening obstacle course along the narrow ribbon of pavement.

"I hope the fire trucks used the main road," Devin muttered, inching around a double-parked car.

A group of people ran in front of the truck, so close she had to stand on the brakes. As she waited for the road to clear, she stared at the inferno, recalling all the nights she'd spent in the ancient barn, feeling surrounded and comforted by the essence of the Civil War soldiers and Depression-era fathers who had also taken refuge there. Her horses had been quartered in the same stalls used by mighty draft animals and fine carriage horses.

The tears in her eyes multiplied the image into several fires.

When she reached the cement pillars standing sentinel at the farm's gated service road, she had to carefully creep between vehicles double- and triple-parked on both sides of the road, barely far enough apart for her truck.

As she fished out the key for the gate, she watched a half-dozen young men scale and scramble over the wrought iron barrier. At least a dozen more shoved past as she pulled it open. Another group surged around the truck as she started forward down the road. The crowd hustled ahead, seemingly oblivious to the truck rumbling behind them. When they turned and squinted into its headlights, their expressions seemed to question why the vehicle was there. Devin honked the horn, and a tall, dark-haired man gave her the finger without turning around.

She backed into an empty spot at the corner of the paddock's high stone fence. Further on, policemen held back the crowd, five and six people deep, that stretched as far as she could see across the paved lot and garage area, all the way to the caretaker's house. The spectators milled about, unearthly shadows in the surreal white-orange light of the fire. To Devin, they were too much like the fleeting images in her frequent nightmares.

The figures moved as one, an eerie surf, surging back to avoid the fiery precipitation of debris and sparks raining down from the roof, then rushing forward to the boundary of hard-hatted volunteers and sawhorses to stay in the front of the crowd, closest to the spectacle.

The field behind the paddock fence was illuminated by the fire and the lights of the rescue vehicles. There, the fluorescent-trimmed hats, coats and boots of the firemen did a herky-jerky dance as their wearers trained their hoses on the flames.

Suddenly a dark horse, a gangly yearling, burst through the barn door, its head covered so it couldn't see the fire. It reared and tossed its head, shaking off what looked like a jacket. The frightened animal turned and dragged its handler back into the burning building.

The barn was supposed to be empty! Devin leaped out of the truck and clambered up onto the paddock fence. She jumped down and ran across the grass field.

A fluorescent cuff grabbed her shoulder. "You can't go in there!" a fireman snapped. "We got one hero already."

"There aren't supposed to be any horses in there."

"Well, supposedly there is one, and somebody's trying to get it out. Don't have much time. That roof's gonna go any second."

The fireman tightened his grip on her arm and jerked her backward as an explosion blew out the wall between what had been two windows. Shivering, Devin pulled her jacket closed and hugged her arms around herself. She backed up even more and hunched down near the driver's door of a fire truck as chunks of rock and burning wood crashed to the ground.

"Who went in for the horse?" She had to shout her question twice before the fireman gave any indication he heard her.

"Don' know. He said the horse was priceless and he had to get it out. An' he was going in whether we liked it or not."

"What did he look like?"

"Lady, we weren't exactly introduced. There's a fire here, y'know? He was going to get the horse or die trying. We gave him a mask, a hard hat and our best wishes. Okay?"

Again the horse lunged through the door, leaping stiff-legged toward the fire trucks and men. It slipped and stumbled among the broken slates, shattered wood, wet grass and hoses, wrestling its handler every step of the way. A broken halter dangled from its neck.

The man on the other side of the horse struggled to stay on his feet and keep control of the terrified animal. As they lurched along, she glimpsed no more than a hard hat and a gas mask. Several of the firemen helped the handler guide the colt toward safety.

She thought she heard the stomping of hooves on a loading ramp, but a noise like the rumbling roar of a train drowned out all others. The barn shuddered and swayed as the overheated stones in its walls grated against one another, making noises like wretched, tortured animals. The heavy slate roof crashed to the ground in a mighty explosion of fireballs and flying, flaming debris. Devin slowly stood up.

In that brilliant flash of light, Devin spotted Wendy's car parked where she always parked beside the barn. Did that mean–? She took several steps forward, but a fireman blocked her way.

"Miss, it's not safe for you to be here." Another fireman tried to shepherd her to the rear of the ladder truck, but she kept side-stepping away from him, her eyes on the flames. "Stay back and let us do our job."

She closed her eyes and leaned against the front of the fire truck for a moment, fighting back tears. *Please let this all be a horrible dream!* But nothing had changed when she opened her eyes.

As bits of burning cinder and wood stung her face, Devin picked her way across the rubble-strewn grass. She craned her head to see over the paddock fence, to her left and then ahead of her, looking for the vehicle that might be carrying the colt saved from the fire.

She paused about fifty yards from her truck to take one long last look at the fire. She gazed at the flames, hands clasped over her mouth, choking on her tears and the hot, heavy air. She stood there several minutes before a chorus of shrill whinnies jarred her back to her immediate, pressing responsibility. "I'm coming, guys."

Back at the truck, she opened a side door and stepped up into the stall compartment to quiet the restive stallions. "Hey, guys, the good news is you'll be out of here soon."

They nickered at her, tossing their heads, moving as much as the cramped stalls allowed. Chief was closest to the door. He nuzzled her pockets and lipped the zipper on her jacket. She stroked his sleek neck. "The bad news is–" Her words caught in her throat.

Beautiful, elegant Apollo, in the center stall, snaked out his head and snapped at her arm. He disliked even the most minute change in his routine, and the past days had been full of them. He pinned back his ears and snapped at her again, catching the fabric of her jacket sleeve and tearing it. The sound startled all three horses, and they reared and pawed.

"Settle down, Pal." She tugged at one of the leather tethers attached to either side of Apollo's halter as she spoke to him. She scratched his chin. "C'mon. Give me a break. None of this was my idea."

Apollo jumped when a vehicle parked nearby backfired as it was started.

Devin evaded the snapping teeth and reached out to rub the velvet muzzle of the third horse.

"How about you, Sammy? Can I count on you to be patient a little longer?"

The white blaze splashed down Shaman's black face seemed to glow in the eerie light inside the truck. Sam the Sham, she called him. He rolled his mismatched eyes, one China-blue, one brown, then kicked the back gate of the truck. Devin knew he'd try to kick his way out if he wasn't let out soon.

"Hang in there, guys. I'll have you out of here as quick as I can." Shaman nuzzled her cheek, then butted her with his head. "I don't have any food, Sammy. I don't even have any cigarettes. How bad is that?"

He snorted in her face.

"I totally agree. Okay, I'll get you out of here as soon as I can."

The crowd had thinned by the time she pulled herself back up into the cab. She had a clear view of the brightly-lit parking area between the barn's fiery carcass and a row of garages. She could see Ian, her former partner, with his brother and parents, standing under the basketball hoop above the center garage door. Ian's girlfriend, Jesse Tyler, was with them.

What were they talking about that was so funny they were doubled over, laughing? Had any of them wondered where she was, or noticed the truck parked there? And what about that horse? The person who brought it out seemed far too tall for Ian.

*Mark?*

She laughed at herself the instant his name popped into her head. He'd be the last person on earth she'd expect to go into a burning building to rescue a horse. Definitely not Mark. He might ruin the manicure on one of his long, tapered fingers.

She grasped the ignition key but paused before starting the engine. Earlier in the day, she had again seen him outside the warm-up ring, just before the jump course in the show ring was opened for rider inspection. When she came back for Chief's warm-up, Ria had confessed, "I have to agree, the person who watches the house definitely isn't Mark."

When she had been given a leg-up onto Chief, and as she settled herself into the saddle, a cold realization hit: Mark was at the only show Wendy had ever missed. And now she was back at her farm, and her barn was in ruins, and someone had rescued a horse that wasn't supposed to be there.

She turned the key and the truck's engine rumbled. A knot of people ambled past. She waited, drumming her fingers on the steering wheel.

*Mark at the show, Wendy missing. A coincidence?*

Had he cut up the truck tires and pulled out the distributor wires? No, the Mark she knew would never do anything to get his hands dirty.

She watched a trio of young men lighting their cigarettes. She licked her lips, envying their enjoyment of that first drag. The men strolled out of her way, under the trees shading the end of the paddock. She clawed through the glove compartment's contents, hoping a pack—or even a single cigarette—had materialized where none had been before.

She looked up from her search as an old Jeep towing a battered trailer rolled out between the trees. The driver had a soft snap-brim cap pulled low over his face. He kept his eyes on the slow-moving people as he steered through them, past her truck.

It had to be another coincidence. She was tired and the lighting was bad. The aristocratic chiseled jaw she glimpsed as the vehicle passed hers had to belong to someone else. Rescue a horse from a burning barn? That wasn't the Mark Frasier she knew.

The Jeep turned right at the end of the lane, onto the paved road. As Devin waited for a car to go by, she again thought of the argument she and Ria had just before Ria left.

*Maybe she was right. Maybe I don't know Mark anymore, either.* She turned left, toward her aunt's house, then mused aloud, "Maybe I don't know anybody anymore."

The truck hadn't moved ten feet before Devin smelled burning rubber. Probably one of the engine belts. She turned on her flashing hazard lights and kept on driving, determined to get to Aunt Aggie's driveway.

A few feet further, the engine banging, clanking and vibrating, she pulled to the side of the road to let a car pass. Its headlights cut through the dense smoke billowing out from under the truck's hood.

She didn't bother to count the vehicles that passed her disabled truck without stopping to offer assistance, and soon she was hacking through the mangled belt wrapped around the fan and hoses. "At least the vandal left me the flashlight."

As she cut away each piece of belt, she wondered if it had been nicked or loosened before she left the polo club or as the truck sat by the paddock during the fire. Or if the belt had just broken.

"Another damned coincidence," she muttered, unlocking a storage bin in front of the stalls where she kept extra belts, fuses, light bulbs and oil. "God, I hope whoever did this left me a belt to put on this truck so I don't have to walk these horses down this road in the dark."

Two belts were there, and the bent screwdriver that made installing them easier. By the time she had the new belt in place, the crescendo of pawing and kicking had risen to a truck-vibrating pounding.

The new belt emitted a short sharp squeal as the engine started. "Just get us home." She patted the truck's dashboard. "I'll make that fit right tomorrow."

As she drove past the darkened manor house, a stately Victorian mansion where her aunt lived, she was thankful Aggie Hall was away on vacation. The old lady had a bad heart and hadn't been well lately. Had she been home, Aggie would have badgered and bothered until someone found Devin that night. Or gone out looking herself.

Two hundred yards behind the house, a small barn's silhouette stood out in front of the fire-brightened sky. It was a scaled down duplicate of the ruined barn. She hoped the horses would be happy to be out of the confines of the truck and settle down quickly.

She stopped in front of the gateless opening in the paddock's stone wall, some twenty yards from the door in the barn's lower level. The space had been built to accommodate a horse-drawn hay wagon, not a twentieth century van. The horses would have to come down the truck ramp in no more illumination than a flashlight's rays.

Devin congratulated herself for leaving a pick-up truck load of hay and straw on the storage floor upstairs. As least she wouldn't have to lug them from the truck before she could ready the stalls. She crossed the dark pasture and unlocked the barn door and turned on every light in the lower level and the single floodlight over the paddock. As she slowly climbed the stairs to the storage floor, she heard, "Will the horses be safe here?" The sentence echoed so loudly in her head she was certain she had spoken it aloud.

Her heart began to pound. Surely her assailant had known about the renovation project in the tack room, the reason she'd planned to move the horses to this barn after the horse show.

As she felt for the light switch, Devin squeezed her eyes shut. She was afraid she'd open her eyes to find an empty spot where she'd left the load of hay and bedding.

Devin opened one eye then the other, then exhaled the breath she'd been holding. Everything was right on the lift where she'd left it. She stepped onto the platform and reached for the switch. Her hand flopped to her side.

Cat Mama's lifeless body was stretched out on top of one of the bales, her head twisted around to an unnatural angle. Devin touched the dead barn cat, her body still warm. The voice rang through her head again: *"How safe is this barn?"*

"Do I have a choice?" she muttered, flipping the switch to move the lift. She sat on the hay bale beside the animal and gently moved Cat Mama's head to a normal position and stroked her fur until the lift reached the basement.

As the wooden platform thumped onto the clay floor, someone called out from the barn door, "Hello! Anybody here?" Devin froze, her stomach fluttering and knees turning to jelly.

Mark Frasier was as she always remembered him: hair gleaming gold in the dim light, body by Nautilus, a god wearing faded jeans and an aged sweatshirt that would look sloppy on anyone else.

"Damn, you look good," she admitted reluctantly.

"You look like hell." He gave her that smile, the one that could melt stone, the one she would have done anything to see each day of the last year and a half. But not tonight.

She leaped off the lift. "Why did you show up this weekend after all the time that's passed?" After a moment's pause, she added, "Should I feel honored?"

The smile disappeared. "Ria tracked me down at the library a couple of days ago, breathing fire, demanding an explanation about why I can treat you the way I do. She threw a bunch of letters at me—"

She jumped on Mark's words. "What letters?"

"They were letters you wrote to me, that I supposedly had the Postal Service return to you. Whoever marked them 'Refused' was a lousy forger."

"Is that why you're here, the letters?" she shot back. "You didn't write, you didn't call–"

"I tried to call." His voice was cold and hard. "The last number I was given for you was an escort service."

"At least someone thinks I have an interesting life." She turned back to the lift and carefully picked up Cat Mama, taking her to the tack room and placing her on a sheepskin saddle pad as tenderly as if the body had been a newborn baby. After stroking the dead cat again, she picked up a pair of work gloves. As she put on one glove, she looked up at Mark, waiting in the tack room door. "As long as you're here, I need some help."

She wanted him to know how he had hurt her by dropping out of her life, but all Devin felt was her own longing to be with him. She put on the second glove, looked up again and met his eyes.

Mark's eyes were hazel, more gold than brown, like a lion's. He wore the slightest hint of a smile. "Ria says you still love me. Is that true?"

"I don't know if the person I loved a long time ago exists anymore." She stepped back into the tack room and grabbed another pair of gloves, slapping them into the hand he held out. "Can you be useful as well as decorative?"

She opened three stall doors and watched in amazement as Mark dropped a bale of straw in front of the center door and broke the bale apart. "When did you become a stable hand?"

He wrinkled his nose as he handed her several pieces of the bale. "I heard it was a great way to pick up girls."

"Where'd you take the horse?"

He gave her a blank look. "What horse?"

"The one you led out of the fire."

He chuckled. Devin looked away as her heart did some rsaults.

"You must have seen someone else. You know me. I wouldn't lead any horse anywhere, much less out of a burning barn." He moved closer and touched her cheek.

Devin abruptly pulled his hand away from her face. "How did you know I'd be here?"

"Where else would you go with your horses?" When she didn't reply, he asked, "What happened to the cat?"

"She's still warm. Somebody broke her neck."

"What's going on?"

She shook her head.

His hand closed around hers, and he took another step closer.

"Don't." She backed away, shaking her head. "The person I know doesn't go to horse shows or touch bales of anything. Your face is familiar, but I don't know you."

He walked back to the lift and she finished spreading straw in the stalls. After he dropped a bale of hay nearby, he said, "You did really well today."

"You stayed till the end?"

"You won first, second and third place, even with a visit from one of Connecticut's finest before you took Apollo in for the jump-off round. And the mishaps. I heard it was the first Grand Prix for the colt. Third is amazing for a debut class."

Devin paused on her way from the tack room, her hands filled with hay nets and buckets for feed and water. "When did you get so knowledgeable about show jumping?"

He smiled slightly. "I overheard someone nearby say it. I've read about it in the paper. You'd be impressed to see all the clippings I have with your name in them." He took the water buckets. "I can fill these for you if you want to start unloading." When Devin opened her mouth to protest, he reminded her, "You don't know me, remember? The other guy doesn't do this, but I can."

The moment of silence that followed was broken by the muffled sounds of pawing and kicking coming from the truck. Devin looked Mark up and down and directed him to a sink in the tack room. "You'll see the brackets to hang them in the stalls."

She jogged across the grass with a lead rope in one hand and a flashlight in the other. *Thanks for the help, God.* She glanced skyward as the prayer ran through her head. *I'm sorry if I don't seem properly appreciative.* She walked around the back of the truck and stopped when she saw the brown station wagon parked beside it.

# CHAPTER SIX

Devin walked around the car, an older Volvo station wagon with a few dings and dents, and all the standard factory body trim where it should be. Massachusetts plates, a Harvard Faculty parking sticker for 1998. And four matching, top-of-the-line, black all-season radial tires.

"I've had it awhile."

Devin jumped at Mark's voice behind her. She glared at him. "I thought you had a Firebird. It was two shades of blue, with the bird on the hood."

"Right. It was stolen about two weeks after you graduated. I bought this car from a friend when the insurance company dragged its feet about a settlement on the Firebird."

"A brown station wagon."

Mark looked confused and nodded slightly.

She wanted to scream at him, recount all the nagging coincidences, but she snapped, "Just stay out of the way."

As she pulled down the loading ramp, Mark asked who she would bring out first.

"Shaman, the spotted one who placed second today. Don't stand near the ramp because he's been known to jump over the side. Tonight he could take off toward the fire with me flapping in the breeze, trying to hold on."

"I'll hold the flashlight for you."

"Just stay out of the way." She reluctantly handed over the light. "Don't say I didn't warn you if he mows you down."

The big horse planted his hooves at the truck door and refused to budge another step.

"C'mon, Sammy," Devin wheedled, tugging the lead line she'd clipped to his halter. "Scared of the dark?"

Mark trained the flashlight on the wide cleated walkway, and the horse hesitantly place one hoof into that pool of light. When Mark moved the light, Shaman moved another hoof. Step by step, precisely in the puddle of light, Shaman made his way to the bottom. Prior to stepping off the ramp, he sniffed the ground, much like a dog, then jerked up his head and looked around the shadow-filled paddock.

"C'mon, Sam," Devin cajoled. "You've been in strange barns before. Think of it as just another show."

Shaman flipped one long black ear at her and nickered. As they crossed the paddock, he shied and jumped at unseen obstacles every few steps. Devin was relieved when she finally closed a metal stall door behind his spotted rump.

Mark looked at the horse through the bars on the top half of the door. "He's one funky-looking animal, with the spots on his butt, white legs, different-colored eyes, and the whisk broom tail. My friends wondered how much Appaloosa blood he has."

"Supposedly he's a quarter App and three-quarters of the bluest of blue Thoroughbred blood. It's amazing the App traits are there at all. We're waiting to see if he throws spotted foals."

"Rather atypical for a show jumping horse, so I was told."

Devin nodded her head. "He and Apollo were part of a consignment package of five horses. The other three horses were nothing special and went back. Nobody wanted Sammy because he looks funny, and both he and Pal were difficult to handle, and still are."

As she and Mark walked back to the truck, he asked, "Does he always act like that when you unload him?"

"Sam the Sham?" She shook her head. "I never know what he's going to do. I didn't know 'walk' was within his capability. He rarely does it."

"What about the next one?"

Devin gave Mark a sidelong glance. This unfamiliar side of him totally unnerved her. "See this?" She held out her arm, with its ripped jacket sleeve, for inspection. "Pal–Apollo, the grey–is not happy today, even though he was the big winner at the show. Usually he only bites me when he's in this mood, but tonight anything might be a target."

Apollo waited with his ears laid back, not a good sign, as she clipped the lead onto his halter. As soon as his head was freed from the short tethers in the van, he bit her hand.

"Hey!" she scolded. "You won today. What's with the attitude?"

Apollo snorted in her face and carefully made his way down the truck ramp. The grey horse placidly walked over to Mark and sniffed his arm, then nuzzled his cheek.

"I thought this was your ferocious, man-eating stallion," Mark commented, as Apollo continued his quiet stroll through the grass.

"He isn't in yet," Devin reminded him.

At the barn door, Apollo took one look, laid back his ears and clamped his teeth around Devin's wrist.

"Jeez, Pal, give it a rest!" Mark grabbed Apollo's lower jaw and squeezed until the horse released his hold on her arm, a trick usually employed to make a horse accept the bit when being bridled.

Devin dropped the lead line and rubbed her wrist. "Who taught you that?"

Mark patted Pal's neck and twitched one shoulder. "Mmm… maybe I saw it on that Canadian station that broadcasts on SportsChannel." He caught the lead rein and walked Apollo to his stall.

Devin watched and shook her head. Wendy was the only other stranger Pal had accepted so quickly. She was wondering what other surprises lay ahead. Not waiting for Mark, she returned to the truck for Chief.

The youngster whinnied as Devin reached the bottom of the ramp. He pitched around in the stall, eager to be out of the confines of the truck. He had twisted himself around in his narrow slot, had the ties pulled so tightly Devin thought she might have to take off his halter to free him.

The lead rope slipped from her hand as she wrestled the horse for a fraction of an inch of slack to unclip the ties on either side of his halter. She barely had time to think "Oh, shit" and grab the chin strap of the halter before Chief realized he no longer was tied in the stall.

Usually Chief was the horse who carefully chose his steps down the ramp, but tonight he made the exit Devin had expected of Shaman, plunging into darkness off the ramp with her hanging onto his halter and a handful of mane for dear life. Mark jumped out of the way as Chief bounded through the gate, tore across the grass to the barn, and galloped through the last open stall door.

"And I wonder why Wendy didn't show up," Devin muttered, rubbing her back and looking for blood. "I'm going to hate the three of you in the morning." The colt nuzzled her shoulder as she removed his leg wraps. He turned to his hay as she pulled off his blanket. "Nighty-night, kiddo."

Mark pushed the door closed as she limped out of Chief's stall. "Are you all right?"

She shrugged. "A day in the life. You wouldn't happen to have any cigarettes, would you?"

"Bad habit there, lady."

"And you're the one who got me started." She checked the latch on Chief's stall. "I'm trying to quit. Some days are better than others." She moved on to Shaman's stall, and rattled the door latch. "Thanks for putting out the hay and feed. I guess you saw that on–uh–SportsChannel, too."

He made a face and nodded. "I watched you do it enough. I thought I could figure it out." He must have noticed her watching as he reached up to the top of one of the stall partition supports and retrieved an unopened pack of cigarettes. As he fished matches from a pocket, he explained, "I put them there when I came in. I heard about the fire on the news, and I knew you'd be driving into it. I guessed you'd need more right about now." He zipped open the cellophane wrapper. "I quit a few months ago, but Ria told me that me and smoking are your two worst habits, and she'd like nothing better than to break you of both of them." He handed the pack to Devin.

He held the match as she lit up.

*He couldn't possibly have been in the fire. He should stink like everything else but I can smell his cologne.*

"Thanks. For the help, for the cigarettes..." She shrugged and gestured with upraised palms.

Mark grabbed her tightly in his arms and kissed her. Devin squirmed and pushed him away. "How can you think you can come back after so long and everything will be fine?" she demanded, taking several steps backward. "Why now?"

"All I've done since I saw Ria the other night is read and reread every scrap of paper she gave me. I can recite some of the letters word for word. Okay, I screwed up. I tried to prove to myself I didn't need you or anyone else and I failed miserably."

"But why did you choose this show, this weekend, to show up?"

"What does it matter?"

"You dropped out of my life for eighteen months. Stuff has been happening to Ria and me that we can trace to the Harvard campus. You made yourself very obvious to me at the only show my groom hasn't attended."

"Devin, I might have seen your groom on TV once, but aside from recalling that she's tiny I couldn't tell you what she looks like. I was surprised to see Ria walk the course with you yesterday, and that was the only reason I went back to the warm-up ring, even though I know you don't want any distractions there, probably less-so today. My friends and I stopped for supper tonight and saw a newscast about the fire on the TV in the bar. That's why I'm here."

"Ria said she made some comment to you yesterday about the security guards at the warm-up ring."

As Mark nodded, Devin pondered just how much she should tell him. "You said you saw the state trooper today."

"So?" He moved one foot, as if to take a step toward Devin.

She put up a hand to stop him.

"You have an old brown station wagon."

"Yeah, I notice a lot of them on the road. What's your point?"

"There's one involved in whatever's happening to me."

"Is it a Volvo?"

"No."

Mark broke the long moment they stared at one another. "Add bad timing to my list of faults then. It's the first weekend I haven't had a Saturday morning tutoring session when the show you were riding in wasn't several states away."

"What subject do you tutor?"

"English as a Second Language at a community center," he snapped. "As if it matters."

Shaman noisily pawed at his straw, and Devin glanced in at him. "I have to close up the truck." She lit another cigarette as she walked out of the barn, and stared up at the paddock light as she took three quick drags. She glanced around as a car door somewhere nearby slammed–maybe at the caretaker's house, or one of the homes in the development across the street–then crossed the wet grass to the truck. She finished the cigarette and flipped away the butt before wrestling the ramp back up into place.

Mark appeared by her side, pushing the balky gate. "I'll help you."

"I don't need your help."

He closed the truck's back door before answering. "I said that too. I didn't love you, I didn't need you, I didn't want you." He seemed surprised at his confession. "I finally realized I can't live without you."

"Right. More of that great timing of yours, I guess." She watched headlights on an approaching vehicle, bumping over the lane between the burnt-out main barn and the small one.

The farm pick-up truck's engine was still rattling and grinding when Ian Marques leaped out and bounded toward them. "Where's Wendy?"

Devin coughed as she inhaled the smoky aura surrounding him. "She never showed up. Why?"

He shrugged. "Her car is up by the barn."

"I saw it when the roof collapsed. She had car trouble this morning and never made it to the polo grounds." Devin was reluctant to share with Ian what little information she had about Wendy's predicament.

"Who took care of your horses?" Ian looked Mark up and down, then turned his back to Mark and jabbed a thumb in Mark's direction. "What's he doing here?"

She glanced at Mark. "He came to watch the fire, like everyone else."

Mark smiled at her reply, his eyes never leaving her face. "She placed first, second and third today, thank you for asking."

As Mark spoke, Devin turned back to see Ian's reaction. Not surprise, just a quick look at her before pursing his lips and looking at the ground. He took a step closer; Devin stepped back.

Ian coughed, loud and exaggerated. "Like I said, why's he here?"

"Ria's worried about Devin's safety."

Ian glanced at Mark as he spoke. "Oh, yeah, right." He was a good six inches shorter than Mark, with the taut, muscular body of a gymnast. "Ria goes home to Mom and Dad, and sends him to the rescue. Did he get here before or after the fire started?" He reached for Devin's hand.

She jerked away and tucked her hands into her armpits for warmth. "You weren't here to help, Ian, so just drop it."

"Being your stable hand was never my job."

Devin tried to interpret Ian's expression as he watched Mark walk away. *Jealousy? Anger? Hate?* Any time they had ever been together around her, they were barely civil to one another. According to Ian, Mark wasn't good enough for her. And Ian had always made her feel like she wasn't good enough for him.

"What was so funny, while you and Jesse and your whole family were watching my barn burn? You were all laughing your heads off." If Devin hadn't been looking at Ian, she would have missed the fleeting scowl and narrowing of his eyes.

"Mom was worried about you. She kept asking if you were back from the show yet."

"Yeah, everybody looked real worried, standing under the basketball hoop, laughing away right after the roof collapsed."

Ian shrugged. "I don't know what you're talking about."

A car door opened and closed. Soon footsteps in the wet grass–and Ian's grimace–announced Mark's return.

Ian looked past her, into the night. "First, second and third, huh? For real?"

"Less than five seconds separated first and third place, with no faults."

"Huh." He ran a hand through his short black hair and bit his lower lip. "What order?"

"Doesn't matter. I took the top three spots without your help."

Ian's eyes narrowed again, accompanied by an ugly look past her as a jacket was draped over her shoulders. The scent of the cologne Mark always wore came up to mask the foul cloud around Ian. She pulled the jacket close to her body as the memory of the only night she'd spent with Mark interrupted her thoughts.

"So who took care of the horses during the class?"

"Ria was there, and the polo club supplied someone."

"Ria helped? I'm impressed." He sounded sarcastic. "Where was Wendy, if she left her car here?"

"I don't know, Ian." She flicked her hand. "Her landlady said she left for the barn at the usual time this morning, but she never made it to the polo grounds."

"I heard she wasn't there last night for Chief's class either."

She frowned. *How does he know that?* "She had a date. She does have a personal life."

Ian let out a little snort. "She probably partied too much and didn't feel like showing up."

Devin ignored Ian's goading. "Well, somebody showed up during the Grand Prix class. Carved up two of the truck tires and pulled out the distributor cap and rotor wires and laid them across the engine block. Nice, neat and deliberate."

Ian grabbed her arm, pulling the jacket off her shoulders. "Why didn't you call me?" He threw the garment toward Mark and stalked to the truck to peer at a tire.

"I called Triple-A and the police." Devin picked up the coat and put it on.

Finishing his inspection, Ian elbowed between her and Mark, turned down the jacket collar and tucked it firmly under her chin. "You should have tried to reach me."

"The partnership's over, Ian. That's how you wanted it. You said if I wanted things my way, I had to take care of myself. So, I did."

Ian made a louder snorting sound. "Whatever. Let's get the horses in."

"It's already done. Mark helped me."

"Now that was a good joke, Devin. Whaddya need, some straw? Some hay?"

"If you had intended to help, you would have been here an hour ago."

"I was talking to the firemen—"

"Well, I'm glad they have your statement. I'm sure I'll get to talk to them tomorrow."

"They were asking where you were."

"I was doing what I had to do. Now, you're going to leave and I'm going into the barn and try to get some sleep."

"Do you want me to stay with you tonight?"

"I'll be here if anything happens," Mark stated.

"You can leave anytime you want," Ian snapped.

"I'm staying."

They stared at one another.

"Enough!" Devin stepped back, hands on her hips, looking from one to the other. "You and your attitude, "she pointed at Ian, then past him at the pick-up, "There's your truck. Good night." He opened his mouth to protest, and she repeated, "Good night." She looked at Mark. "If you insist on staying, you sleep in the van."

"I don't sleep in trucks." Mark's angry expression matched his tone of voice.

"You will tonight, if you want to stay."

"Fine." As he turned away, he asked, "Where do you want my car?"

"It's fine where it is."

"I don't want my tires cut up or the engine taken apart."

"Whatever." She let out an exasperated sigh. "I'll open the doors so you can put it in the upper level of the barn."

As Mark walked to his car, Devin climbed the banked approach to the wide front entrance. Ian trailed her like a puppy. He fidgeted and jingled his keys as she unlocked the big sliding doors.

Ian touched her arm. "You're sure you don't want me to stay?"

She rubbed her eyes until she saw a kaleidoscope of colors. "Ian, I just want to get some sleep. Maybe things will be better in the morning. Just please go and leave me alone." She leaned hard against one of the eight-foot-tall doors to move it back along its track. As Ian struggled with the other one, she flipped a light switch and illuminated the stacked hay and straw in the otherwise empty space. Devin slumped against the wall, studying the post-and-beam framework above her head as Mark steered his car through the opening.

"I'll be back in a minute." Ian ducked outside.

Mark turned off the Volvo and climbed out as Devin strained to close the door she had opened. He crossed the expanse of rough-hewn floor to the opposite wall, leaned down and picked up something.

Ian returned and tossed two packs of Marlboros at her. "Here. These should hold you till morning. I'll lock the doors."

"Go for it." Hands shoved into her pockets, Devin watched Ian close the second door. She listened as the heavy frames thumped together, and the hasp scraped over the staple and the lock clicked, watching Mark walk toward her, examining whatever he had found.

"What is it?" Her voice echoed in the huge open room.

"Who else has keys to this building?"

Devin hesitated. "I have a feeling there's more than mine. Why?"

"Can the doors be secured on the inside so keys can't work?"

"What did you find?"

In the palm of his hand was a scrap of stamped metal, the plain block letters NT, broken from the middle of a word. "Can you lock the doors from the inside?"

Devin ignored the repeated question. "What's that?"

"A couple letters."

She made a face. "I can figure that one out. Lisè–she does errands for Aunt Aggie–is an artist trying to find her muse, and, at one phase, did some metal sculptures from car parts up here."

He raised an eyebrow. "At one phase?"

"I haven't seen any of the sculptures, but Aunt Aggie has several very nice sketches and paintings."

He put the scrap into one of his pockets. "I better keep this for posterity then. When she has her one-woman show at one of the trendy galleries in The Village, we can wander among her *objets d'art* and match it up. Then you can brag about how you knew her when." He twitched an eyebrow, then winked. "Posterity, y'know."

He was here after so long, as handsome as ever, standing too close to her. The person she had loved since she was twelve. Her heart pounded so hard he must have heard it.

"WHAT?" Mark demanded so sternly Devin jumped.

"What?" She wondered if she had been thinking aloud.

"You're looking at me like I'm an axe-murderer or something."

"At least with an axe-murderer, there's no doubt what's on his agenda."

"Trust me, there are no bloody axes up my sleeve or in my car. I'm not even sure there's a tire iron in the car." He rubbed his forehead. "I'm here to help however I can. Ria says you don't trust anybody anymore—"

"Oh, really? I'm surprised she talked to you."

Mark shrugged.

"She thinks you're involved. Wants me to have you arrested."

"Call the cops." He sighed. "Right now, I'm going to walk you through the barn and make sure all the doors are locked and it's just you and the horses in here."

She didn't move.

"Are there any other doors up here?" Mark sounded as if he was struggling to be calm and patient.

Devin walked to the small entry door beside the big truck doors. She lifted one end of the heavy strip of metal fitting into brackets on the inside of the metal door and resting against the inside of the door frame. "As long as this bar is in place, this door doesn't move." She dropped the bar into its bracket. "And, yes, the windows are locked, even though all of them can only be reached by a ladder."

"Now, one more time, can you secure the big doors on the inside?" This time, Mark's voice had an edge to it.

"I put a new lock on the outside before I left Tuesday morning." She thought of Cat Mama's warm body on the hay lift. "Obviously, it wasn't enough." She returned to the big doors and flipped a rusted hinge over a toggle-style latch. As she turned the toggle, she indicated a second one near the floor with her foot. "It's not the greatest solution, but it's all there is."

Mark shook his head. "If you're planning to stay here alone tonight, let's check the other doors and windows." He went down the steps.

She paused at the top of the stairwell, taking another look around the storage floor before turning off the lights. On her way downstairs and back to the stall area, she thought of the trim piece Mark had tucked into his pocket.

*What had it told Mark that bothered him so?*

She found him, glowing flashlight in hand, carefully inspecting the multi-paned windows on the lower-level door.

"Do you think I'll be safe here tonight?"

He pointed to a deadbolt at the top of the door. "Are there slide bolts like this in the stalls?"

"Those doors are all nailed shut, as are all of the windows down here. Have been for years."

As he peered at the windows on each side of the door, she asked, "What are you looking for?"

He shook his head, not answering as he walked toward her. He leaned close and said in a low voice, "I got a whiff of perfume when I came down, and it isn't yours. Or mine."

Devin sniffed several times, but smelled nothing but the horses and the sweet scent of hay…and Mark's cologne. She shrugged. "You came out after I did."

"And I latched the door. So someone *was* in here."

"Mark, I won't leave these horses alone tonight."

"Did you call the police yet?"

"Oh, right." She pretended to hold a telephone with one hand. "Florian Police? I found a dead cat in my barn, and my friend smelled perfume." She dropped the hand. "They already think I'm paranoid."

"Ria said you're keeping a log–"

"And I'll make notes in it as soon as you leave." She went to the tack room for a blanket and froze at the door. "Cat Mama's body is gone."

"Now you're calling the police. Where's the closest phone?"

"Up at the house."

"Lock up here. I'll walk you up."

She began to shake. "What if–"

"Whoever was here must have gone out while we were upstairs." He nodded toward the stalls. "Do they seem all right?"

She entered each stall and closely inspected each horse, its food and the stall itself. When she finished, Mark asked softly, "You must be freezing. I have another jacket in my car. We can stop for it on the way to the house."

She nodded, then woodenly followed him out the door and turned the key in the lock. As they crossed the paddock, she noticed the smoky halo swirling around the paddock light had thinned somewhat, but the stench of the fire hung in the air.

Crickets and other night creatures had resumed their nocturnal serenade.

"Like nothing ever happened," Devin mused as Mark walked to his car and retrieved the promised jacket, then walked around the front of the truck, out of her sight. When he emerged on the opposite side of the vehicle, he had something in his arms.

"Here." He held out something bundled in a tweed jacket. "This was on the hood of the truck."

Devin looked down at the bundle and saw Cat Mama's body wrapped in a greasy University of Massachusetts sweatshirt.

# CHAPTER SEVEN

*I hope you're ready for a long night. When you were talking about that freak show horse of yours, I was so close I could have reached out and touched you. And you never knew it. I may be locked out of the barn right now, but I'm not done with you yet. Mark is right–he <u>won't</u> be sleeping in the van tonight. We'll make sure of that.*

As Devin closed her eyes and buried her face in Cat Mama's soft multi-hued fur, Mark commented, "You really should have a cell phone."

She lifted her head to look up at him. "I did. At one show, it only worked when I stood on the roof of the truck, and it was so static-y that I couldn't hear the caller. At another one, if there was a single cloud in the sky, it didn't work at all. And out here at the farm, it's like a black hole. I barely get radio reception, much less a cell tower signal. It's in a drawer in my office."

Mark lifted an eyebrow. "Where's the closest phone?"

"In Aunt Aggie's kitchen."

As she and Mark waited for the police to respond, standing on the gravel lane between Aggie's house and the paddock, she stroked the cat and tried to imagine what pain or torture

Wendy had endured to get her prized sweatshirt so dirty. *Had she been forced to cut the truck tires or vandalize the engine?* Devin let out a short laugh at that thought.

Mark stopped his pacing and peering around into the darkness. "It's good to hear you laugh, if that was a laugh." When she didn't reply, he asked, "What's the significance of the sweatshirt?"

"Wendy's boyfriend gave it to her. Someone must want me to think Wendy was wearing this when she vandalized my truck."

"You sound certain enough that Wendy wouldn't do that."

"Wendy knows horses. Things mechanical are hopelessly beyond her scope."

Mark was looking toward the road in front of the farm. "Car in the driveway."

Moments later, a tall thin uniformed man climbed out of the car, chewing a toothpick. "I hear y'all had some more problems today." He looked at Mark. "Care to tell me about it?"

*Oh, yippee, the redneck who treated Ria and me like we were complete idiots.*

Mark pointed to Devin. "You need to talk to her."

"Someone killed my cat," Devin began.

The cop cut her off. "You called us because someone killed a cat?"

"Yes. My barn burned down tonight, after someone vandalized my truck while I was at a horse show. My groom disappeared under suspicious circumstances." She held out the sweatshirt-wrapped body. "This is her sweatshirt, which she never got dirty. This cat's body was warm when I found her, and her neck had been broken. When we looked for her a few minutes later, her body was gone. Mark said he smelled someone's perfume, but it wasn't mine. He found the cat's body on the hood of the truck, which wasn't where I'd put it."

The cop transferred the toothpick to the other side of his mouth without saying anything.

"I see you don't have a notebook," Mark observed. "Don't you plan on taking any notes?"

"Far as I'm concerned, this is another nuisance call from someone who seems to get off on making them," the policeman replied.

"What's happening to me is a nightmare!" Devin shouted. "The police don't seem to care! I want your name and badge number."

He leaned against the unmarked vehicle. "A *Law & Order* fan, eh?"

Mark stepped up beside him, stood over him. "Do you have paper and a writing implement somewhere in that car?"

The cop looked up at Mark. "You threatening me?"

"Give me your name and badge number and get your useless ass out of here."

After making a big show of producing a notepad and pen, the cop scrawled something and shoved the paper into Devin's jacket pocket.

She pulled out the paper and glanced at it. "Skyler, 628. I'll be making a complaint about you. That's a promise."

"You think a complaint's gonna do you any good?" he sneered as he slid back into the car.

"Get off my property."

He rolled up his window, started the car and turned around, spinning up gravel and grass as he gunned the engine and drove away.

"What the hell was that?" Mark demanded.

"That's the treatment Ria and I have been getting. He's responded three times when we called and never took a single note. Someone named McChesney came to the cottage last week. He said there were only two reports filed about our complaints, even though we've called–" She shrugged. "I don't know how many times we've called the police."

Mark shook his head. "What happened to 'protect and serve'?"

Devin shrugged. "Officer McChesney said that the person or persons doing this to us haven't broken any laws because I can't prove anyone has entered my home uninvited, and I haven't been threatened." She hugged the dead cat closer to her as a tear trickled down one cheek.

Mark nodded towards the barn. "Go in and try to get some sleep. Do you want me to walk through the barn again?"

She shook her head. "It should be all right."

After fumbling with the deadbolt locks, Devin gently put the cat back on the counter in the tack room. She slumped into a corner of Chief's stall with a blanket and flashlight. "Like I'm really going to sleep tonight," she told the horse as he sniffed at the blanket and slobbered on the end of the flashlight.

Devin closed her eyes, and the image of Wendy's face popped into her mind. There had to be some other explanation for the grease on Wendy's prized sweatshirt! When she received it, a ring with a tiny diamond had been pinned to the center of the University of Massachusetts logo. Whenever Wendy thought she might get dirty, she removed the sweatshirt, carefully folded it and set it in a safe place. The ring never came off.

She drifted into sleep, enumerating Ian's litany of complaints about the groom he so detested: "We don't know where she came from. She's homeless. She never knew her old man. She has to stand on a box to groom and tack up the horses. She has to stand on a box...stand on a box...stand on a box...."

Someone trained a bright light on Devin's closed eyes and shook her shoulder. A woman said, "I knew we'd find her here." She heard thumping and heavy footsteps upstairs. She put her hands over her eyes and peeked through her fingers into the darkened stall.

*Another bad dream.*

Chief stood over her, looking out his window. She could see Apollo, in the next stall, in the same position. She heard footsteps outside.

She inched up to the window, afraid when she could see out she'd be face-to-face with someone. Instead, Mark was a few feet away, his back to the barn, looking around the enclosure. After a few minutes he walked toward the gate.

She had to check the barn. Had those noises upstairs been part of the dream? She played the beam from her flashlight across the open area in the basement. Nothing had changed there since she had turned out the lights.

She crept up the stairs, listening for any noise out of the ordinary. The horses pawed their hay and straw. The soft swish of wings high in the rafters–birds or bats coming in to their nests. Crickets predicting the next rainfall. Tiny feet scampering along and tiny squeaks–she stopped on the next-to-last step, leaning against the dusty wall to catch her breath when she remembered Cat Mama wouldn't be around to chase those mice.

She took the last step. The paddock light illuminated the storage floor. She inspected each window again, rechecking the locks. She peered out one of the windows overlooking the paddock and thought she saw a shadowy figure melt into the trees beyond the wall.

*At this point I could see Santa Claus and swear he was Charles Manson.*

Her footsteps echoed in the emptiness of the storage area as she crossed the uneven floor to the windows on the opposite wall. The thin sliver of moon turned the weathered fencerow and trees in the pasture below into black silhouettes against the dark-grey grass. A dog or fox trotted across the field and disappeared in the tree line.

Devin stopped in back of Mark's big boxy station wagon near the barn doors, listening. Someone walked past, slowly and cautiously, and continued down the bank to the rear of the barn, away from the paddock.

*Can that person also hear me moving around?*

In the basement, one of the horses nickered, a greeting usually reserved for someone familiar to them. Upstairs, Devin placed each foot carefully as she crossed the room. She kept to the side of the stairway, avoiding the steps that creaked as she descended.

By the time she reached the stalls, the horses were dozing or nosing at their hay. She went back to her blanket in the corner of Chief's stall, hoping to sleep for another hour or so.

At the grey light of dawn Devin was awakened by the horses' whinnying and pawing. All three horses were watching at their windows. The panes were streaked with dirt, making the person outside a bobbing shadow.

The latches rattled on the boarded-up outer stall doors. Chief barely missed stepping on Devin's leg as he pitched around in the stall. She jumped for the door when she had the chance.

Even in the dim light, through dirty window glass, she recognized the big man who had followed her around the mall. Stringy blond hair hung around his ears in greasy clumps. He wore a torn, shapeless maroon sweatshirt and black sweatpants. And black gloves.

He loped across the grass to the gate, the ungraceful, shambling waddle of someone not accustomed to much more than walking. When Devin fumbled open the deadbolt and two slide locks on the door and yelled, "Hey, you! Stop!", he never looked back. She ran after him but he disappeared as soon as he went around the paddock fence and the back of the van.

She tried to open every door and compartment on the truck, but all were locked. No one hid under the van. *Well, he didn't vanish.* She stood in front of the truck, wondering what to do.

After a few moments, Devin saw Mark running over the banked drive in front of the barn. When he was several yards away, he slowed down. She folded her arms across her chest. "You better have a damned good explanation for all this."

"Are you all right? I heard the horses and–"

"You lying bastard!" Devin slapped Mark across the face as hard as she could, knocking off his glasses. "You wanted to see me, you said. Did you stick the disguise in the van at the polo grounds when you vandalized my truck?"

He bent down to pick up his glasses before he looked at Devin. "I don't know what you're talking about."

"Nobody ran past you as you came up the bank?"

"No. Why?"

"My stalker was at the barn, knocking on the stall windows. He ran off past the van–he just disappeared." She noticed his faded old jeans and sweatshirt, spotless the night before, were now dirty and torn.

He inspected the glasses and put them on before replying. "At least two people dressed in black have been around the barn and fence all night long."

"I saw you out there before, but just now someone in a maroon sweatshirt was right outside the barn windows."

"They were wearing black. And they stayed outside the wall most of the time."

"Sure. I bet if I go down the hill, I'll find a pile of clothes."

"So go look, if you're so sure."

They stared at one another for a few moments before she averted her eyes and brushed past him. She took only a few steps before she heard a loud thud and the sound of smashing glass coming from the barn.

The breeze blowing through the broken window brought the stench of wet ashes into the musty storage area. A smooth, round black stone the size of a grapefruit lay among shards of glass scattered across the floor in front of Mark's car. Rubber bands crisscrossed the stone, securing a folded paper.

Devin picked up the rock, a souvenir from a trip her aunt had made to northern California's gold fields. Before it disappeared from the desk in her office, Devin had used it as a paperweight. Today it bore a message like the one she had found in her car, letters cut from newspaper ads, assembled to say "Are you starting to see things my way?"

As she looked down at the field below the window, hoping, maybe expecting, to see someone staring back at her, Mark inspected his car for damage.

"Somebody has a good arm."

"Did it hit your car?"

"No."

"One of the people you saw running around the barn?"

"Maybe." He reached for the stone, but she pulled back. "No, it might have fingerprints on it!"

He gave her an annoyed look. "Whoever heaved it up here from down there must have been a baseball pitcher or shot-putter."

A wispy female voice drifted up the stairs. "Hello! Where are you?"

"Aunt Aggie! When did you get home?" With Mark behind her, Devin clattered down the steps to greet her aunt.

Nearing seventy, Aggie Hall was barely five feet tall and slight, with a cloud of white hair and emerald-green eyes like her niece. She flung her thin arms around Devin and applied a bear hug that took Devin's breath away. "Are you all right?" Not waiting for a reply, she released her grip and held Devin at arm's length. "You look terrible! What's going on?"

"You don't want to know, Aunt Aggie. It's a nightmare."

Mark gently squeezed Devin's arm as he edged around her. He whispered in her ear, "I'll be outside."

Lifting an eyebrow, Aggie said, "I heard about the fire on the way from Sikorsky Airport. I hoped it wasn't true, but there was a police car in the drive when the cab dropped me off a few moments ago."

"The big barn's gone." Tears stung Devin's eyes and a lump formed in her throat. "It's gone."

"Oh!" Aggie gasped. "That's terrible! Was anyone hurt?"

"We can't find Wendy. She might have been in the barn."

The tiny lady pulled herself as tall as she could and jabbed a finger in the air to emphasize each word. "I'll bet that little weasel has something to do with that. He never did like that little girl."

"'Little weasel'?" Officer McChesney echoed, stepping up behind Aggie.

"That's what my aunt always calls Ian," Devin explained. She turned to Aggie, but was cut off before she could say a word.

Aggie stamped a foot for emphasis. "Well, he deserves it since that riding stable fiasco last fall."

McChesney turned on a cherubic smile and asked, "And what might that have been, Miss Hall?"

"There was a riding stable here, and that little weasel made everyone so miserable the owner just packed up and left."

Devin shook her head. "I think Susan Holt was able to take Sleeping Giant Stable up more than a few notches by moving. She's out near the park now, close to all the riding trails there. Her boarders didn't have as much room here."

Aggie shook her finger in Devin's face. "You mark my words. When you find out who's been causing all these problems for you, you'll find that little weasel in the thick of it."

"So far, we can't link anyone to anything," Devin replied.

"Mark my words. You heard it from my lips." Aggie glanced from Devin to the cop. "I'm going to go make you some coffee while you talk with this policeman."

"A cup of coffee would be great, Aunt Aggie. Thank you." As her aunt bustled past the stalls, Devin noticed the cop was leafing through papers in his notebook. "I'm glad you're here."

"I understand there's been more trouble since the fire."

"I just heard a window break upstairs."

"Okay. I came to show you a picture we received from New Haven this morning, but let's take a look at that window first." He looked at the narrow, steep stairs and whistled.

Devin directed him to the platform. "We'll take the hay lift up." As they made the bumpy ride, she pulled a crumpled wad of paper from her jacket pocket. She smoothed it out and held it out to McChesney. "I want to file a complaint against this cop."

McChesney looked over the paper and shook his head. "Who's that? I know all the Florian cops. He's not one of ours."

"He came out last night when I found another of my cats was killed."

He shook his head again. "I'll check it out, but I don't recognize the name or badge number."

"He's responded three times before. He drives an unmarked car."

"Do you know what kind of car? What color?"

"A dark blue Crown Victoria."

"Our only unmarked car is a Malibu, and it's in the shop for a brake job."

"He's been here three times, always in that Crown Vic."

The cop seemed to be mulling something over, then shook his head again. "Orange doesn't use a Crown Victoria either. Huh. No wonder there weren't any other complaints logged." He put the paper into a pocket on the inside of the folder he was carrying. "Did you call the same number you've used before?"

Devin nodded.

"What phone did you use?"

"In my aunt's kitchen."

"And you said you called because another cat had been killed?"

"The mother of the kittens that were killed last week." She looked into McChesney's blue eyes. Her chin quivered. "Her body was still warm, like someone waited till I got to the barn to kill her and leave her body for me to find."

"Did it disappear, like the others you saw?" The cop didn't smile as he made notes, then walked to the broken window. "Wow, it's pretty far to the ground from here!"

"This was on it." She showed him the paper. "And, no, I don't know what it means"

He rolled his eyes and shook his head. "What about the cat?".

"I found her when I came up to get hay and bedding for the horses. I put her in the tack room, then a little later Mark and I were up here, checking the doors and making sure everything was locked. He came down before me and said he smelled perfume. I went into the tack room and the cat was gone. Then Mark found her body on the hood of the truck, wrapped in my groom's sweatshirt."

"What did you do with the body and the sweatshirt?"

"I put them in the tack room down by the stalls."

He pulled a faxed photograph out of his notebook and handed it to Devin. "Is this your groom?"

Devin gasped. "Oh, Wendy, sweetie!" She studied the grainy image of a face with closed eyes, lips slightly parted, revealing the biting edges of the top teeth. The person's hair was matted and slicked down on the cheeks. "Is she dead?" Devin whispered.

"Is that your groom?"

"Yes." She leaned forward. "IS SHE DEAD?"

McChesney's eyes darted across a paper in the notebook. "She was alive when we were called."

Devin grabbed his arm. "Where is she? What happened to her?"

He consulted his paper again. "According to the information we received from New Haven, the victim was found this morning outside a men's dormitory on the Yale campus, babbling and incoherent, apparently under the influence of drugs. She had no identification on her."

"Where is she?"

"The Medical Center in New Haven," McChesney replied, sounding weary. "They said they were pretty sure she'd recover."

"Can I see her?"

He nodded. "What can you tell me about her, in relation to what's going on?"

"She was supposed to take care of my horses at a show near Norwich yesterday. At 6:30 yesterday morning, she called the office at the polo club where the show was being held, and left a message that she had car trouble and would get to the show as soon as she could."

She paused, remembering how the message had been delivered, and shook her head. "No. I was told that someone called about Wendy, but the person who took the call couldn't tell if it was a woman or a man."

"Last night, when did you get back from—where did you say you were? Norwich?"

"Ten? Ten-thirty? I don't know the exact time. Just before the barn collapsed." Devin turned toward the sound of footsteps on creaky stairs.

McChesney also looked toward the steps as Mark came up. "So you don't know if anyone was here, in this barn, yesterday."

Devin shook her head. "During the class I was riding in, a state trooper came and said they'd found a license plate from Wendy's car on a wrecked stolen car, an SUV. Later, someone cut up two tires on my truck and disabled the engine."

"I did get reports on both of those incidents." He whistled. "And you came home to the fire."

He shook his head as Devin said, "During the fire, I saw her car by the barn where she always parks."

"We'll be impounding it for further inspection. And I'll need to take that sweatshirt as well." He held out a hand for the photograph. "Where can we reach you if we have any more questions?"

"You have my home phone number. I check the voice mail often when I'm out and pass a phone." Devin handed over the pictures. "Can I bury my cat?"

He nodded. "But I'll need to take the sweatshirt."

Mark stepped forward. "What about the man she saw at the window, and the two people I was chasing all night?"

The cop clicked his ballpoint pen in and out several times. "And you are?"

"Mark Frasier."

"Where were you last night?"

"I'd been to the horse show with some friends from Orange. We were having drinks and chatting after supper when we saw the fire on the news."

"What time was that?"

"Eleven, I guess."

"You're still a student at Harvard?"

"Yes. And I teach." He paused. "Shouldn't you be looking for prowlers?"

Stan McChesney carefully slipped his pen into his shirt pocket before answering. "Miss Marques has been complaining about a tall blond man bothering her, and you fit the description. Why don't you stop by the police station in a little while and give us some fingerprints?"

"You aren't even going to walk around the barn?" Mark snapped.

"Why don't you and I stroll around the barn, Mr. Frasier?" The cop imitated Mark's tone of voice. "See what we can see."

They stared at one another for a few moments before Mark walked to the steps without waiting for the policeman to follow.

Devin stayed in the barn, feeding the horses, wondering what had happened to her aunt and the promised cup of coffee. *That walk around the fence is taking an awfully long time.* As the horses munched and pawed, she went upstairs and unlatched the big doors behind Mark's car. As she returned to the stall area, she heard voices outside, and hurried out to the paddock.

Aggie stood in the fence opening with an insulated Hartford Whalers mug in one hand. In her other hand she clutched a straggly blond wig. Draped across her arm were a maroon sweatshirt and black sweatpants. As Mark and the cop approached, she held out the clothes. "I found these over there near the fence, under one of the bushes."

"How could you?" Devin looked from the clothes to Mark. "Damn you!" To the policeman, she said, "Please take him away."

Mark, who was six and a half feet tall, looked at the size label in the sweatshirt. "Before you have me hauled away," he said, holding up the garment, "I want you to see something." He stripped off his light blue sweatshirt and struggled into the maroon one. "How did this fit on your prowler?" The sleeves fell several inches short of his wrists, and the waistband was at least an inch above his belt. "Tell me, Devin, how did he look?"

She gasped. *That sweatshirt would fit Ian.* Then she recalled hearing her horses whinnying when there were prowlers outside the stalls. They knew Ian.

She shook her head, unable to speak.

"It wasn't me, Devin! What do I have to do to prove it?"

"Where did he go, then? The truck doors were locked and I couldn't see anyone under it."

He grabbed the sweatshirt at the neck and ripped it apart, then shrugged it off. "I'm not your stalker." He flung the pieces to the ground, picked up his blue sweatshirt and walked away.

When the policeman cleared his throat, Devin looked up. "Can I come help someone make a composite sketch?"

"You can, but we don't have a lot to go on. The fingerprints we took from your house last week came up as a match for an AWOL soldier who allegedly died in a fire two years ago."

111

The officer gestured at the wig Aggie held. "And obviously, we're dealing with people who like to play dress-up. Without something to point us in the right direction, we can do nothing."

"Can I come look at mug shots?"

He shook his head. "I told you before, Miss Marques, this isn't *Law & Order*, and we aren't going to be done in an hour."

"The cop last night asked if I was a *Law & Order* fan." She paused, shook her head. "Can't you do anything?"

He stared her in the eye for a moment before responding. "What were you thinking when Mark put that sweatshirt on? Something crossed your mind."

She waved a hand. "One of those random thoughts out of nowhere that just popped into my head. It was nothing." Pause. "Except he did say the people he was chasing were wearing all black, and that one was maroon."

He nodded. "Maybe the lighting made them look different. But a bit of advice from someone who's been around too many blocks in his day: don't ignore those random thoughts, especially since it looked to me like it was more than nothing. With what's going on, maybe there's some truth in it. Meanwhile, we'll send patrols around your house and farm, but that's all we can do. Are you keeping that log I told you about last week?"

She gave her head a slight up-and-down twitch.

"Keep it in a safe place." He smiled, curling the corners of his mouth, but putting no emotion in it. "I'm sorry. I have a wife and two kids. If any of them were in your place, I'd pray to God someone else would get the bastard bothering them before I did." He took several steps toward his patrol car, pausing in front of Mark. "I'll see you later today for fingerprints, won't I?" He didn't wait for an answer.

Aggie handed Devin the Whalers cup. "I hope this coffee isn't cold by now. If you're done with the horses, why don't you come up for breakfast? It looks like we have a lot to catch up on."

"Thanks, Aunt Aggie, but I'm not hungry. I have to go up to the–where the fire was."

Aggie looked at the retreating policeman, wrinkling her nose and fanning the air in front of her face as the odor of his freshly-lit cigar drifted back towards them. "You do what you have to do. Stop by later so we can chat."

"I'll go with you," Mark offered after Aggie left.

"Leave me alone."

"I can hold your hand."

"I needed you to hold my hand when the strange phone calls started. I needed you to hover over me and tell me you were worried about me when someone was getting into my house. I don't need you now."

"I need you." He moved closer to her.

She backed away. "You don't need anyone. You told me that so many times, I lost count."

"I was wrong."

"You don't make mistakes."

"Yes, I do. I walked away from you, didn't I?" They stared at one another for several seconds. "I can prove I wasn't following you last Monday."

"How?"

"I'll get you the name and phone number of the lab where I was taking some tests that afternoon."

"What kind of tests?"

"What do you care?"

"I love you, remember?" She ran past the van to the upper barn entrance. She fumbled with her keys, trying several before she was able to open the lock. She looked back at the horse van as she heard one of its heavy doors slam. Mark put something into his pocket as he approached the barn.

*He probably picked up something he'd left in the truck's sleeping compartment.*

She clung to the door frame, suddenly numb and weak.

*Wasn't that door locked when I tried to open it a little while ago?*

She pushed open one big door, then the other, and looked at Mark's car through tear-blurred eyes. He couldn't be part of this conspiracy against her! She loved him too much! She backed the car out of the barn and wiped her face as he closed the doors. She couldn't let him see her crying.

She moved to the passenger seat and he slid behind the wheel.

"Are you all right?"

She folded her arms across her chest and shook her head. "How'd you get into the truck?"

He started the car before answering. "The door was open."

"It wasn't before."

At the site of the fire, Mark stopped the car at a yellow police barricade tape. He whistled softly. "Jesus Christ, look at that."

Devin couldn't reply. She struggled to keep from crying as she surveyed the remains of the barn.

The wreckage was worse than she had imagined: a stinking, smoking pile of broken rocks, charred wood and slate shards. She set down the mug of coffee Aggie had given her and climbed out of the car. Staring in disbelief, Devin stood behind her door, clutching it so tightly her knuckles were white.

Ian walked over; he had been talking with a guard whose jacket proclaimed he was from the fire department. "The police checked out Wendy's car this morning and found gasoline-spattered clothing and an empty gas can, and one of the license plates was missing."

"Yeah, I already know about the license plate. Did Officer McChesney come up and talk to you?" Devin's eyes never left the burned-out building as she spoke.

"He just left. He told me about Wendy." He cleared his throat. "High on drugs." He shook his head. "You knew what she was when you hired her." He paused. "What was she doing at Yale?"

"I don't have answers for anything that's happening, Ian." She glanced across the parking area to Mark, leaning against the hood of his car, arms folded across his chest, a stony expression on his face. His mirrored sunglasses made her shudder.

"I hear there was more trouble at the barn overnight." Ian cocked his head in Mark's direction. "I'll bet he's involved."

Devin looked him in the eye. "Some people think you are." His body stiffened and he scowled at her. She turned toward the fire site and walked slowly around the blackened ruins, wrinkling her nose at the smell.

A sporty red car entered the parking area, the driver shrilly singing, "Born to be wi-i-i-i-ild," Steppenwolf's pounding music blaring out the windows. The driver honked the horn as she backed the car into a spot beside Ian's truck.

"Devin! Yoo-hoo!" the new arrival bellowed over the loud music. Grasping the door frame and grunting, she hoisted herself from the car and tottered across the asphalt in red mules with three-inch heels. "Devin, how are you? I know your aunt would have been so worried if she had been home." The woman struck a pose, hand on hip, at the edge of the pavement. "Have you heard anything about Wendy?

With her too-red chin-length bob, long, blood-red fingernails, too-tight stretch pants and knit tunic, she reminded Devin of a character from a Fox TV comedy. Tall, beefy Lisè Logan had arrived.

Ian tried to steer Lisè back to her car. "Yes, we heard about Wendy. We're trying to get information from the hospital. Why don't you leave Devin alone right now? She's a little spazzed by everything that's happened."

Avoiding Ian, she "yoo-hooed" in Devin's direction again and waved a plump arm covered with charm bracelets. "Devin, is there anything I can do to help?" Her voice carried across the wreckage as clearly as if she used a microphone.

Devin waved but didn't look up. She feigned great interest in a part of the corner foundation. "Please leave me alone. Please stay away from me," she muttered over and over, under her breath.

Unsteady in her stilettos, Lisè returned to Ian's side. "The horses must have kept her up all night in that strange barn!" She waved her hands, making the bracelets tinkle like wind chimes. "Will you have this bulldozed now?"

"That isn't on today's list of things to worry about, Lisè," Ian replied, taking her arm in another attempt to guide her back to her car. "You really shouldn't be here while the investigation is going on. I don't know how you got past the fire police at the road."

"Oh, Ian," she cooed. "A little leg, a smile, a wink– I can do anything I want. Now, if I can't be here, how can that gorgeous specimen over there–" she pointed to Mark–" be here?"

"You know who he is, and you know why he gets special privileges. C'mon, Lisè. Just leave things alone today, okay?"

Lisè turned her attention to Mark. "Now why don't you and I go somewhere for coffee while they sort this mess out?" She beamed her brightest smile at the stone face.

As Devin watched, she decided Lisè had to be admiring her twin reflections in his sunglasses.

Lisè was close to six feet tall, plus the three-inch heels, and weighed at least two hundred-twenty pounds. Devin knew Lisè didn't threaten or intimidate Mark–no one did–but she was in his space. And his face. Yet he seemed to act as if Lisè wasn't there.

Lisè looked Devin's way and waved as she asked, "How's she taking this? She must be so upset!"

"Like Ian said, leave her alone."

"I just want to help her."

Ian joined them. "Why don't you try just backing off?"

Lisè smiled up at Mark. "Only if he 'backs off' with me." She linked her arm through Mark's, but he pushed her hand away.

Devin had begun picking a careful path right into the center of what had been the roof.

"D, don't go in there. Let it cool off first," Mark pleaded, taking a few steps toward the barn's remains.

"I think I see the weathervane." She poked around in a lump of debris. The pieces of slate were still hot and she had no gloves, so she used a sneakered toe to push through the rubble. The mangled object finally came free, a deformed lump of patined copper with one part ending in a drooping "S."

Lisè pranced back and forth along the edge of the asphalt, holding her arms out from her sides as if for balance. She took two tentative steps out onto the grass, stopping when her spike heels stuck in the turf. "Did you find it, Devin? Is that the weather vane?" She looked back at Mark and gushed, "It was so unique! Oh, show it to us, Devin!"

"Just stay put and keep your mouth shut," Ian ordered, grabbing Lisè's arm.

Mark tromped around rubble in the grass, into the crumbling foundation, stepping over a charred beam and slipping on damp wood and slate. He crouched beside Devin and put his arms around her. "Come on, lady, Ian has everything under control. We're getting out of here."

She waved Mark away as she held up the mutilated weathervane. "Whoever is responsible better take notice," she announced in a loud voice, raising the artifact over her head. As she faced one direction, then another, she continued, "I don't know who you are or why you're doing this to me, but I'm done being scared." She marched out of the wreckage, directly to Ian and Lisè, looking from one to the other. "Neither of you belong here. Leave."

Lisè made an exasperated sound and stalked to her car. She peeled out of her parking spot and rocketed down the drive.

Ian blocked Devin's path back to Mark's car. "I live here. Where would you have me go?"

"You have no reason to go anywhere near either of the barns."

"So I'm a suspect?"

Devin nodded slightly. "I know where I was yesterday when the fire started. What about you?" She brushed past him.

"What about him?"

Devin glanced back to see Ian pointing at Mark.

"His next stop after dropping me off at my car is the police station." She climbed into the passenger seat of the Volvo, keeping her eyes on the weathervane.

Mark slid behind the steering wheel and slammed the door. He started the car, moving onto the bumpy lane between the barns before he spoke. "I saw the broad in the red car stop by that stand of pine trees down by the road and pick someone up."

# CHAPTER EIGHT

*You silly girl. I'm not trying to scare you. I'm going to bring your world down around you and destroy you.*

Wendy Hilliard didn't have as many tubes and wires attached to her as Devin had expected. "They took most of that stuff off already," the girl whispered, putting on a brave smile. "I'm sorry, Miss D. I don't know what happened!" Tears welled in her eyes.

Someone knocked on the open door.

Smiling, Officer McChesney shook his head as he approached Wendy's bed. "We gotta stop meeting like this. The guys back at the office are starting to talk."

Wendy pulled her blanket around her chin as he came closer to her.

"He's okay, sweetie," Devin reassured her. "He's one of the good guys."

McChesney cleared his throat and smiled at Wendy. "I hope I can live up to that. I have to ask you about what happened, and I have to ask Miss Marques to leave."

"Oh, no, please let her stay!" Wendy grabbed Devin's hand and arm and held on tenaciously.

"It's okay, Wendy. I'll be right outside the door."

"No, please, please don't leave me!"

Devin noticed Stan look back and forth from her to Wendy.

"Okay, here's the rules." He gestured at Devin. "Miss Marques can stay, but she can't say anything. If I think she's influencing what you're saying, or you look to her to approve of anything you're saying, she's out of here. Only you can answer my questions, without her help. Can you do that?"

Without hesitating, or so much as a sidelong glance at Devin, Wendy softly said yes.

The cop smiled and nodded. "Can you let go of her arm?" He winked. "I think you're cutting off the blood supply to her fingers."

Wendy giggled and let go with a little squeaky "Oh!"

Stan pulled the rolling bed table in front of him and placed his notebook on it. "You need to tell me what happened. Start whenever you're ready."

"Ian's girlfriend, Jesse, called me and—"

"Jesse?" Devin couldn't believe her ears. "Are you sure it was Jesse?"

Wendy nodded. "I've talked to her on the phone lots of times. She said you called from the horse show and told her you didn't need me."

"You're sure it was Jesse." Devin stepped back, shaking her head.

McChesney shook his finger at her as he questioned Wendy. "Miss Wendy, what time did you get this call?"

"It was about six in the morning. I was up. I was getting dressed to go to the horse show." Wendy licked her lips and blinked.

"She said you'd–" Wendy quickly looked at the policeman. "Jesse said Miss D had told Ian she'd cancelled the work in the tack room, and I needed to get the stalls ready for when she got home from the horse show."

"What was being done in the tack room?"

"They were going to make it bigger after moving the stalls for Devin's horses to another section of the barn."

"Were you alone?" the officer asked.

Wendy looked up. "Tony, my boyfriend, said he'd go with me, but I told him I'd be okay. I was going to go to the horse show after, "she glanced at Devin, "even though supposedly Devin didn't need me. There was a car race on TV I knew Tony wanted to watch, and I'm not much of a car race fan."

Stan nodded as he scribbled some notes. "I can relate. My wife feels the same way about fishing shows. What happened when you got to the barn?"

"I brought over a bale of straw and started with Chief's stall. It's right by the tack room. I put out the straw and left the rest of the bale by Sammy's-Shaman's-stall. And I did the same with the hay. I filled the water bucket in Chief's stall. When I went back to the tack room for water for Sammy's stall–" She inhaled heavily and reached for Devin's hand. "All of a sudden, this great big arm clamped around me from behind, and the person put something over my nose and mouth."

"Did this person say anything?"

Wendy shook her head. "Not at first. When he put his arm around my neck, I smelled gasoline and something musty like something when it's stored wet. Whatever was on the rag or whatever he put on my face made me really queasy."

"Did you see this man?"

"He was strong. And bigger than me. Real big." Wendy looked up at Devin, who smiled and patted her hand. In a whisper, Wendy added, "But everyone's bigger than me."

McChesney smiled slightly. "Did he say anything?"

Wendy shook her head. "Not at first."

"What happened next?"

Wendy shrugged and shook her head again. "I guess I passed out. When I woke up, my arms were tied behind me."

The cop wrote as he spoke. "Were you still at the barn?"

"I'm not sure where I was then. Everything was kinda fuzzy."

"What happened then?"

"He said he was glad I was awake, so I'd know what was going to happen."

McChesney set down his pen and stepped back from the table. "Did you ever see the person's face, or recognize his voice?"

Wendy shook her head. "He always stayed behind me, even when he held a needle in front of my eyes and asked if I knew what it was. And I said yes. He called me a mutant half-breed freak and told me I took his job." Her face crumpled and she began to cry.

Raising an eyebrow, McChesney glanced at Devin. "He said you took his job?"

Devin shook her head as she handed Wendy a tissue.

"Why do you think he said that?"

"I don't know, but he said it several time." Her squeaky voice trailed off into a wail. "He laughed, then stabbed me with the needle."

The room was silent except for Wendy's sobbing. After a few moments, she collected herself enough to continue, stopping frequently to blow her nose. "Whatever was in it burned like fire when he put it in my arm. He said–he said–" Tears trickled down her cheeks again. "He called Miss D the rich bitch. He said he was going to put me back where I was when you," she looked up at Devin, "when you gave me his job." She looked at the cop. "But I didn't know what he meant."

Devin handed her another tissue and walked over to the window, wondering who Wendy's attacker might have been.

"Please don't be mad at me, Miss D!" the girl begged. "Don't leave!" Sobbing harder, she pulled her blanket over her face.

"I'm right here, Wendy. I'm not going anywhere." Devin looked between the mini-blind slats.

The policeman gently pulled the blanket off Wendy's head. "I only have a few more questions. Do you remember anything after you were given the shot?"

Wendy blew her nose and took a drink of water. "Things got all weird. I'm pretty sure he put me in the trunk of a car. I passed out again. I don't know how long. I think it was dark when I woke up, but it could have just been dark in–wherever I was."

"What was it like?" The officer's pen stopped briefly.

"There wasn't much air and I was on my back with my arms tied behind my back, and the movement made me real sick, and I threw up." She paused, furrowing her eyebrows and looking around the room. "I was cold, because my sweatshirt was gone."

"I'm almost done." McChesney smiled. "You're doing fine. Did you hear any sounds?"

"My head was roaring. I don't know what I heard. I was so queasy and mixed up, I don't know."

Devin leaned down and kissed her forehead. "It's okay. I'm not mad at you."

Wendy gave Devin a weak smile. "Everything was gray, like at dawn. I don't know where I was or what time it was. He gave me another shot when he pulled me out of the car. That one was different from the first one. I started having hallucinations and I couldn't stand up."

"But you didn't see him, and you didn't recognize his voice?" Stan scribbled a few more words and set his pen down. "Miss Wendy, I know you're tired, and I know you had a bad experience, but I want you to really think about this person who attacked you."

Wendy sniffled and dabbed her eyes. "When I saw him when he took me out of the car, he was all hazy and distorted. A big dark blob."

"You said several times it was a man, and he was bigger than you. Do you think he was as tall as me?"

She looked from Devin to the policeman. "I don't know. He was big and strong, but fat. I grabbed his arm when he first came up behind me, to pull it away. It was—like squashy or spongy. Not like—" she grasped her own forearm. "I can't describe it. It felt funny, maybe padded. But not like a real arm."

"Okay, Wendy. One more question – do you remember taking your sweatshirt off? You said it was gone when you woke up in the car trunk."

She shook her head, biting her lips together. "No, but I hope you find it."

"Thank you very much, Miss Wendy. If you think of anything else, there's a policeman out in the hall. Tell him you need to talk to me." He smiled at her. "Better yet, here's my card. You call me and talk to me, not anybody else. Okay?"

Wendy nodded, her eyelids drooping.

"I need to talk to Devin now."

"You've been a big help, sweetie." Devin patted Wendy's hand and smoothed her hair. "You'll be going home in no time."

The sick girl looked up through half-closed eyes, mumbling, "You'll let me come back to work after this?"

"Of course! You didn't do anything wrong! I'll see you tomorrow."

Devin followed McChesney into the hall. Ria leaned against the opposite wall, and, as the cop had told Wendy, a uniformed policeman stood by the door. McChesney paused beside the guard. "Until I come back, no one is to go in that room. No one." As the guard nodded, McChesney motioned to the big window at the end of the hall. As they started walking toward it, Devin heard Ria call out something about going downstairs for coffee.

When they reached the window, the policeman quietly asked, "Who do you think she was referring to when she said the assailant told her she took his job?"

"I don't know. She wandered into our barn at a horse show at the Expo Center in Springfield. My horse Apollo doesn't like anybody, and he was nuzzling up to her in no time." She raised her arms, palms up, frustrated. "There was no Help Wanted sign up. We hadn't been advertising for any stable help–"

"You said we. I take it Ian–I think you said it was Ian–was still part of the farm–" He gestured, apparently fishing for the right word.

Devin nodded. "Oh!" She closed her eyes and let her head drop back. "Oh, shit."

"You sound like the proverbial light bulb came on." The cop had a hand poised above the pen in his pocket.

"You asked the other day when the phone calls started, and I could only say maybe a year ago, maybe around Easter. The show at the Expo Center was in June, and that's when I hired Wendy. And right after that the calls started."

"You were very surprised when Wendy said Ian's girlfriend called. Or was that one of your random thoughts?"

Devin shook her head.

"Tell me about the girlfriend."

Devin rolled her eyes. She conjured up a mental image of Jesse. "I don't know what to say. Ian's been seeing her–I don't know–a year and a half, maybe? Something about her just sets me off."

Devin slowly shook her head as he asked, "Something she does? Something she says?"

"This sounds stupid, but it's the way she looks at me, like she's examining me. Every so often, out of the blue, she asks questions about my family, what I own–" Devin paused, groping for words. "The kind of questions you don't expect from someone you don't know, like, 'What's your mother's brother's name?' or 'How much did you inherit when your father died?'"

"You mentioned that both of your parents had passed."

"Yeah." Raising her eyebrows, she sighed. "Not long after Jesse asked me about my inheritance, the collage Mark did for me with a rubbing and a photograph of my father's name on the Viet Nam memorial wall in Washington–it hung in my bedroom–it was damaged." She looked up at Stan. "It's since disappeared." Tears welled in her eyes. "His medals were in it, and one of the few pictures that exist of him holding me."

"Huh." McChesney stared out the window. He finally asked if she knew Jesse's last name.

Devin opened her mouth to answer, then reconsidered.

He looked surprised. "I didn't think it was a hard question."

"When I first met her, we were in a big college class together and I'm pretty sure her name then was Jamie Schuler. When Ian started to date her, he introduced her as Jesse Haver. When I said something about the other name, she told me I must have her confused with someone else."

"Did you?"

"I don't think so. Jamie was part of a group of us who studied together and went out for coffee. She was always part of the conversation. Very intelligent."

McChesney opened his mouth, as if to say something, but Devin added, "She's going by Jesse Tyler now. Allegedly a name change after a messy divorce."

"You don't sound convinced."

"After all the time he's dated her, Ian doesn't even know where she lives or works, aside from some part-time jobs while she's in school. But he doesn't know which college. I asked once, and he got hostile about me questioning anything about her."

"Do you know where she lives?"

"Somewhere in West Haven. At least that's what she said when she heard that my cleaning lady lives in West Haven."

"Any idea where?"

Devin shook her head. Then she thought of something Wendy had said. "Have you talked to Mark yet?"

"Before I came here. We had a nice chat. Why?"

"I have *three* horses. Wendy said she was told to get the stalls ready for my horses, but she was attacked after she finished one stall. I would swear that, at the fire, I saw Mark driving a Jeep towing a horse trailer after a horse was taken out of the burning barn, and there weren't supposed to be any there."

"He said nothing about that. But if I have reason to talk with him again, I'll ask." He opened the notebook and took out a battered envelope. "Does this mean anything to you?"

Devin studied the smudged cream-colored envelope, pointing as she spoke: "It's from Mark, that's his handwriting, and that was my address when I was at MIT. It's postmarked two days after Christmas, the year I graduated. How did you get it?"

"Wendy said a security guard where she was dumped had it. He said to be sure you received this letter. We'll check to see if said security guard exists."

Devin gave him a puzzled look. "Well, that's weird enough." She pulled out the crumpled pages from the envelope. Some of the pages were ripped, the torn-off pieces shredded into multi-colored confetti that fluttered to the floor. Other pages had words cut or blacked out.

She looked from page to page, turning them over and over, trying to put them in order. "These are from different letters. This page is marked with a '2' and this one is marked '3,' but what he's saying from one page to the other isn't a continuation. It's like everything else that's happening–I don't think it's supposed to make any sense."

She finished reading the first side of the last sheet of the letter, and flipped it over to finish. Under the signature, "Love, Mark", someone had arranged newspaper letters to spell out "He doesn't see me either."

She held out the battered letter. "Please find who's doing this to us."

"We will. Until we do, all of you are getting police protection. Even Auntie. Real cops." He winked. "I'll pick 'em myself." He took two steps away from Devin, then stopped. "Tell me again—why do you live in that little house in Florian while your aunt is all alone in that big mansion at your farm?"

"Does it matter?"

"I don't know yet, but something tells me it might."

"Till I left for MIT, I lived at the Hale House—that's the mansion's name from way back when my something like four greats back grandfather on my father's mother's side built it. I was on the road for horse shows a lot, so my aunt had some hired help and a couple tenants over the years. There didn't seem to be room for me there when I was done at college and moved back to Florian, so I bought the beach house. Aunt Aggie enjoys being the lady of the manor, with her errand people and cleaning lady and such. So long as I come for tea now and then, she's been happy with that arrangement."

McChesney nodded, cleared his throat. "Ready to tell me about that random thought about that sweatshirt yet?"

"No. I can't." She paused. "And Wendy's sweatshirt disappeared again."

"Do they have any clues about the fire yet?"

Devin joined Ria in the hospital café and reached for a container of creamer. "Nothing yet, like they'd tell me anything anyhow. It's totally weird, Ria. Someone was in and out of the barn while I was getting the stalls ready and bringing the horses in, like someone was in and out of the house when you were packing to leave. But they're never there when the police show up."

"I heard Wendy say that whoever attacked her was so fat he was squashy."

"She was whispering! How did you hear that?"

"I was right by the door till that cop came and made me move." Ria tore open a pack of sugar and poured it into her coffee with exaggerated care. "That lets out Mark, because anyone can tell he doesn't have an ounce of fat on him." She moved her head left and right, an exaggerated negative head shake. "Definitely *nothing* spongy or squashy about that body!"

Devin sipped her coffee. "Kinda blows your theory out of the water, doesn't it?"

"Do you still think Mark's innocent?"

"He says he can prove he was somewhere else last week when I was being followed around."

"Do you believe him?"

"Part of me wants to scream 'How can you ask such a stupid question?' and the rest of me never wants to see him again."

Ria looked up, past Devin. "That second part of you isn't going to get its wish. He just walked in the door."

Devin kept her eyes on the table when Mark stopped beside it. When she finally looked up, she asked, "Do I have a homing beacon on me?"

"I went up to ask about Wendy. They told me at the nurses' station you'd just left, and might be here. May I sit down?"

Ria gestured to the empty chair beside her. "We were just talking about you."

Mark didn't immediately take the seat he was offered. "I doubt you were discussing my finer qualities."

"Do you have any?"

In response to Ria's question, he sat down.

"Why are you here?" Devin demanded.

"I told you when I dropped you off at your house I'd get in touch with you tonight."

"Ready for your exam?" Devin sipped her coffee.

"I'm not looking forward to it, that's for sure."

Ria stirred and stirred her coffee, an indication of her annoyance with someone, and a habit that drove Devin crazy. "What course was it in?"

Mark shook his head and gave Ria an angry look. "It's a follow-up series to the tests I was taking last Monday when I wasn't stalking Devin at the mall, okay?"

Ria set her spoon on the table with great care. "Whatever."

He turned to Devin. "They said Wendy was doing better."

"She doesn't know who drugged her and dumped her," Devin replied with a sigh. "She's afraid I'm going to fire her now."

"You wouldn't do that, would you?" Mark asked softly.

Devin shook her head. After a moment's silence, she looked into his eyes. "When you were taking me back to Aunt Aggie's a little while ago, you never answered when I asked why you didn't follow Lisè's car."

"You needed to wash your face and get your car so you could come see Wendy."

"It could have waited."

He looked from Devin to Ria. "I have my reasons. I'd rather not explain now."

Ria stood up. "Am I one of your reasons? Should I leave?"

They stared at one another. "Like everyone else, I don't know who to trust. Let's leave it at that."

The next morning, after cruising up and down the streets in Devin's beach-front neighborhood, Mark didn't see her Thunderbird parked near the cottage and decided she probably on her way to her farm. He pulled to the side of the street, a couple houses up from the cottage, the car engine idling, mulling his next move, when he saw Ria tugging at the reeled garden hose as she walked, barefoot, to the front of the small house. He moved the car slowly up to the cottage and turned off the engine.

Water spattered onto Ria's feet when she dropped the hose reel on the sidewalk to attach it to the outside faucet. Mark heard her mumble something as she fumbled the end of the hose onto the faucet. Water sprayed out around the threads of the improperly attached coupling when she turned the handle.

She shrieked and jumped up. "Oh, man! I don't need this! I didn't even plant the damned flowers!"

She turned off the water and fiddled with the hose and faucet again, turned the water back on and aimed the spray head at the plants.

"Stupid flowers!" she muttered, tugging the hose behind her as she approached another plant. "You all must be happy I don't do this every day. You'd never grow."

Mark walked up behind her. "I don't think they like that tone of voice."

Ria jumped and turned around. "Devin isn't here."

"I thought you went back to Cambridge to Mom and Dad."

"She gave me my house keys back, but I stayed with some of my Dad's friends in New Haven last night." Ria yanked the hose and moved a few feet away from him. "I thought you had important business somewhere else today."

"That's later today. I thought I'd come aggravate you this morning."

"What do you want?" She flattened the flowers to the ground with the force of the water sprayed on them. "Why didn't you write her? Why didn't you call her?"

"You asked me that before. I did write to her. I don't know where the letters went because they never came back. I used the farm's address, her aunt's address, Ian's–I even sent a few via General Delivery in Florian."

Ria didn't look at Mark as she coiled up the hose. "She got nothing from you until yesterday when parts of a couple of your letters turned up on Wendy. Nothing. Zip. Zilch. Nada."

"I sent her a birthday card in November. I thought for sure I'd hear from someone after that. I have something for her I have to move before much longer."

"What is it?"

"It's a surprise. I want to keep it that way. Anyhow, I told you yesterday–I don't know who to trust, either."

"Why didn't you come see her?"

"It was easier not to. I was fine when I didn't think about what happened."

Ria looked puzzled. "What happened when?"

"Not long after I started at Harvard."

"What do you mean?"

"I was told she had an abortion." They stared at each other a moment before Mark looked away.

"You wouldn't see her because you thought she had an abortion?" Ria's voice rose as she finished her question.

She looked around before continuing in barely more than a whisper, "She had some kind of cyst removed."

Mark shook his head. "That's not what I heard."

"You weren't living in my house. You didn't see how much pain she was in, or how weak she got from bleeding as long as she did before Mom dragged her to a doctor." When he made a face, she added, "You don't get incisions from abortions, Mark. Ask her to show you her scar sometime."

"She could have called me and told me about it."

"Information wouldn't give out your unlisted phone number, and the carrier pigeon couldn't figure out which of the thousands of dorm windows was yours. How was she supposed to reach you, Einstein?"

"She could have called my uncle in New Haven."

"No. You should have called her." Ria turned off the water and reeled up the hose, then disconnected it from the faucet. She turned the water back on and rinsed her hands, shook them off and wiped them on her behind. She twisted the handle and took it off the spigot head before replying, "Mark, my best friend's heart was broken, and she cried and cried. You'll have to excuse me if I seem a tad hostile toward you."

"What about you? You left."

Ria picked a dead twig from a shrub and spent blossoms from the flowers beside the sidewalk. "I didn't turn my back on her like you did."

"Didn't you?"

She whirled around and planted herself in front of him. "I don't like your tone of voice and I don't think you deserve an explanation."

"You came to me, remember? You said I had to help somehow. You told me I owed it to Devin."

"It's gotten real scary living here. To the point I got sick every day when I drove home from work. Last week I came across a list of suspects Devin had made–a list SHE said she knows nothing about–of everyone she knows–me, you, her aunt, Wendy, Ian and his girlfriend Jesse, Devin's uncle and grandfather in Florida. Some names I didn't recognize. Those must have been horse-show friends or other people who worked for her."

"You told me about that before, and the list of what had happened, and the phone messages. When you found out the police couldn't help, you bailed. How convenient." He crossed the small yard in three long strides.

"Oh, look who's talking!" she shouted after him. When he stepped off the curb, she called out to him to wait, and crossed over to the front walk. "This isn't helping Devin one bit. Do you have any idea what to do next?"

"I have to go back to Cambridge for another doctor's appointment now, but I'll be back tomorrow. I don't have a master plan yet, but I know I'll have time to think about it this afternoon." He pulled his sunglasses from his pocket.

"And what's happening this afternoon?" Ria's question had a sarcastic tone.

He stared at her for a moment. "I'm getting a camera put where no human body was designed for a portrait sitting." He paused. "Satisfied?"

She seemed to wilt a little. "But you'll be back tomorrow?"

"That's what I said."

Ria took a step and looked down as she curled her toes over the edge of the curb. "When we talked last week, you said Devin cared about you when you didn't want to live any longer."

"She cared about me when I hated her more than I hated myself. I'm just returning the favor."

"Why did you try to commit suicide?"

"I'm not sure that's your business."

"Devin says I don't know anything about you, but you understand about not being wanted." Ria folded her arms across her chest and stood as tall as she possibly could. "Which, I was rather pointedly told, I knew nothing about. Enlighten me."

He pulled off the sunglasses and stared at her a few moments before saying, "I was five when my father first told me he didn't want me and didn't love me. Did either of your parents ever say that to you?"

"Never!"

"I regularly got dumped at his parents house, sometimes days at a time. They liked little boys. Couldn't keep their hands off me. I'd get mauled and pawed, touched, felt up, had to touch them, and every day I begged him not to take me back. He told me he didn't care. In his eyes, I wasn't there."

Ria cringed, made a disgusted face. "Ewwwww. Is that why you tried to kill yourself?"

He tried to keep his voice even. "I wanted the nightmares to stop."

The cold blank mask of his face frightened Ria.

"I can't stand being touched. I still have nightmares. All the pills the psychiatrists prescribed, and all the drinking haven't made them go away. All that has kept me here is knowing Devin loves me."

"Do you love her?"

"She's the only thing that matters to me in the world." Mark put on his sunglasses and opened the driver's door. He put one foot inside, stopped and looked at her. "Y'know, Ria, after I gave Devin her birthday present at the park that day, she was crying when the two of you walked past my car. I know you saw me because you gave me a dirty look. Devin never knew I owned a brown station wagon, but you did."

Ria leaped off the curb, shouting, "I TOLD you, Mark, I'm not involved in what's been happening to Devin!"

"Someone you know is."

"How dare you—" Ria stared at him, her face inches from his.

He didn't move. "Remember when Devin built her Thunderbird? How she got the body parts to finish it?"

Ria backed away, then looked away. "All those ugly car parts, they appeared one by one on our carport. She acted like she was getting diamonds and gold." Ria's voice softened. "I always suspected you sent them. You did, didn't you?"

"Since your father was helping Devin with the project, he gave her aunt a list of the necessary parts. Aunt Aggie gave it to me. Whenever I located a piece, I checked it off the list and indicated the date I had it delivered."

"Salvaged car parts. To me, they were so many pieces of junk. You should have seen her face." She looked back to Mark and smiled. "She said I didn't know anything about you. Nobody thought you were a nice guy."

"I'm not a nice guy, Ria." He wore the expressionless mask that went with the mirrored sunglasses. "By the way, do you remember my Firebird?"

"Was that the blue car you had, with the bird on the hood?"

"That's the one."

"It was beautiful! Why'd you trade it for that ugly thing?" She pointed to his Volvo.

"The Firebird was stolen right after I moved to Cambridge."

Ria shook her head. "Did you call the police?"

"They got a laugh out of it."

"What's funny about having your car stolen?"

"It's coming back to me piece by piece, in the same order I had the Thunderbird parts delivered to your house."

# CHAPTER NINE

*You better get round-the-clock protection for that ugly little freak. Once I'm done with her the next time I find her alone, you'll never let her near your precious horses again.*

That afternoon, after Devin had delivered Wendy into the over-enthusiastic ministrations of her landlady, she stepped out onto the porch to find a Florian policeman parked outside.

"Are you one of Officer McChesney's real cops?"

"Real as it gets, Miss Marques. Stan'll have my badge and probably a few body parts if anything happens to the girl or the landlady while I'm on the watch."

Devin wrote down his name and asked his badge number. "Just in case."

"We're always happy to give them to you. Anything to help you feel safe till this is over."

"I hope you guys don't scare easily. Whoever these people are, whatever it is they want, they seem hell-bent to get it, whatever the cost."

He shrugged. "Keep an eye out. Don't be afraid to ask the guy to check your house before you go in, or walk through the barn or whatever. That's what we're here for."

"Thanks. Tell Officer McChesney I said thanks too."

In a few minutes, she parked in front of her cottage, and watched her rear-view mirror as the teal Ford pickup that had trailed her from Wendy's house parked in front of a neighbor's house.

"Well, that's real inconspicuous. I'm sure the bad guys will just never notice that pretty teal truck sitting where there's never been one before." She shook her head and climbed out of her car. If the bodyguard was going to be parked out front, she might as well leave the Thunderbird sitting out where he could watch over it as well.

She paused and took a deep breath before opening the screen door. "No dead cats today, please."

She pulled the door open a few inches, peeked inside, and sighed with relief. She unlocked the main door and swung it in over the day's mail delivery. As usual, the mail had fanned out across the slate floor, at least a dozen envelopes, a bulging white packet, some sale flyers. None looked as if it might contain a note composed of letters cut from newspaper ads.

She set the unwieldy stack on the small half-circle table by the entryway, and opened a large manila envelope marked "Photographs Do Not Bend." Devin flipped through six 8×10 black-and-white photos taken by a press photographer at a show in Tampa, Florida. She enjoyed his work because his camera's eye saw more than awards presentations and the winning jumps. His pictures recorded the joy of victory, reflected in the smiles of the grooms and stable hands who made the horses happy to go into the ring and compete.

A lone envelope she had missed beckoned from halfway down the hall. It bore no return address, postage or postmark. Inside was a single piece of Kodak paper with "He's mine, bitch!" scrawled across it. She flipped the picture over.

"What?" she shrieked, when she saw Mark and a nude woman in a shower stall. She studied it closely, trying to decide if the woman's blurry face, a partial profile shot, belonged to anyone she knew. As she reread the note on the back, a knock on the door made her jump. She peered through the peephole to see Ian, and opened the door. "How'd you know I was home?"

He came inside without waiting for an invitation. "Who else in Florian has a candy-apple red 1956 Thunderbird with the removable white top, and would park it in front of your house?"

"Point well taken. So what brings you here?"

He looked around the foyer, and into the dining and living rooms. "Just wanted to know if you were all right."

"I'm fine, Ian, I'm—" She thought of Wendy's revelations about Ian's girlfriend, and stopped herself before telling about the police protection. "Everything's under control."

"I saw guards out at the barn." When Devin didn't respond, he continued, "They wouldn't let me in to check on the horses."

Devin continued to stare at him.

"Hey, I'm trying to help." He took a backward step, then gave her an ugly look. "I don't like what you're accusing me of."

"Should I be accusing you of something? You wanted out; you're out, period. Nothing at the farm is your responsibility anymore." She bit her lips together to stop a harsher reply, holding her breath. "What's with you, Ian? Since you started seeing Jesse, you've become an entirely different person from the one I knew. And I'm not sure I like this new person."

He opened his mouth, but she added, "And don't say you don't know what I'm talking about.

"Well, I don't."

"Is Jesse worth changing who you are to be with her?"

"She cares about me. You didn't."

"I never didn't care. I just wasn't interested in anything more than a professional relationship with you."

"We were partners till you decided you had to run the show, making all the decisions and acting like you knew what was better for Hightower than I did."

"I knew what the horses could do, and it wasn't what you had in mind. You're the one who insisted if we weren't winning, there was no point in even riding into the ring."

"Devin, you wouldn't even try three-day eventing. What were you, scared?"

"Huh! Never."

He shrugged. "I never thought I'd see you backing away from a challenge."

"I'm going for a bigger challenge, competing at the Olympics."

"You have a better chance of making the US equestrian team in eventing than show jumping."

"I know that, Ian. And I know Shaman and Apollo would do well in both the cross-country and jumping events, but I'm not sure either of them would settle down for the dressage portion. I think Chief could be a good eventing horse, but he won't be old enough to compete internationally, even by the time for the try outs for the 2000 games."

Ian shook his head. "You'll probably miss your chance, just like your old man did when he went to Viet Nam instead of the 1968 games in Mexico."

"He had a choice. Apparently he felt being a medic was more important than going to some riding competition."

Ian made a face. "What if you don't make the team?"

"Who knows what two, four, even six more years will bring? But everybody needs dreams, Ian, and making the Olympic team is one of mine."

"And I just don't fit into your other dreams anymore."

Devin pulled the door back as far as its hinges allowed, and nodded toward the opening. "You weren't part of any dream of mine unless it involved where Hightower and its horses were going."

He glanced around the foyer again, not quite meeting her eyes. "In your opinion, I sold out. Now you're jealous since I finally found someone who loves me for me."

"I'm not jealous of Jesse. I hope you're happy and you two have a wonderful life together."

"Right." He shifted from one foot to the other. "Before you kick me out of your house – and life - which is what I sense you're doing, a stable hand from Corbin Hills Farm brought some hay and straw today."

"That was kind." Devin glanced at the pile of envelopes she'd set on the hall table.

"He insisted he saw Wendy at the show on Sunday, working on the horse van."

"Corbin Hills? They were in the same barn and helped get mine ready to haul. No one mentioned seeing Wendy or anyone else working on my truck."

"Devin, this guy swore it was Wendy."

She picked up the batch of mail and pretended to study one envelope. "You know Wendy's a mechanical moron, Ian. It must have been someone else."

"Remember all the grease on her sweatshirt?"

She slowly lifted her eyes from the mail to Ian's face. *How does he know we found a greasy sweatshirt?* "Grease on a sweatshirt doesn't mean Wendy was wearing it. Did he talk to her? Did he see her face?"

"He said he saw Wendy." He scratched his neck as he looked at Devin. "Stay right there. I have something for you in my truck."

"I'll walk out with you." She set the mail back onto the table. As Ian stepped in front of her on his way out the door, he reached out and flipped the stack onto the floor.

Ian cut across the lawn to his truck and pulled a bulging plastic grocery bag through the open passenger window. He took a few steps toward Devin, then tossed the bag to her. "I found those stuffed in one of the storage compartments under the van." He dug in a pocket. "And here's my keys for the barns and both of the farm trucks, since I'm not supposed to be trespassing on your precious property anymore."

He threw the keys onto the grass and stalked to his truck. Closing the door with a mighty slam, he gunned the engine and spewed gravel as he peeled away from the curb.

As Devin leaned down for the keys, the policeman on guard duty approached. "What was that all about?"

Devin waited, not answering until he stood beside her. "I need to talk to Officer McChesney right away."

"I'll radio him. Your telephone should be ringing in a couple minutes."

As she waited for the promised call from McChesney, Devin collected the mail once again strewn across the foyer floor. The bulky white envelope had split open, spewing out dozens of snapshots.

Mark was in every single picture. Mark and that woman at a horse show... Mark alone...Mark and that woman in the shower... Mark and that woman...

Devin knelt among the colorful scenes, a lump in her throat, feeling hurt and betrayed.

That face! She grabbed the black and white Tampa pictures. There the woman was, in the background of four of them. Staring right at the camera. "Look at me; I'm here." With the slightest smirk on her face. She had been in Tampa in February, when the calls to Devin's motel rooms had started.

Devin closed her eyes and slumped against the door. Who was that vaguely-familiar person? Worse yet, who was she to Mark? And who took all those pictures? Not Lisè – she had been caring for Aunt Aggie after she had foot surgery earlier in the year. Definitely not Ian, as jealous of Mark as he was – no way would he allow a girl he was seeing to be photographed with Mark, anywhere, much less naked in the shower.

She carefully placed all the photographs into the torn envelope they had arrived in and set them on the dining room table. The bag Ian had thrown to her sat by the living room door. Inside was a maroon sweatshirt and black sweat pants. She picked up the shirt, holding it out by the shoulders to marvel at its "XXXL" expanse. As the phone rang, she noticed the sweatshirt had the fresh smell of line-dried laundry, not the leather, liniment and oil of the horse van. She also noticed several red hairs on the neckband. She grabbed up the phone before it could ring a second time as she pulled a pair of sweat pants from the bag, and stretched the waist of the pants, also labelled "XXXL", out as far as the tightly-knotted drawstring allowed.

McChesney didn't wait for her to say hello. "I understand someone stopped by and upset you. What happened?"

"Ian was here. He knew we found Wendy's sweatshirt, and it was covered with grease. He'd already left when Mark found it with the cat's body."

She heard a sigh on the other end of the phone, followed by a few moments of silence. "I guess we'll need to talk to Ian again. Anything else?"

"He said he talked to a stable hand who claimed he had seen Wendy working on my truck at the horse show. The horses from that stable were right beside mine, and their grooms were helping with my horses. They knew Wendy wasn't there. Ian also threw some clothes at me he supposedly found stuffed in one of the compartments in the truck, but they smell all fresh and clean, not like stuff in those compartments. A huge sweatshirt with red hair on it, and an equally large pair of sweat pants. The sweatshirt is maroon – Mark said he only saw people wearing black that night."

"Fold the clothes carefully and don't touch the hair. Anything else?"

She glanced at the pile of pictures, but said "no".

"You need to stop here at the station to pick up all your new keys, because all your locks have been changed and I was given the keys for safekeeping. You can drop off those clothes then, and I'll hand-carry them to the lab."

"I can stop on my way to the barn." She paused, choking back tears. "Thanks for caring. And thanks for the people outside."

"We're doing what we can. I hope it's enough."

As Devin hung up the phone, she heard footsteps on the concrete stoop, and the screen door opening. The person knocked, two tentative raps with the brass knocker. She leaned against the door and squinted through the peephole. She didn't recognize the man waiting there, looking around. Nervously, impatiently, she thought.

"What do you want?" she called through the door.

"I'm looking for Devin Marques."

"Why?"

"I need to talk to her about the fire. About the horse."

When she opened the door, he stepped up onto the threshold. "Wait a minute!" she said, trying to push him out.

"No, please! I'm not here to hurt you! The cop outside knows me. I'm the fireman who tried to get you to stay behind the truck where it was safe." He looked up and down the street again. "Please? Just give me a minute?"

She threw up her hands. "Why not? Everyone else has something new and interesting to tell me or show me today."

He came in and pulled the door closed behind him, appearing relieved to be out of public view. "I'm not supposed to be talking to you while the investigation is going on, but you got there when the windows were blowing out and the horse had just gone back into the barn. You asked who went in for the horse, and what he looked like. And you were cold. Your teeth were chattering."

"Okay, so we watched the fire together. Do they have any idea yet what started it?"

"Arson, probably. But you didn't hear that from me."

She nodded. "What did the person who went into the barn for the horse look like?"

He shook his head. "All I saw was a huge barn fire. He was a voice bothering me while I was concerned about the safety of the other guys and getting equipment where it was needed."

"The barn was supposed to be empty–"

He nodded. "You said that when you first got there, and that's what we were told when we arrived."

"Who called in the alarm? Who told you the barn was empty?"

"I don't know who called in the fire. An older lady at the scene said nothing was in the barn."

Devin figured he must be referring to Ian's mother. She waited for him to continue.

"When we got there, the barn was pretty much engulfed and ready to collapse. At that point, our job was protecting the house and the idiots who were there to see the show. Five minutes later this man showed up, telling us a horse was in the barn and he was going to save it or die trying. He said it didn't matter if he died because no one would miss him, but the horse was priceless, absolutely irreplaceable."

She cocked her head to one side, intrigued.

The fireman continued, "He said he knew exactly where the horse was and every second he argued with me shortened its life. I have a ten-year-old daughter who would have disowned me if she found out I let a horse die, so I handed him some gear and–" He shrugged, and looked into Devin's eyes. "I prayed for a miracle."

She looked him up and down and nodded.

His eyes darted around the foyer. "Look, you don't have to believe me." He opened the front door.

"Actually, you're the first person I've talked to who was at the fire and admits seeing someone rescuing a horse."

The man pushed the screen door open, and turned back to her. "He said something I didn't catch about a little red-haired girl. That's all I remember."

"Thank you for coming." Her voice was barely a whisper.

She closed the heavy wooden door behind the fireman and slowly walked toward the staircase. Mark called himself Charlie Brown, after the comic strip character whose love interest was a little red-haired girl.

She climbed the steps like a very small child, one foot on a tread, then the other, very slowly. The fireman's story convinced Devin that Mark had been the person rescuing the horse. A "priceless, absolutely irreplaceable" horse. That's what he had supposedly said to the fireman. Why had Mark lied to her about being there?

She shook her head as she stepped off the top step into the hallway. "It must be one special animal for him to make that sort of comment about a horse, then walk through fire to rescue it."

The sound of her voice echoing in the hall startled her. She looked into Ria's empty room, then her bedroom as she hurried to her office at the opposite end of the hall.

A red button was flashing on the telephone. Four messages, according to the Caller ID display bar. Three of the calls came from friends at other horse farms. When her aunt's number appeared on the screen, she called the voice mail system to hear her messages.

The time announcement indicated the message had been left an hour earlier. Aggie's tiny wavering voice pleaded, "Devin, if you're there, please pick up." A pause. "Well, I guess you're not home yet. Please call me, dear. There are some important things I have to discuss with you. Call me or come see me as soon as you can." Another pause. "This is your Aunt Aggie. It's very, very important. I'll talk to you soon. Good-bye."

*Probably wants to know when I'm coming to have tea with her.*

Devin closed the door and moved on to her bedroom. She again glanced into Ria's room as she passed its open door. When would life go back to how it was when—when what? Devin had forgotten what normal was. She just wanted her life and her friend back.

She sat on the edge of her bed and dialed Aggie's number, looking around the room, taking inventory as she counted telephone rings. The phone dropped from her hand when she saw a picture taped to her vanity mirror, a picture of her and Ria, arms around each other's shoulders, except Ria's face had been blackened out, and a picture of the woman in the shower pictures glued over it. A piece of paper with letters to spell "What do you THINK now?" was taped beside it.

Devin wasted no time to get to the police station for keys. She soon stood in front of Stan McChesney, throwing the picture and note on his desk, stammering, "I know I locked and bolted the kitchen door and locked the front door. I know I set the alarm at the beach house before I left. I even changed the security code." She also dropped the clothes onto his desk.

"There's a car at the farm right now. I'll let them know you're on the way. If there's anything else wrong, someone will be right there." He handed her an envelope containing the new keys. "Get going. Your aunt needs you."

She sped out to Hightower, weaving in and out around slower cars, and barreled up Aggie's drive, skidding to a stop behind a dark-blue Plymouth Reliant, the kind of car one of her aunt's friends might drive, a no-frills econo-box.

She would have ignored the car if the rear license plate hadn't been missing and the nameplate on the right rear corner of its trunk lid hadn't been broken. The letters "N" and "T" were missing from "Reliant." Devin ran her fingers across the spot where they had been attached. The paint was gouged as if the trim work had been pried up, rather than breaking and falling off through normal wear and tear. But she wasn't sure if the remaining letters were the same size and type style as the scrap Mark had found in the barn.

After a quick look at the front of the car–also void of a license plate–she unlocked the back porch door and called her aunt's name several times. Instead of a reply from her aunt, she heard a sweet, wavering soprano voice singing Bizet's aria from *Carmen*, "*Si je t'aime, prends gard à toi! L'oiseau que tu croyais surprendre battit de l'aile et s'evnola….*"

Devin followed the voice to the powder room next to Aggie's sitting room, to find Lisè, paintbrush in hand, carefully touching up the edges of a delicate faux lace border painted above the chair rail and wainscoting. The music Lisè sang to was so loud Devin could clearly hear it through the headphones she wore.

"Lisè." No response. "Lisè." Slightly louder, still no response. Devin went into the kitchen, where she found a note on the counter from Aggie, its corners held down by her camera and her journal. "Bella and Doris picked me up for a movie and supper. We might play bridge afterward. I'll let you know." She picked up the note, journal and camera, and turned toward Aggie's sitting room.

"*L'amour! L'amour! L'amour est enfant de Bohéme,*" Lisè sang on, her voice stronger as she performed the aria's chorus.

Devin froze in the middle of the kitchen when she spotted the sitting room's door wide open, pushed all the way back against the wall behind it, the padlock hanging open on the hasp. Months ago Aggie had stamped her foot and demanded the padlock because, she claimed, "The old skeleton-key lock isn't enough."

She had straightened her tiny frame to its full height and, with a shake of her fist, stated, "My things have been disturbed." Since the padlock had been installed, she never left the door unlocked.

Devin moved back to the powder room door, and waited till Lisè had pulled her brush away from the painting, to avoid startling her and perhaps causing a disaster when she touched her arm. "Lisè, that's lovely!"

The big woman jumped and jerked around, pulling down her earphones. She had been crying. "Oh, Devin, hi! My music's so loud, I never heard you come in."

"I enjoyed listening to you sing. Your French is quite good." Devin noticed Lisè's foundation and blusher were more heavily applied than usual. "That bruise on your cheek looks like you walked into a door."

Lisè seemed to shrink back against the wall. "I'm such a klutz."

"We all have our moments." Devin nodded. "Where did you learn *Carmen*?"

Lisè dropped her head and looked up at Devin through her bangs. "I sang that aria in a school recital. I wanted to be a voice major in college and sing opera."

"You have a beautiful voice."

"Yeah. My father said fat girls don't get scholarships, so–"

"Does your father follow sports?"

"You name it, if it's on TV."

"Well, at some time he must have heard that phrase 'It's not over till the fat lady sings.'"

"That's about Kate Smith singing 'God Bless America.' I wanted to sing opera." She reached for a tissue and blew her nose.

"It *is* about opera. Back in the '70s, a sportswriter coined that phrase during the NBA playoffs. Basketball games aren't over till the final buzzer. An opera isn't over till the lead female character sings her aria. And the female lead is usually a very sturdy woman, who needs that power for her voice to reach the back of the balcony."

"No matter. My old man wasn't going to pay for me to go to college. He said I better find a cheap school or a job with a salary I could live on, because once I graduated high school I was out on my own."

"But you–"

Lisè flipped a hand. "I took art classes instead, and sang in the college choir. I just finished my associate degree and found a job at an art gallery in SoHo. I'm leaving next week."

"How exciting!"

Lisè gave her a tiny smile. "Maybe I'll get to be an extra in a Broadway play in the chorus."

"Now THAT would be exciting!"

Lisè turned back to her painting.

"How did you do that border?"

"It's a surprise for Miss Hall. She saw the lace painting technique in a do-it-yourself magazine, and was going to pay someone, but I wanted to do it because she's always been good to me." She flicked back her bangs and tugged at her t-shirt, looking Devin in the eye for an instant, then back to her artwork. "The lace was off a bridal gown I found at a thrift store. Where I want the lace, I paint the wall with a paint base–the stuff you use when you want paint custom-mixed. It's clear. I press the lace onto the wall, let it dry a few seconds, then paint over the lace with white paint and carefully peel it off. And you get the lace effect. And to finish it, I go around the edge very carefully with a tiny brush to make a crisp edge, like lace has."

"That's absolutely amazing! Aunt Aggie will love it!"

Devin had never seen Lisè smile, so she was surprised how it transformed Lisè from an over-painted caricature to a beauty. And how quickly Lisè dissolved into tears.

"I'm so sorry! What did I say?"

Lisè wiped her eyes with the back of her hand, careful not to touch the wall with the end of her paintbrush. "She hardly looked at it before she went out a little while ago. I think she's angry I'm leaving."

"No, Lisè, that's not how Aunt Aggie is. She loves the paintings and charcoal drawings you gave her. She has the landscapes in her sitting room and the sketches of children on the landing where she likes to sit and read."

Lisè gave a slight nod of her head. "She did wish me luck, and when she was leaving she told me to keep in touch. She left a note for you in the kitchen."

Devin waved the paper. "Was she upset when she left?"

Lisè's eyes darted from Devin's face to the floor. "I was listening to my music and singing, and she had to tug on my shirt to get my attention. She seemed in a hurry." Lisè stepped back to admire her artwork. "There. I'm done. I need to get going."

"It's beautiful, Lisè. You're truly talented."

Lisè nodded as she closed the paint can and wrapped her brush in a plastic sandwich bag. She side-stepped Devin in the narrow powder room door and left the house without a backward glance.

Several steps away, leaning against the sitting room's doorway, Devin opened the journal as she gave the room a cursory inspection. She flipped the pages: lunch dates, comments about movies, Danielle Steele's autograph and Aggie's comments about a "lovely sky-blue gown." Nothing about "things being disturbed" or who might have been disturbing them. She returned the journal to its place on the table beside Aggie's little blue upholstered rocker.

The camera belonged on the second shelf of the bookcase below the window. She plopped the camera into the chair when she glanced out the window and saw Lisè, head down, plodding toward the barn. Ian's truck and Jesse's red and white Volkswagen Cabrio were parked by the paddock fence. Blocking the entrance was a Florian police cruiser. Gesturing wildly, Ian appeared to be shouting at the uniformed cop. Jesse stood close by.

Devin locked Aggie's room and hurried out through the porch door, rattling it to insure it, too, was locked. She ran to the paddock, directly up to Ian. "Wasn't it like–an hour ago, I told you I had things under control and you didn't need to check up on me anymore?" She glanced at Jesse. "You don't belong here either."

Lisè took a step forward. "I have some things in the barn."

Devin shook her head. "I don't think so, Lisè."

Jesse smiled. "How do you know, Devin?"

"Because I know." Devin slowly circled Jesse, looking her up and down. Jesse was shapely and leggy, much taller and more muscular than most of Ian's previous girlfriends. Jesse reminded Devin of the favorite porcelain doll in her collection. Her face was delicate and fragile-looking, with large light-brown eyes fringed with long lashes, perky upturned nose and a pouty mouth. Her hair was a waterfall of highlighted dark-brown curls. And, like that porcelain doll, Jesse always had every hair in place and wore an outfit that seemed to have been made just for her.

*Almost unreal in her perfectness.* The thought made Devin catch her breath.

"What are you doing?" As Jesse pressed close to Ian, Devin smiled and turned her attention to Lisè.

"By the way, Lisè, where's that red Sunbird of yours?"

Lisè glanced toward Jesse before answering. "That old blue wreck, that ugly Plymouth thing up by the house, is a loaner till my Sunbird's done being inspected." She kept the bruised side of her face turned away from Devin.

Devin looked from Lisè to Ian to Jesse. "It's time for all of you to leave. Lisè, if I find anything of yours, I'll be sure to have my aunt get it to you."

"Oh, Devin, how sweet!" Jesse cooed, in her breathy, little-girl voice. She patted Devin's arm as she brushed past on her way to her car. "Lisè just wanted to get her things since the old lady told her to pack up and leave. How nice that you'll take care of that."

"Well, the story I heard didn't include 'the old lady' telling Lisè to pack up and leave, but something must have happened to her, because she was really upset when she called me a couple hours ago."

As she flounced to her car, Jesse tossed her head and looked back over her shoulder, an ugly scowl on her face. Lisè followed a few steps behind Jesse, turning to give Devin quick look and almost-smile, and a little wave of her hand. They both climbed into the red and white Cabrio, Jesse behind the wheel, driving toward the site of the fire and the caretaker's house.

She turned her attention to Ian.

"And you, Ian, the next time you lie to me, try a little harder to make it seem true."

He stepped closer to Devin. "What do you mean by that?"

She didn't flinch or back away. "Who planted those clothes in the van?" Looking into Ian's eyes, she added, "If they were in the van."

Ian looked away. "They were in the compartment, just like I told you."

"They weren't there long."

"How do you know?"

"I've been seeing a dirty, greasy slob. The clothes should have reeked of body odor and hair oil, or the empty motor oil bottles and funnel that, since Saturday, have been in that compartment where you said you found them. But guess what, they smelled like they'd been dried in fresh air and sunshine."

"I don't like what you're accusing me of."

"That's the second time you said that. Are you guilty of something I should be accusing you of?"

They stared at one another till Ian looked away.

She made a slight motion with her head. "There's your truck. Get in it and go." Her eyes never wavered until he did as ordered and drove away.

She walked over to the patrolman. "How long were they here?"

"McChesney had just radioed me that you had had an altercation with Ian at your house when the tall babe showed up."

"The one that just left?"

"I was talking on my radio, parked up by the house, when she walked around from the front yard."

"Was that red and white Cabrio parked at the paddock fence?"

"No – uh, yeah. She and Ian were talking."

"I thought you said she was up walking around the house. And you were parked up there. And no one else was here?"

"I thought I saw your aunt looking out a window."

"Not my aunt. According to Lisè, she left an hour or so ago, which would have been some time before Ian was at my house."

The cop shook his head. "Huh-uh."

"The note she left said her friends picked her up for dinner."

"I haven't seen any cars come in except the red and white car and the pickup truck that just left."

"How about the blue car?"

The cop shrugged. "It was by the house when I came on shift at three. I thought it was your aunt's."

"Didn't you notice it has no license plates?"

He looked around the paddock and back at Devin. "No, I didn't."

"Did you see my aunt leave?"

"No. Just someone driving the little red car."

"What little red car? And just when exactly did Ian and his truck come? When did Jesse show up in the red and white Cabrio they just left in?"

Devin turned at the sound of a car in the driveway and walked toward the house. She watched Ria's Honda round the corner between the house and garage.

Ria stopped and stuck her head out the window, shouting, "Did you talk to your aunt?"

"No," Devin called back. "And she's not here." She jogged up to Ria's car as the policeman followed her in his car.

"I saw your car turning the corner when I got to the cottage, and the phone was ringing when I went in. It was Aunt Aggie."

"Did she say what was wrong?"

"Just that she wasn't feeling well, but she was with her friends and she'd see you later. Then she hung up without saying goodbye."

Devin felt cold. "Something's wrong. That's not like her at all." She turned to the cop. "Did the two women who just left come together or in separate cars?"

"I dunno. I didn't know the redhead was here. Maybe she's the one I saw in the window. And like I said, the tall chick drove off in a little red car, but not the one they just left in."

"She left in a little red car a while ago, then just happened to come back in the Cabrio. Is that what you're saying happened?"

He stared at her without answering.

"I want that blue car impounded." She thought of the letters pried off the nameplate, and the ones Mark had found in the barn. "It's important to have the police look at that car."

"The big redhead just said it was her loaner."

"Not even - it doesn't have plates on it."

The cop shifted his weight from one foot to the other. "Like I said, it was here when I got here."

"And you didn't notice there were no license plates on it."

He shook his head.

"Well, it has no plates, so it's not Lisè's loaner. I want it removed from my property."

"I'll make the call."

Devin opened up the cell phone she'd received when she stopped at the police station for her keys and to drop off the clothing Ian had delivered. "Mark says you need this," McChesney had told her.

She dialed a number. "Here. Use my phone so I know you're actually calling the police station and requesting a tow truck."

He gave her an ugly look as he took the phone from her and made the request.

"I hope you warn the cop watching the house overnight to keep an eye on your car so nobody hurts it," Ria cautioned as she shut her car door.

"At least that one's a real cop. The one here watching my horses isn't."

"Is there anywhere else you can take the horses?" When Devin shook her head, Ria exclaimed, "You gotta be kidding!"

"No place Ian wouldn't be welcome."

Ria rolled her eyes in response.

"Come with me. I need to take a walk through the barn. Lisè was just here and said she'd come to get stuff of hers out of the barn. And I need to bury Cat Mama."

"Who?"

Devin stopped. She turned toward Ria, but looked across the paddock instead of at her friend. "Remember the kittens that were on the door last week?"

"The dead kittens?"

Devin nodded. "They were Cat Mama's babies. Somebody killed her after the fire Sunday night and left her body on a pile of hay for me to find." She continued on toward the barn, sorting through the carefully labeled key ring McChesney had given her.

As Devin unlocked the barn door, Ria said, "Some guy in a teal truck – a guy in a *teal* truck - asked me for some ID when I was unlocking the door at your house this morning. What's that all about?"

"McChesney had guards posted there, here at the barn – supposedly here at the barn, and where Wendy lives. And I – Ria, what am I supposed to do? That guy's not a cop!" She hesitated, looking toward the house, before she swung the door open, to a trio of nickers from the horses. "Hey, guys!"

She looked back to Ria, who was shaking her head.

She followed Devin inside. "What are we looking for in here?"

Devin rolled back each stall door, spoke to each horse and looked around each stall before replying. "I have no idea. I don't recall seeing anything that might have belonged to Lisè here or in the house, except maybe a jacket right by the back door, either yesterday or when I was just up there." She considered her answer and added, "She said she just got a job at an art gallery in The City, and she's moving there next week. If she left anything here, it's not out in the open, so it has to be something small, inconspicuous or concealed."

"Any or all of the above," Ria responded. She stepped into the tack room. "Is that the cat you were going to bury?"

Devin was almost relieved to hear the body hadn't disappeared again, after someone – she suspected Ian - had dumped it into a trash can and took Wendy's sweatshirt. She picked up a shovel and walked to the opposite end of the barn, an open area used to walk horses in bad weather. She began digging in a corner.

"You're burying it in here?" Ria sounded incredulous.

Devin moved two more shovels of clay before replying. "Somebody was in the cottage again this morning. I know I changed the password and set the alarm before I left. I have a feeling if I bury this cat outside I'm going to find her on my bed or in the refrigerator or in the shower or something. Maybe whoever's been watching won't be able to see me bury her here."

As Devin finished her task, Ria busied herself opening feed bins in the tack room. "Could it be hidden in the horse food?"

"Your guess is as good as mine," Devin called from her back corner. "Stir it up with the scoop and see if anything turns up."

They poked and sorted through the tack room for about fifteen minutes before the loud rattling of a diesel truck engine cut through the silence. They looked at each other and, at the same instant, asked, "Tow truck?"

They both leaped for the door. Devin took two giant steps toward the paddock gate, then turned back and locked the barn door. *Gotta get used to doing that.*

After she moved her car to let the tow truck haul off the old blue Reliant, Devin showed Ria the envelopes of pictures. "Take a look at these and tell me if you recognize anyone aside from Mark."

"We didn't get done with our search in the barn."

"You look at those while I search. No, start with these." She handed Ria the Tampa pictures that included Wendy and the spectator gallery. "Who do you see?"

As they walked back to the barn, Ria glanced at each picture, and returned to the first one. As Ria held the photo out for Devin to see, she pointed to a woman at the edge of the crowd. "She took a couple classes with me at college. She dropped out a month or so into the semester because of a family emergency, so I heard."

Devin bit her lip. "She's in three other pictures from that show, and reminds me of somebody in one of my classes, too. Dropped out for the same reason. Do you know her name?"

Ria shrugged. "There were about a hundred and fifty people in the class. She was one of the hundred and forty-seven or so I didn't know. Why?"

"Somebody sent me a lot of pictures of her." Devin inhaled, a noise that sounded like a sob. She held out the white envelope. "Her and Mark."

Ria looked surprised. "Together?"

Devin didn't reply right away. She didn't want to start crying. "They're in the shower together in one of them."

Ria shook her head as she took the package. "It must have been a set-up. He stopped by this morning after you went to the hospital. I never thought Mark had any feelings until he was talking about you. Either he's a damned good liar and actor or–" She tucked the envelope under her elbow and looked down, picking at her nails before lifting her eyes to meet Devin's. "I hope I find someone who loves me as much as he loves you." She quickly looked away.

"What about all these pictures?" She thought of the desecrated picture she'd found on her mirror at the beach house. She was afraid if she described it to Ria, she'd leave again.

Ria gestured toward the barn. "They say pictures don't lie, but they're only telling the photographer's version of the story.

"She looked back at Devin. "I'll take another look at them, then let's try to find whatever it is in the barn Jesse says belongs to Lisè."

As Devin aimed her key at the new deadbolt on the barn door, she remarked more to herself than Ria, "Maybe there's nothing here. Maybe she wanted to leave something, or take something." She turned the key, softly adding, "Or open a door or window to come back later."

# CHAPTER TEN

Early Tuesday morning Mark flew into New Haven's Tweed Airport. He stood in line to rent a car because he figured everyone in Devin's neighborhood would be looking for a brown station wagon.

He checked his watch and glowered at the chirpy rental clerk. The drive from Tweed would take at least forty minutes. Devin was usually at the barn by 7:00.

*Christ, could the girl behind the counter be any slower?*

Too many minutes later, he eased his car, a black Camaro with black-out windows, into the press of commuter traffic. He glanced at the camera, telephoto lens and note pad on the seat beside him. He fingered two rolls of thirty-six-exposure film. He'd be ready if he found the person he was looking for.

"I should have flown into Bridgeport," he muttered as he crept along a traffic-clogged street that eventually took him to the Connecticut Turnpike, Interstate 95. Traffic was always heavy on I-95, but rush-hour turned it into an irritable animal ready to crush an unwary or timid driver. This morning, the beast crawled past the remains of an earlier accident, crowding into one lane, then spreading into three just beyond the tow-trucks and police cruisers.

He hoped all the troopers assigned to patrol the turnpike that morning were working at the accident. If he did seventy until he reached the exit near the farm, maybe he'd catch Devin before she left her house. At the end of the exit ramp, he turned toward Florian.

Along the way, he watched for her bright red Thunderbird. At the town's green he turned left at the intersection and saw the red car traveling in the opposite direction on the other side of the green. A brown Toyota station wagon followed Devin.

Mark cut through a side street and the wrong way through a one-way alley to get behind the Toyota. As Devin drove under a yellow-turning-red traffic light, the brown wagon skidded to a stop. Mark watched in amazement as four medium-sized dogs and at least as many children climbed from seat to seat inside the waiting car.

He wrote down the Toyota's license plate, and noted its *I ♥ Square Dancing* bumper sticker. "Four dogs and five kids." He laughed. "That lady doesn't have time to run around burning barns and terrorizing people!"

He bought coffee and a newspaper and returned to Devin's neighborhood. She had said her stalker apparently knew her schedule and habits. Mark cruised her street from one end to the other. A battered brown Toyota was parked across from her house, and a large person was perched on the top rail of the fence around the steps that led down to the beach.

Mark parked near a clump of scrubby trees and screwed the telephoto lens into his 35mm camera. He hoped the small evergreens would provide enough cover for him.

He focused the camera on the hands holding chunky government-surplus field binoculars, then noticed the end of a flesh-colored undergarment's sleeve sticking out beyond the long sleeve of the person's blue sweatshirt. "What is that?"

Several pictures and additional focus adjustments, and he still wasn't sure.

The shutter clicked and the film advance whined as he snapped the person's head covered in frazzled, spiky blond hair. "Our man has a new 'do," he mumbled, "if it is a man. He must think that's how I look on a bad hair day."

He studied a small area of cheek, which appeared to be dirty rather than unshaven. Charcoaled or made up? He changed to a higher-powered lens. Definitely some kind of face paint. A glued-on mustache hung askew on the upper lip.

"Trick or treat was over months ago, pal. And I never had a 'stache." He pressed the button twice. "What are you looking for? She's not home."

The watcher on the rock lowered the binoculars and put on the lens covers. Mark snapped the profile shot. "Come on! Look this way!"

The man leaned down to pick up a dropped lens cover. As he bent over, the breeze caught the back of his sweatshirt and lifted it. *What's under that sweatshirt, a back brace?* Mark took two more pictures, then several more as his quarry stood up. Tall guy, staring at the house.

Mark glanced at the cottage to see what the other man found so interesting. Devin's cleaning lady, vacuum cleaner in one hand and a tote full of cleaning supplies in the other, trudged up the walk. She opened the door and disappeared inside. The man ambled across the lawn and knocked on the door.

The domestic opened the inside door but not the screen. Mark could see her shaking her head as the man tried to enter the house. After the door closed with a thud, the man took long loping strides to the old brown Toyota. The small car shook as he plopped down behind the wheel. As the car sped away, gravel pelted the windshield of Mark's Camaro.

He trailed the Toyota past several large apartment buildings and houses near the green, then up and down side streets and alleys. When the other driver shot through an intersection under a red light, Mark said, "I have all day and a full tank of gas, Ace. I'll find you."

Ten minutes and several blocks later he found the decrepit car parked in front of a three-story house. A wooden stairway jutting out at the rear of the building indicated a third-floor apartment. He parked and noted the address, took several pictures of the building, while mentally playing "eenie meenie" to decide which doorway to approach first.

A few minutes later a tall slim woman in an ill-fitting tweed suit and low-heeled brown shoes clopped down the wood stairs. She had short brown hair, wore oversized sunglasses and bright red lipstick. Mark took two pictures of her as she walked to the Toyota and climbed in.

"Well, well, well. I think I've seen this babe before." He took more pictures and checked how many shots remained on the roll. "Let's see where she goes."

Mark followed the woman to a three-car garage in an alley. He wrote down the street name and its approximate location as she opened one of the doors, backed a green Taurus onto the street and parked it. Quick picture of the Taurus, focusing on the license plate.

He thought he saw a red car inside the windowless garage. "And what's behind door number three?" he wrote, followed with a quick snapshot of the garage as the woman drove the brown car into the open stall. He looked up as she returned to the green car. She looked in his direction and gave him the finger before getting in, precisely as Mark had the camera focused in on her face.

"Same to you, sweetheart," he replied, and pressed the shutter button.

After her one-finger salute, Mark didn't bother keeping his distance as he trailed her through Florian's streets. The woman turned left into the lot for a suite of offices. She parked and ran into the building. When Mark reached the lobby, it was empty except for a directory.

*Does she work in one of these offices, or is she hiding somewhere, waiting for me to leave?*

He carefully read the directory, touching the suite number for a third-floor office. He recognized the name of the security system whose signs were posted at Devin's beach house and Aggie's big mansion.

Mark returned to the shabby apartment building and asked a grubby kid in the neighboring yard if he knew where the landlord lived.

The child pointed to the house with the wood stairs. "Good luck! She's MEAN!"

"Thanks." He winked at the boy. "I won't tell her you said that."

The woman who answered Mark's knock had a head full of rollers and crooked yellow teeth that desperately needed a dental hygienist's attention. A shapeless, stained housedress covered her bloated body. She smoked a thin cigar.

"Whaddya want?" Blue-frost eyeshadow filled the space between her eyebrows and heavily mascaraed lashes. Pale blue eyes squinted at him through the rusted screen door.

"Are you the landlady for this building?"

"Who wants to know?"

Mark pulled his hands out of his pockets and let the folded bills in his left hand show. "I'd like to see the third-floor apartment, the one with the wooden stairs." He looked beyond her, into her flat. He smiled when he saw a palm frond draped over the edge of a framed picture of the kneeling Christ.

"It's rented." She kept her eyes on the money.

"I don't want to rent it. I just want to see it."

"You from the housing authority?"

Mark fanned out five twenty-dollar bills. "A hundred dollars to open the door and forget I was here."

The woman looked from the money to Mark's face, and back to the money. Her eyes quickly returned to the mirrored sunglasses. "I know you! You're the college boy in the pitchers! Take off that hat and those glasses!"

Mark didn't move. "What pictures?"

"You wanta see the room or dontcha?"

He slowly lifted his New York Mets cap, ran his fingers through his hair, then pulled off his sunglasses.

"Yeah, you're the one. I was wonderin' when you was going to show up." She looked him up and down. "A hunnerd dollars, cash, for jist openin' the door. What ya think you'll find up there?"

"Some answers. Maybe a name to give the police."

The woman threw back her head and let out a lusty laugh. "The college boy wants to bribe me for a name!"

Mark spoke slowly and distinctly. "Does she have a name?"

"Elizabeth Logan, Liz, I call her. She's okay. But her cousin moved in and I ain't so sure what her real name is. I seen papers addressed a few different ways."

"What other names does she use?"

"Jewell Watts, Jules Walter, JayJay Tyler. I can't remember the other names I seen. Jamie or Jerry or something like that."

"Like what?"

"Look, college boy, you said a hunnerd dollars to open the door." She unlatched the door and opened it a fraction of an inch, holding out an open hand, wiggling her fingers. She grabbed two bills he slipped through the gap in the door. "Answerin' questions is extra."

"I figured as much." He gave her another bill and waved two more as he asked, "What other names does she use, and what kinds of papers have you seen?"

"You're a smart one, college boy. You learn fast. I seen bank statements, rental forms, stuff like that. I go up now and again to check things out."

"Does she have a boyfriend?"

"Ain't nobody payin' rent but Liz. This cousin's been stayin' with her 'bout six months now, an' Liz pays some extra for her. And some guy visits now and again. He's been around about a week lately."

"Some guy was driving her car–"

She puffed on her cigar. "Yeah, he was jist here, but he left jist before she did. But you look like you could handle jist about anyone who come along." She cleared her throat. "Like I said, I gotta see more money before I take you up there."

He offered her two more twenties. "That's a hundred. No more till I'm in the apartment."

"Follow me." The woman swung her door wide and motioned him in. She led him through her home, modest and shabby, but tidy and clean. "If you wasn't in all those pitchers, I wouldn't do this." Her kitchen door opened near the bottom of the wooden staircase. "Liz ain't here, and we ain't got a lotta time."

"I followed the cousin, if that's who you say it was, to an office out near the hospital. Do you know where she works?"

"I don't ast no questions." She briskly climbed the first run of steps before continuing. "Liz pays cash money, on time, an' like I said, some extra for the cousin. I ast security and two months rent up front, and she paid it when she looked at the place. She ain't no trouble, but the cousin's strange, and so is that boyfriend. I don't know nothin' about the two of 'em but they're scary strange." Mrs. Smith turned the corner on the landing and continued to the top, where a green corrugated plastic awning sheltered the door. She unlocked and opened it.

"Why don't you stay? I might have more questions." He stepped into the tiny kitchen.

"I tol' you–answers is extra."

"They better be the right ones, then." He glanced from the stained sink to the two-burner cooktop, across chipped Formica counters to a small breakfast counter. "I'm not–"

Above the counter, he saw a poster-sized picture of himself and a woman, both naked, in a shower. "Jesus Christ, where'd that come from?" He reached up to rip it down, then hesitated.

"That's the cousin. That's Jules."

Mark turned to the landlady, saw her eyes move from his face to the poster. "What else is there?"

"I been wondering about you, a rich college boy, and her. It don't figure. Been going with her long?"

"I don't 'go with' her." He scowled at her. "May I ask your name?"

Mrs. Uh–Smith. And you?"

"Mark Frasier."

"I wondered if you'd use your real name."

"How do you know my name?"

Mrs. Smith smiled. "I'll show you in a minute. Why's she got all these pitchers of you if you ain't together? What's she to you?"

"She's been bothering me and terrorizing a friend of mine."

"Oh? That Marques woman, the one who had the fire?"

He gave her his full attention. "How do you know about her?"

Mrs. Smith nodded her head. "You'll see. Th' fire's been on the news, college boy, and in the paper. I got lotsa things to show you, but we ain't got a lotta time."

She gestured toward the barren living room. A weathered-grey electrical line spool served as a table beside a brown tweed recliner. Against the opposite wall, a 25-inch television sat on a cheap wheeled metal cart. Light came through a curtainless window with a view of a brick wall.

Hundreds of photographs of all sizes were attached in some way to each of the peeling, crumbling walls in that room. Jules at a horse show, Jules at a tennis match, Jules at a rowing meet. There may have been many other people in the photographs, but, in almost every grouping, she stood close to Mark. One collage was composed of photos of him alone: reading in the library, in his car at a traffic light, in the cafeteria, in the gym.

The landlady followed him. "Things was different before Jules moved in. Liz painted, sang, played opera music. All her stuff was in the trash the day after the cousin came. Liz was at school, come home and saw the stuff on the curb, picked it all up then sat right down and cried, all her art stuff in her lap. She begged me to keep it for her till she found someplace to hide it till she was done at school." Mrs. Smith shuffled across the room. "All them pitchers showed up then. That Jules, she sorta took over."

"How long ago did Jules move in?"

"Before th' holidays. I missed how it was las' year, when Liz played her Christmas music and made cookies an' had a tree an' all. This year, nothin'. Liz tol' me a couple days ago she was movin' to New York City nex' week. Got herself a job in an art gallery. I tol' her good for her! Get away from Jules and her creepy boyfriend."

Mark looked from picture to picture, identifying a location or event here, cursing there, as he moved from one side of a wall to the other.

Mrs. Smith directed him to a bedroom. "She's got other stuff in here."

She pulled back the blanket stapled to the woodwork of the only window, letting light pour into the dingy room. The bed was a mattress on the rough wooden floor. Paperback books replaced a missing leg on a three-drawer dresser, its white paint chipped and peeling. A crazed and blurry mirror was perched atop the dresser.

If the living room was Jules' photograph gallery, the top of the dresser was her trophy display area. Dangling from a nail to the left of the mirror were the remnants of the maroon sweatshirt Mark had ripped up. Mrs. Smith touched it. "That's new. It wasn't here–" She glanced at Mark and quickly stepped away. "I was up Satiday and it wasn't here."

"She must have been at Hightower Farm Sunday morning. That's where it came from." He looked at the garment hanging on the other side of the mirror, a grey t-shirt labeled "Harvard Crew."

"That's yours, ain't it? You're wearing it in some of them boat pitchers."

"I'm on the rowing team at school. The shirt disappeared after the last meet."

He studied the collection on the top of the dresser. Propped against the mirror was a Connecticut license plate, FCT 897, its registration stickers scraped off. He picked it up. "She stole my Firebird!"

"Liz ain't no car thief! I had her checked."

"This plate was on my car when it was stolen."

"Want me to call the police?"

He put the plate down and picked up a small trophy. "They'll hear from me." He looked at the gold statue of a shot-putter, its base bare except for the remains of the glue that had once attached a name plate there. "Oh, yeah, they're going to hear from me." He set the trophy back on the dresser and moved on to inspect another of Jules' prizes.

A coat was nailed onto the wall at its shoulders and the cuffs of its outstretched sleeves. It was made of denim and leather, now reduced to shreds. The tattered designer label said "Tara's Threads."

The jacket had a quilted silk lining, with the quilting pattern of straight lines alternating with the words "Zannie-Annie." Devin's middle name was Anne, but Zannie?

Mrs. Smith was at his elbow. "You know whose that is?"

He nodded his head. "Devin was wearing it the last time I saw her before she graduated from MIT." He pointed to the label. "That's the name of a sportswear line from the design house one of her friends owns."

"It's more cut up every time I come up here."

Newspaper articles about the fire were taped to the wall around the jacket. Notations in the margins stated where each had appeared: *Elm City Citizen, New Britain Herald, Stamford's Advocate, New Haven Register"*

He looked closely at a color photo. "'Front page, *Connecticut Post.'" She probably had an orgasm when she saw that.*

He glanced around the room again as he wrestled open the balky closet door. The musty compartment held nothing more than two stark business suits and a rumpled raincoat. He coughed as the smell filled the room. Then he noticed a grease-covered U-Mass sweatshirt on the floor.

"Huh. That was fulla clothes the other day!" Mrs. Smith looked into several dresser drawers. "I guess Liz packed up. She paid till the end of the month, but these're empty, too!"

Mark closed the closet door and took a few steps toward the mattress when Mrs. Smith tugged at his arm. "I gotta show you something."

"There's something else I want to look at."

"C'mon! We gotta get outta here!" She shuffled to the kitchen with Mark firmly in tow.

She pulled open a drawer and pointed to the envelopes filed there. "I never read 'em, but I happened to see 'em one day, and I wondered how they got there. They're all to that Marques woman."

He scooped them out of the drawer and looked through the envelopes. Two Valentines, a dozen or so letters, and several cards, including the one he had sent for her last birthday. "Do you know where she keeps her writing paper?"

"Here." She opened another drawer and pulled out a tablet.

Clutching the bundle of mail intended for Devin, Mark scribbled a note for Jules: "I know where you live. I know where you work, and I know where the brown Toyota is. And I'm the meanest son-of-a-bitch you ever met." He folded the paper in half and dropped it into the drawer where the letters had been. Then he ripped the poster off the kitchen wall.

"Wait a minute!" Mrs. Smith protested.

Mark silenced her by holding out five more twenties. "You just got the worst case of amnesia in medical history. You don't even remember what daytime story you watch on TV." He leaned over her, scowling. "You weren't here. You don't know anything. Do we understand each other?"

As she tucked the money into her ample bosom, Mrs. Smith asked, "How do you know I won't call the cops?"

"Don't worry – that's my next stop."

She nodded. "We better get outta here. That Jules woman is strange, a creepy kinda strange. I don' want her livin' here."

Mark followed Mrs. Smith down the steps. "Hey, thanks a lot," he told her, as she entered the back door of her apartment. "It was a big help."

"You wait jist a minute. I got sumthin else."

The screen door banged in Mark's face as Mrs. Smith disappeared inside. He heard her rummaging around, and she returned with something in a brown grocery bag. "This was in the garbage a coupla days ago. You wasn't here an' I do' know nuthin." She shoved the bag into his hands and gave her head a little nod. "I gotta run. Hubs and me are goin' outta town for a few days. Goo' bye, and goo'luck." She went back into her home and closed the door without a backward glance.

After his abrupt dismissal, Mark waited until he was in his car to look into the bag. After a quick glance, he banged his head on the headrest. "God, if you don't want that bitch to die, let someone else get to her before me." He reached in and pulled out a smashed picture frame containing a picture of a section of names on the Viet Nam Veterans Memorial.

A car drove up behind his. As it idled, Mark glanced up at his rearview mirror to see a small red car.

Its driver waited, letting the car run. Mark started his Camaro and put it into gear. Maybe he was in a tenant's parking spot. Or was it the car Lisè was driving when she visited Hightower the morning after the fire? Or in the garage where he watched Jules put the brown Toyota?

When he drove away from the curb, the other car followed. It stayed right behind him when he went to the Hummingbird Photo drive-up window to drop off his film. The driver went through a red light at one intersection and swerved wildly to avoid rear-ending Mark's car when he stopped at the next traffic signal.

The red car clung to his bumper until he turned into the parking lot of the Florian Police station. He pulled into a space and watched the other car speed past. He wrote down its plate number and decided to wait a few minutes to see if it circled back.

As he waited, he thought about red shoes. Not the open-back mules Lisè had been wearing the day before. No, red shoes with stiletto heels and open toes. They had been beside the mattress on the splintery floor in the bedroom, partly covered by a pilled olive-green blanket. They seemed out of place in that shabby apartment. He'd seen Devin wearing shoes like that.

What else had he seen, just before Mrs. Smith—or whoever she really was—tugged at his arm? She showed him the letters, and whatever it was faded from memory. Only a small piece had been visible, but that split-second glimpse had been enough to make the hair on the back of his neck stand up.

# CHAPTER ELEVEN

*You think new locks will keep me out. You think making Ian go away will keep me out. You think you can make me go away. Not a chance. And don't count on those policemen that are everywhere around you to protect you. They're easy to buy.*

Devin was two blocks from her house, enroute to the farm, when a brown Toyota wagon turned onto the street behind her. She held her breath, repeatedly glancing at the car in her rearview mirror, keeping a white-knuckled grip on her steering wheel.

A golden retriever poked its head out the window behind the driver. Devin saw several more dogs milling around in the rear cargo area of the car. Three or four small children bounced on the back seat. She exhaled. The head barely visible above the Toyota's steering wheel wasn't her big, burly stalker. Besides, this car had most of its chrome trim—even if some of it was held on with duct tape.

She didn't look in the mirror again for about a block and a half, when tires squealed behind her. A black Camaro shot into traffic from an alley between two storefronts. "Everybody's in a hurry today," she mumbled, scanning through the radio stations.

Even though the Toyota didn't seem to pose a threat, Devin went through a yellow light as it changed. The black Camaro was too close to the little car's rear bumper–and its driver *had* been going the wrong way in that alley.

*When will I stop seeing something suspicious in every little thing?*

Maybe, she decided, when she could get a good night's sleep again. Aunt Aggie had called from the movie theater at the mall at midnight, not five minutes after Devin had gone to bed. Aggie had said she would be staying with one of the friends who had rescued her earlier in the day, and could Devin pick her up at the theater and take her to her house so she could pick up some things for the night.

*"My friend who rescued me."* Her aunt's comment had been on continuous loop in her head as Devin was driving to the mall.

Aggie had stared out the window in silence all the way to her house.

"Don't make me go in there alone," the frail little lady had begged as Devin parked beside the back door. Once inside, Aggie had flipped every light switch she passed, hurrying upstairs to her bedroom, then her bathroom and back downstairs, stuffing things into a tote bag, constantly glancing behind her to make sure Devin was still following.

Aggie didn't say another word until she said good night at her friend's front door and hugged Devin. "It's late, and you need your rest," Aggie had said. "We'll have tea tomorrow."

A small car's horn bleated behind Devin. She didn't recognize the vehicle, but there was Wendy, staring at her from the driver's seat.

As they parked in the paddock, near the barn door, a patrol car pulled across the open gate. Wendy climbed from her car and stalked over to Devin's, a dark scowl on her usually sunny face. She stood at the Thunderbird's front fender, staring at

Devin until Devin left her car. Wendy glanced in the direction of the paddock gate and demanded, "Who was that person at my place last night? He said he was a cop sent to protect me."

"Officer McChesney assigned them."

"I didn't see a uniform, only a badge."

"I didn't request it, Wendy." Devin glanced at the uniformed policeman standing a few feet away.

"They better not be there tonight." Wendy's squeaky little voice was unusually harsh. "I don't want somebody knocking on my door when my boyfriend's over, asking who he is and why he's there."

"Wendy, don't you know you could have been killed by whoever attacked you? I was happy to know you were going to be safe."

"My boyfriend will protect me."

"I'll talk to Officer McChesney."

Devin fumbled the new keys into the new locks. "Isn't it just like Mark to have them install two deadbolts where only one cheap lock was before?" she muttered when the first key wouldn't fit the upper lock.

Out of the corner of her eye, she saw Wendy watching in silence a short distance away.

Devin stepped back to let Wendy enter ahead of her. She waited to speak to the approaching cop.

He smiled. "Good morning."

Devin rolled her eyes. "It's morning."

He raised an eyebrow. "I heard the young lady had a few choice words for the patrolman at her place last night."

Devin put up a hand to stop him. "I think I can use my imagination to fill in the blanks about the intrusion."

"Would you like me to do a walk-around inside?"

Devin waved toward the door. "Please do."

Inside, Wendy was chattering away, fussing over the horses. Devin followed the policeman upstairs, peering here and there for something, anything out of place, something that might be what Lisè had returned to claim.

Ian had already left a message on her voice mail that morning, telling her that he'd seen someone at the barn, repairing the broken window pane on the second floor, as well as the locksmith at work. And, again, he'd been refused entry into the barn.

As she stared out that newly-set pane of glass, at the rubble of the big barn, she recalled her fleeting random thought about the maroon sweatshirt Mark had tried on being Ian's size. Maroon, when Mark insisted the two intruders he chased wore black. And Wendy's statements about Jesse.

"Does everything look all right up here?

She jumped as the policeman's voice boomed in the relatively quiet space. He waited at the top of the stairs as the lift rattled up from the ground floor and Wendy came into view. Devin gave a quick nod. "Everything seems to be fine, thanks."

He said, "I'll be down by the door till you come lock it" at the same moment Wendy announced, "I need some hay and straw, Miss D."

"Oh? I just saw some beside the tack room."

Wendy hesitated before conceding, "There is, but we could move some more down." She watched the policeman disappear down the stairway before asking, "Did you find my sweatshirt?"

The edge on Wendy's tone and her attitude annoyed Devin. "Why don't you tell me about your sweatshirt, Wendy."

"What do you mean? Did you find it?"

Devin took a deep breath and looked at the dusty floor before looking back at Wendy. "During the show on Sunday, two tires were cut on the horse van and its engine was vandalized. Someone told Ian you were working on it."

"No!" Wendy vigorously shook her head. "I told you what happened. What I remember anyhow."

"Were you wearing your sweatshirt when you came out to prepare the stalls Sunday?" As Wendy nodded, Devin asked, "Do you remember taking it off?"

"No. And I remember being cold when I got pulled out of that car. And the hospital didn't give it back, so I guess I didn't have it there."

Devin motioned to the window. "Take a look at what's left of the big barn."

Wendy moved to the window and stared out, her mouth hanging open, shaking her head. When she slowly turned to face Devin, tears rolled down her cheeks.

"It was on fire when I got back from the show. When I got here to put up the horses after the roof collapsed, someone had killed Cat Mama and put her body on the lift with the hay."

"I'm sorry," Wendy whispered.

"The body disappeared, then turned up a little later on the hood of the truck, wrapped in your sweatshirt, which was all greasy. Yesterday morning, you were found in the state you were in." She looked over at the girl, then back out the window. "They've terrorized my aunt, and Ria's so scared she moved back home. They could have killed you. Don't give me attitude because the police are trying to protect you."

"Please don't fire me, Miss D." Her voice was a faint whisper.

"I have no intention of firing you, Wendy. Just drop the attitude." She paused. "Was there a horse in the barn on Sunday when you got there?"

"A horse?" Wendy shook her head. "I–no." She screwed up her face, fidgety little Wendy again. "If there was, it wasn't in any of the stalls by the tack room. I didn't go anywhere else in the barn before–"

A shadow crossed her face. Her chin quivered as she looked at Devin. "Was it–did you get it out?"

"Someone did. No one seems to know who, or where it is now, or even where it came from."

"Not even Ian?"

"I'm not sure what Ian knows, Wendy, and that scares me. Especially since you were dead certain it was his girlfriend who told you to go out to the barn."

After a moment's silence, Wendy asked, "Are we–uh, you going to that show in New York this weekend?"

Devin shook her head. "I had trouble concentrating on Sunday." A bird flew overhead, and Devin watched its flight to an uppermost beam. "Besides, it's just not safe. For you, the horses or other people."

She thought of her walk back to the barn after picking up her ribbons on Sunday, past the row of security guards. "Not till this is over, and I hope that's real soon."

As they rode down with the straw and hay, Devin said, "I hope you aren't planning to camp here overnight."

"Why not? It's my job."

"No. I don't want you staying here at night. You feed the horses twice a day and let them out to move around a little."

"Can you be here Thursday morning?"

Devin frowned, trying to recall that day's schedule. "I would have to be here to let you in."

"Chief has a farrier appointment in the morning. You know he won't let the blacksmith touch him unless you're there."

"I think I'll reschedule that appointment. There's just too much going on right now."

"Do you want me to call him for you?"

"That would be a big help, Wendy. I'd appreciate you doing that for me."

With the uneasy feeling of eyes upon her, Devin walked the perimeter of the barn and paddock, expecting at any moment to discover someone watching her. The same questions continued to plague her: safety, security, were the Florian police patrols enough?

As she approached her car, the question that bothered her most ran through her mind again: What was Ian's connection to everything?

She took a bag of apples and carrots from the passenger seat and, after a moment's pondering, the little phone Mark had given her and tucked it into her jacket pocket. She settled herself in a sunny spot on the paddock's stone fence to watch her horses as Wendy brought them out. Chief was first. He dropped to the grass to roll not far from the barn door. He got up, trotted a few feet, sniffed the ground and rolled again. He repeated the sniffing and rolling in two other places before going to Devin and nuzzling her face.

His jet-black coat glistened and rippled in the sun. Devin brushed a few blades of grass from his back and out of his long wavy mane. He sniffed the apple she offered but jerked his head around, ears pitched forward, staring intently beyond the opposite paddock wall.

Chief whirled around, watching some spot in the distance. Wendy led Apollo out. A few feet from the door he froze, gazing in the same direction.

Devin felt the hair on her arms and neck stand on end. *What do they see? A bird or animal, or something I really need to worry about?*

Whatever had caught the horses' attention soon disappeared. Chief returned and gently lifted his apple from her fingers. Apollo tried to bite through the plastic bag for the lone red apple in it. "Be patient, Pal. I'll get it for you." He licked her face as she spoke.

As Shaman pushed between the other two horses for his treat, Wendy asked, "Did you see anything where they were looking?"

"No, but it could be anything."

"Should I put them back in the barn?"

"No, let them stay out. Just keep your eyes open."

They watched the three stallions mill around the paddock, paw, roll and nibble at the grass. After a few minutes, Wendy whispered, "I'm sorry about being mad about the policeman, Miss D."

Shaman came up and nuzzled Devin's cheek. As she stroked his neck, she replied, "I can understand why you were upset, Wendy. But I'm glad he went up to investigate, rather than–" She stopped, not wanting to consider another scenario.

Devin waited until Wendy was satisfied the horses had had enough exercise and attention and were safely back in their stalls, and made the promised call to the farrier. After Wendy left and the patrolman said it was time for his drive around the farm perimeter, she drove up to the house. She hoped to find some clue to her aunt's distress the night before. She climbed the front steps to the verandah that wrapped three sides of the big brick mansion and walked across its wide moss-green floor.

As she opened the ornately-trimmed wooden screen door, she turned and admired the sweep of lawn and neatly-tended gardens shaded by huge oak and maple trees. "It's so peaceful here," she mused. "So beautiful. Why is someone trying to destroy it?"

She unlocked the double oak entrance doors with their leaded, beveled glass panels and stepped into the large foyer dominated by a soaring cathedral ceiling and dramatic open, curving staircase ending in the middle of the inlaid hardwood floor. She leaned back against the doors to close them. The *clunk* as the doors closed reminded her to flip the lock behind her.

In the center of the foyer, suspended from the ceiling by ropes of faceted glass cubes, was an immense crystal chandelier. As a small child, she had helped one of her grandmother's servants clean the chandelier and had been told it was "one of Madam's favorite things in the house."

Devin gasped. "What would Madam think of it now?"

This morning, the fixture was festooned with panties, bras and pantyhose. She circled under it, shaking her head.

She sidled into the formal living room, sank onto a nearby couch, staring, mouth open. Bright-red paint was splashed all over the fieldstone fireplace as high as the vandal could reach. She clapped both hands over her face.

*What else is there to find?*

Her eyes settled on a gouge in the dining room door jamb. About a yard up from the floor, the brittle, multi-layered old paint had a circular indentation in it. As she hurried over for a closer look, she stepped over a few slivers of glass scattered on the polished oak boards. Crunching underfoot were pieces of some kind of black metal cylinder and the bent remains of the slotted film spindle from a camera.

In the kitchen, the trash can sat in front of the sink cabinet instead of its customary place under the sink. As Devin opened the door to replace the can, she found the remains of her aunt's 35mm camera, entangled in a roll of film torn from its spindles. Also in the can were the partially-burned cover and crumpled and shredded pages of Aggie's journal. The pages looked as if they had been torn out one by one as someone read the book. She reached in and picked out a page, asking aloud, "What was here, Auntie, a picture in your camera or notes in your journal about what scared you?"

She jerked her hands away. "Evidence. I'm tampering with evidence." She turned toward Aggie's sitting room to see its door flung wide open and books and magazines strewn across the floor. The rocker was up-ended. Not a single thing remained on the small bookshelf under the window. Lisè's stretched-canvas oil paintings of spring and fall at a local stream had been reduced to splinters and fabric shreds.

She turned around to look into the powder room. Lisè's beautiful border had been totally destroyed; the plaster where it had been painted was smashed down to the lath, all the way around the chair rail.

She slumped against the door jamb. "How could they?"

She took a moment to inventory Aggie's medicine bottles on the shelf above the sink, three brand-new prescription bottles, their safety-seal tapes intact. Devin supposed her aunt had taken the older, almost-empty bottles along in her handbag when she went to her friend's house the previous night.

She grabbed the phone handset, but her fingers froze over the keypad. *What if this phone is bugged and the person who responds isn't a real Florian policeman?* She set it back on the counter and dug the little phone from her pocket.

She hurried down the hall, past the staircase, stopping to unlock the front door then dialing her own phone number. *Thank God Ria agreed to stay one more night.* The call went into voice mail. *She must be in the shower.*

The answering machine beeped in her ear. "Oh, God, Ria! The house was vandalized and Auntie's room was destroyed!"

She thought she heard a *thump* from somewhere upstairs. "Somebody's here, Ria!"

She sidestepped into the parlor, a small stuffy room tucked behind the staircase, just inside the front doors. She heard a muffled squeak, then another. Someone on the back stairway, on the landing where it made a right-angled turn around the powder room. The person moved slowly down the last three steps, then took several hurried strides into the kitchen and then out to the mud room. The back door banged shut.

Devin took several giant steps and yanked open the front doors. As she pushed open the screen door, she saw someone with dark hair sprint past the big willow tree near the end of the driveway and disappear into the evergreens clustered at the edge of the lawn.

She ran out to the driveway, dialing 911 on the way. "Please send somebody out to the Hale House!" she blurted out to the operator. "It was vandalized and I think someone's still inside!"

"A car is enroute. Your friend called a few minutes ago and told us the house had been entered overnight. She said she was on her way too. Just sit tight, okay?"

Devin knew the drive from her home in Florian took fifteen minutes; she was relieved to see a cruiser turn into the driveway in less than ten. Soon a second police car parked behind the first. Officer McChesney climbed out and consulted with the other policemen.

One headed for the front of the house, and the other went to the kitchen. McChesney turned to her. "Did you go through the whole house?"

"Only the first floor. Then I heard someone on the back steps and ran out."

As he nodded, she added, "Ria and I walked through yesterday afternoon, maybe five-thirty, six o'clock, after my aunt called my house, all upset."

"And everything was fine then?" As Devin nodded, McChesney continued his questions. "Is Miss Hall all right?"

"She called around midnight last night from the mall, and we—Aunt Aggie and I—came out so she could pick up a few things and stay at her friend's house." She looked McChesney in the eye. "She wanted to go to her friend's house, she said, because she was afraid to be here or at my house. I'm really glad she wasn't here."

"So am I. Was Ria with you when you came out with your aunt?"

She shook her head.

"Was the house in order at midnight?"

"I don't know. I could barely keep up with Auntie while she scooted upstairs to her bedroom and bathroom collecting her things. I think she was terrified to be here."

"Have you talked to her since then?"

"I never call her this early. And it's way too early to call her friend's house."

"Are you okay with going back inside?" He headed for the front steps.

She nodded slightly. "You guys are here now." She paused. "Officer McChesney."

He stopped on the top step and looked toward her in response.

"I saw someone running across the yard."

"It sounds like you know who it was."

"I think it was Ian." Her face crumpled and she struggled with her tears.

He nodded. "That random thought about that sweatshirt – was that about Ian?"

"I thought it would fit him."

"Do you think he's responsible for this?"

"I don't want to."

He motioned her inside and looked around the foyer, then whistled and pointed to the chandelier. "That's new."

"That's only the start."

As Devin stood below the lingerie-draped chandelier, McChesney went to take a closer look at the fireplace.

"I'm calling in for some more help." He turned back to her. "What else?"

Devin pointed out the debris on the floor and the marred woodwork on the door jamb as they entered the dining room.

"What else?"

"There's a mess in the kitchen. And Auntie's sitting room. And the powder room."

In the kitchen she gasped when she looked at the counter. Aggie's three medicine bottles that had been on the shelf above the sink now topped another cut-and-paste note on the counter. "You haven't seen the last of me yet."

"That wasn't here before!" She looked around the kitchen. "The trash can's been knocked over." She pushed past McChesney and another policeman. "I can't stay in here."

Standing in the middle of the driveway, surrounded by police cars, Devin lit a cigarette. She took a long drag, exhaled, threw back her head and shouted, "I don't know who in hell you are, or why you're doing this, so how will I know you when I see you?"

When the cop reached her, she took a deep breath and exhaled, a loud exaggerated "Huh. I guess I picked a bad week to give up smoking, didn't I?" she asked as she crushed out the cigarette and pulled out another.

McChesney nodded, sighing. "Been there, done that." The cop waited as she lit up again. "After Miss St. Amont called and the first car went out, I tried to pull up your file on the computer but nothing was there."

She blew smoke rings, wiping away tears as she watched the wispy rings dissipate. Halfway through her smoke she asked, "Not even last week's complaint you promised me would be entered and followed up on?"

McChesney slowly shook his head.

"Not even the fire?"

A slight lift of McChesney's eyebrows was his only response. "The computer record, the evidence file, the file with my notes–everything I had set up was gone."

She looked across the lawn to the woods and back at the policeman. "That means one of the cops here with you now could be an accomplice, like that guy that came out that you said wasn't one of yours. And the one who was here yesterday."

"He never showed up today for his shift. He hadn't been with us too long. I shouldn't have trusted him." McChesney sounded as if he was talking through clenched teeth. "I can't say much more than–" He shook his head. "Access to our filing system is limited, but files just don't disappear like these did. Let's just say I -" He paused again. "I don't know how much my error in judgment might have hurt you."

They stared at one another. She didn't attempt to wipe away the tears running down her face. "I can't deal with this any longer. God knows what happened to my aunt before she called her friend to take her away."

The policeman sighed. "Are you ready to go back inside?"

Another policeman met them at the back door. "Miss Marques, we need you to check the library and tell us if anything's missing." He held open the door for her and McChesney.

As McChesney passed the other policeman, he said, "On our way."

Devin led the way to the front stairway, noting someone had taken the lingerie off the chandelier.

As the other cop started up the stairs, McChesney paused at the living room door. "Jesus." The word echoed in the high-ceilinged room. He followed Devin up the steps and along the wide hallway that overlooked the living room like a balcony. A ballroom was at the end of that hall.

Devin pushed open the ballroom's double doors and squinted at the sunlight pouring through windows usually covered with drawn velvet drapes.

"What is this?" McChesney asked, pointing to the brilliant, multi-colored confetti littering the polished wood floor. Devin knelt to scoop up a handful. Bits of satin ribbon.

She looked across the floor to the back of the room as she let the scraps of ribbon flutter from her hand. Flowers lay like water lilies among the confetti. Not flowers, she discovered, but rosettes from horse-show ribbons. She grabbed another handful of the confetti and saw gold and silver lettering on some of the ribbon bits.

Devin picked up a blue rosette and turned it over to read the back card. "'Mystic Chief, Intermediate Jumper Class, Tampa Invitational.'" She held it up for the cop to see. "Chief's biggest win so far this year." She wandered around, picking up the rosettes, and stepped on something amid the ribbon confetti. Chunks of shattered crystal lay among dented silver dishes and cups and wooden trophy bases. A few feet away, in a pool of sunlight under a window, a piece of broken cut glass cast rainbows around the room.

Devin picked up a small jumping horse trophy that had escaped destruction. As she caressed the figure, she said, "This must be every ribbon and every trophy we had in the tack room at the big barn."

*Were they collected before or after Wendy was drugged, or was Wendy forced to cut the ribbons up?* Devin shuddered at the thought.

She glanced down at the little statuette she held and read the engraved nameplate on its base. "'First Place, Junior Jumper Championship, Devon, PA. Ian Marques.'" The event had taken place twelve years earlier, not long before he was in a car accident that ended his competitive riding, and her career in the sport took off.

She set the trophy and rosettes on a windowsill and hurried out of the ballroom, toward the grand staircase, anxious to see if her aunt's bedroom had been disturbed.

McChesney followed, "What else is on this floor?"

"Two bedrooms, my aunt's and one made up for guests. And a bathroom."

Devin led him to the door of the guest room, which appeared untouched. She slowed up as she approached her aunt's door. "I don't think I'll be able to handle it if her bedroom's trashed."

He stepped ahead of her and tried to open the door. "Do you have a key to this?"

"It's not locked."

"It doesn't open."

She looked at the bottom half of the door where the paint was chipped and someone had left a half-dozen black shoe prints. "You have to know how to do it." She put a hand on the doorknob, pulled up on it and pushed, and the door opened. After a quick glance at her aunt's tidy bed, she added, "Good. They didn't."

The bathroom across the hall had also been spared, so they continued along the hall to a small alcove and sitting area at the bottom of the steps to the third floor.

She stopped, shaking her head. The floor was littered with smashed glass, splintered picture frames and colorful confetti made from photographs and Lisè's drawings.

Devin looked up at untouched pictures and photographs on the walls and back to those shattered on the floor. "Why?" The word came out in a small, strangled voice.

McChesney shook his head, and they continued up the carpeted steps.

"And what's on the third floor?"

"Two bedrooms that had been servants' quarters. They're used for storage now. And what used to be a much larger library."

The library was a shambles. Every book had been pulled from the shelves and ripped apart. The heavy Stickley table had been smashed against one of the empty bookcases, breaking the shelving and one leg of the table.

"What in God's name was this person looking for?" McChesney demanded.

Devin leaned against a wall. "I haven't a clue."

"Would you know what was here, and if anything was missing?"

A policeman carrying camera equipment entered the room.

"These are just–" she shrugged, "old books, novels, atlases, encyclopedias. Nobody ever looked at them, but my aunt refused to part with them. The only thing of real value in the room was the broken table."

"Was there something here of value at one time?" The camera-carrying cop looked around. "Someone obviously thought so."

Devin turned away, bumping into McChesney. "Aunt Aggie said Lisè had been–"

"Lisè, you said?" He pulled out a notepad. "You talked about her before."

"Lisè Logan. She house-sat and ran errands for my aunt. Yesterday she was painting the powder room downstairs and said she was moving to New York City for a new job. She thought my aunt was mad at her for leaving."

"When was this?"

"I think she talked to Auntie not long before Auntie called my house, when I said I thought she sounded upset. That would have been before Ian showed up yesterday."

"And what were you saying about your aunt talking about Lisè, not yesterday, but some time ago?"

"I think I told you Aunt Aggie found Lisè looking through all the family history books. Not long after that, Lisè started asking about wills and deeds and such, and I guess my aunt was bothered by her sudden curiosity. Not that it really sounded like something Lisè would do. But she and Jesse are together a lot, and those were the kind of questions Jesse asks about my family that irritate me."

"What did your aunt do?"

"She made a big deal about wanting to redecorate, and took down all the pictures and artwork and took all the family history books, journals and house plans off the shelves up here, and gave all of that stuff to me for safekeeping at my house. And then she began collecting paint chips and fabric samples and dithering over the decorating scheme."

The cop glanced around the room. "Do you think Lisè did this in retaliation?"

"Not Lisè. When she was painting yesterday, she said she wanted to do it for my aunt because my aunt had been good to her. She was singing *Carmen*, and someone had given her a black eye. That beautiful painting she did in the first-floor powder room–it's totally destroyed."

She cocked her head to one side. "She left the house and went down to the barn to meet Ian and Jesse. Said she wanted to get her stuff out of the barn, but to my knowledge, there was nothing of hers in the barn. The only thing I had seen of Lisè's at that time, here in the house, was a jacket on the dryer. I remember it because last night Auntie put her coat on the dryer, right beside Lisè's. But I don't remember seeing it when I came in a little while ago." Her voice trailed off. "I need some air."

Uniforms seemed to be all over the house. Devin counted five between the library on the third floor and the landing at the top of the grand staircase. She hurried down the wide, curving steps, her heart pounding in her ears. All those policemen looking for clues, but no one could answer her single question "Why?"

She stepped out onto the verandah and stared across the swath of manicured lawn, looking towards the road where she'd seen Ian disappear into the pines near the end of the driveway.

McChesney opened the door and joined her. "I'm sorry we haven't been able to move ahead on this and stop this destruction."

"You told me more than once you can't do anything till you know who you're looking for."

"The people we can find have alibis. Your cleaning lady won't open the door for us, not that she has to when we don't have a search warrant. One of her neighbors told us she's terrified." He paused. "Something about the kids being threatened."

"I know. She was going to take her kids out of school and go away for a few days. She planned to clean today at the cottage before she left, even though it wasn't her usual day." Tears welled up again. "I'll have to ask Ria if she came."

"You say you talked to Lisè yesterday. We haven't been able to find her."

Devin shrugged. "She did have an apartment in West Haven, but I don't know the address."

The policeman nodded. "Devin, I feel like they're always a step ahead of us, like someone is sitting back, laughing."

"You said the guy who came out the night of the fire wasn't a Florian cop."

He gave her a slight smile. "We're working on that, and more patrols." The policeman rolled his eyes as one of the other officers called to him from the front hall. Before he went inside, he cocked his head slightly. "That looks like Ria's car turning up the driveway."

She watched as Ria threaded her way around the police cars parked along the pavement.

Ria rolled down her window and called out, "Sorry I took so long. The phone rang as I was leaving. I stopped to answer–"

Devin went down the steps to the Honda, and Ria hugged her after she climbed out. "There isn't anything in the house they didn't–" She stopped, close to tears, a loss for words.

Ria gently took both of Devin's hands into hers. "I would have been here sooner, but *your* phone rang as I left the cottage. I went back and answered because I thought it might be–" Ria bit her lip and looked away from Devin. "Someone from the emergency room in Florian Hospital called. I'm so sorry!"

Devin pulled away from Ria. "What happened? What did they want?"

"I stopped by the hospital to make sure it wasn't a prank before I came out. I'm so sorry, Devin." She cleared her throat. "I'm so sorry. Your aunt collapsed and died a little while ago when she and her friends were having coffee."

# CHAPTER TWELVE

*I was a nurse in another lifetime, another identity. I specialized in putting suffering people out of their misery. I never got caught, because I only used undetectable methods, like altering the content of a heart patient's pills. The truth would never show on an autopsy! But Stan McChesney and the other Florian cops <u>will</u> find some of the capsules and artificial sweetener residue–and another little surprise–in <u>your</u> bathroom...*

*But I didn't mean to kill the old lady.*

*Not yet.*

Devin jerked away from Ria's grasp and took several steps backward. "No!" She held her hands in front of her like a shield as Ria came closer. "It has to be a bad joke, like that cop that wasn't really a cop!"

"Your aunt's friends were there, the Hat Lady and the Jewelry Lady."

*Ria's nicknames for Aggie's best friends. The Triplets, they called themselves. Aggie, Doris and Bella, always together.* Devin hung her head and covered her face as the tears began.

"It can't be true! They were just going for breakfast like they always do on Tuesday!"

She sank to the driveway. "I was going to make sure I found time today to have tea with her so I could find out what was wrong!" She curled into a ball, her forehead touching the gravel, sobbing. "It's my fault! It's my fault! I didn't protect her! I didn't make her stay somewhere else!"

Ria knelt beside her, wrapped an arm around her. "Hey, that's not true! You know she had a bad heart, and hasn't been feeling well lately. Her friends were right there. Honey, she wasn't alone, or here with whoever's been scaring her standing over her, laughing at her."

Devin shook her head. "Some thanks for all the years she took care of me." She slowly stood up and brushed off her clothing. She stared into space, seeing nothing, then looked around at all the police cruisers scattered along the driveway. "I have to go see her."

Ria hugged Devin. "I'll go with you. Is there anything you have to do here?"

McChesney was talking on the phone in the living room when Devin and Ria entered, and hung up as they approached. He opened his mouth to speak and closed it again. He looked at Devin. "I just heard about your aunt. I'm so sorry. And I know you have a lot on your mind now, but I just need a few minutes. That little sitting room behind the stairs seems quiet."

Trailed by Ria and the policeman, Devin turned and walked across the hall, then dropped into the first chair by the door, eager to be on her way to the hospital, certain Ria was wrong.

"I won't take too long." The policeman opened his notebook. "I just wanted to bring you up to date on some things that have come to light in the past two days."

Devin nodded, half-listening.

"The SUV that had Wendy's license plate on it has been missing almost a year, as was the owner. We found his remains yesterday in a storage locker in North Haven. The Plymouth Reliant we towed from the driveway yesterday disappeared about the same time its owner died suddenly under circumstances similar to your aunt's death."

Devin gave the cop a quick look. "Do the owners have anything in common?"

"Both people were cancer patients with home-care nurses."

"Did you find anything on the Crown Victoria, or that fake cop?"

He looked from Ria to Devin. "We're working on it. "He paused, took a deep breath. "As for the Reliant's owner—it was discovered that his medicine had been tampered with, so the meds in your aunt's purse are being analyzed. I'm to collect anything here that she may have been taking that might also have been adulterated." He paused. "I also need to fingerprint you, since you might have had access to any medicine Miss Hall may have ingested."

Devin opened her mouth, too stunned to speak, but Ria jumped up, shouting, "You've *got* to be kidding! Devin wouldn't—you're kidding, right?"

He shook his head. "I'm sorry." He spoke softly, but in a no-nonsense tone. "I have to do my job."

Devin's voice shook as she replied, "Aunt Aggie never let me touch her meds, but you do what you have to do."

Ria reached over and patted Devin's hand. "Sir, by any chance do they have pictures of the nurse or nurses who took care of the cancer patients?"

"We're waiting for them to be faxed over. You can stop by the station later for those fingerprints. Right now, you need to take care of your aunt's arrangements."

The explosion Devin anticipated from Ria came the moment Ria turned her car from the driveway onto the road as she drove Devin to the hospital. "How dare that cop accuse you of poisoning your aunt, after all that's been happening!"

"Ria, he said it's routine–"

"He has to know there's no way you'd hurt her!"

"He's probably seen stuff you and I can't even imagine one person doing to another." Devin looked out the window, not really seeing the passing landscape. "Maybe now it makes sense," she mused, almost to herself. "Aunt Aggie always took brand-new bottles of medicine with her when she went away. She would get three months at a time–that was what her insurance allowed–but she had the pharmacy put each month's supply in a separate bottle, then put a sealing tape on each bottle."

"I remember you commenting about it when she started doing that last year."

"I didn't think anything of it then because she had her thing about me touching her medicine. She'd be fine when she was away, but would start having bad days right after she came home. Sometimes–sometimes–" She paused a long time before continuing. "Sometimes I got mad at her because I thought she was pretending about not feeling well, just for attention. But Officer McChesney just said home care nurses were involved with those people who had disappeared. Maybe her medicine was–do you think she saw Lisè mess with it or something?"

Ria shrugged. "I can't see Lisè being a nurse. An aide maybe, the person who empties bed pans."

"You saw the painting Lisè did. She said she worked in a print shop, an artist." She thought for a moment. "We never did find anything she might have left in the barn, and the jacket we saw yesterday that I said was hers was gone this morning."

Ria nodded. "I think you were right when you said they probably intended to unlock something or open something to come back later."

"Someone must have come in while I was there with Auntie last night."

"Why do you say that?"

"Everything was locked, Ria. The cops checked every window and every door yesterday. Today, when I found the house vandalized, I thought I saw Ian run across the yard. He could have come in while Auntie and I were upstairs and gone to the basement, and I never would have known."

She watched Ria slowly nodding. "I don't know why they had to kill Aunt Aggie." She burst into tears again.

As they approached the hospital, Ria wondered, "Should I go to the emergency entrance or the front entrance?"

"I don't know. I've never come here to visit a dead person before. But I would probably go to the emergency room."

When they entered the waiting area, Devin spotted her aunt's friends, now two bedraggled lumps on chairs closest to the door. The two older ladies simultaneously got up to meet her. They embraced Devin as one and wailed, "Oh, we're so sorry! There was nothing we could do!"

She tried to extricate herself from the web of arms, murmuring, "It's okay. It's okay," as she patted a hand here, an arm there. She looked from one forlorn soul to the other, then tried to smile. "I'm grateful my aunt was with you, and you stayed with her. You did what you could, I'm sure. Thank you."

Bella Paige had been Aggie Hall's closest friend as long as Devin could remember. She had offered her guest room the previous night, when Aggie had refused to stay home alone. She was a tall, vibrant, white-haired woman who favored bright colors and big, chunky jewelry. She dabbed her eyes and sniffled. "We'd just been served our coffee. Aggie said she felt sick, then her eyes rolled back and she slumped over. The waitress ran and called 911."

Doris Baker loved hats and cats, and, in Devin's mind, was something of a drama queen. Today Doris turned her most pitiful face to Devin, sighed heavily, and whimpered, "The poor dear was gone almost instantly! There was a doctor in the coffee shop, and he came over to check her pulse. Oh, it was terrible!" She threw herself onto Devin and broke into huge, noisy sobs.

When Doris calmed down, Devin kept an arm around her. She looked from one woman to the other. "I'm going to see what has to be done now. Thank you for staying here and waiting for me. I'll let you know as soon as I know what the arrangements are."

"She had preplanned some things," Doris offered, dabbing at her eyes.

Devin nodded, turning a forced smiled at her. "I know. I have that information at home." She shook her head, not wanting to cry again, not wanting to set Doris to tears again.

"You'll let us know if you need anything?" Bella asked.

"Of course."

Bella engulfed Devin in her arms. "If there's anything we can do–"

Devin smiled through tears. "Would you like Ria to walk you out?"

"Oh, no, dear! You need her here with you!"

The ladies shuffled away, turning to wave at Devin and Ria as they approached the automatic doors. Devin watched them, leaning on one another, arm in arm, as they crossed the driveway to the parking area.

Ria elbowed her, pointing to the chairs where Bella and Doris had been sitting. Devin had to smile at the circle of used tissues in front of one chair that had apparently fallen from a lap as one of the ladies had stood up.

*Probably Doris.* She leaned over and picked up the litter.

She couldn't delay the moment she'd been dreading, and approached the emergency room desk.

The woman in white scrubs smiled. "You must be Miss Hall's niece. Those two ladies kept telling me you'd be here shortly. I'll get someone to take you to her."

"Whenever you're ready," the aide quietly instructed, her hand on the doorknob. Devin leaned against the wall and closed her eyes, wanting the scenario to be another bad dream. But she was still in a hospital corridor when she opened her eyes and looked around. She nodded to the aide and turned to face the door, taking a deep breath before she stepped inside.

Ria waved a hand, shaking her head. "I'll be *here* if you need me."

"The medical examiner will be here in a moment," the aide said. "He has a few questions."

Aggie was on a table, covered with a sheet, looking as if she were taking a nap. Devin touched Aggie's hair, smoothing it away from her face. "They can't frighten you anymore, Auntie," she whispered.

The medical examiner approached. He reminded Devin of one of her math professors, very tall and thin, with slicked-back brown hair and a pen clipped to his shirt collar. He extended a hand and cleared his throat. "I'll need to do an autopsy. It's state law when someone passes as suddenly as your aunt. We know from the meds in her purse that she had a heart arrhythmia. Were there any other conditions we should be aware of?"

"She had high cholesterol. She took Lipitor for that. But it was normal the last time she was checked, which I think was February." She blinked rapidly, again close to tears. "She said her doctor told her she was in great shape for a sixty-eight-year-old."

The man nodded.

"How soon–?" Devin didn't know how to complete the question.

"Autopsy results may take a few weeks. But you should be able to lay her to rest by the weekend. There are papers for you to complete, and we'll release the body to the establishment handling the arrangements as soon as we can." He cleared his throat. "I'm sorry for your loss."

She turned back to the small, still figure laying on the table. The medical examiner was instantly by her side, discreetly lifting the sheet, exposing Aggie's arm. "Why don't you hold her hand while you say goodbye?"

Devin did as he suggested, gazing at Aggie's face. "I'll probably never know what they did to upset you so yesterday, Auntie. It'll be a long time before I forgive myself for not protecting you better." She stroked a cold cheek, twirled a grey curl around her finger. She leaned down and laid her cheek against Aggie's, and kissed her forehead. "I'll make sure you look your best and have the right dress for your send-off." She patted the cold hand she held. "I promise to keep Doris's remembrances short."

She studied Aggie's face again, then looked at the man patiently waiting near the door. "Thank you. Take care of her."

He nodded and opened the door for her.

Devin and Ria walked back to Ria's Honda in silence. They left the parking lot before Ria asked, "What now?"

"The medical examiner does tests, he releases the body to the funeral home, and they do whatever they do before the viewing and burial." She paused, swallowing. "He said I could probably bury her by the weekend."

"Will you need a special permit to bury her in the private graveyard at Hightower?"

"I'll have to find out. The funeral home should know. I know she'd want to be with Grammy and Ashley."

"I heard the Hat Lady say your aunt preplanned her funeral?"

"Someone they all knew died, and they were all up in arms about how they thought the service was all wrong and not at all what their friend would want. Aunt Aggie must have spent a week flipping through a hymnal and her Bible. She picked some songs she wanted, and some Bible verses, and even wrote part of her eulogy, and who she wanted to read what verse and sing a certain song."

"Did she write her own obituary too?"

"Oh, yes. She probably felt I'd be too busy, so she wouldn't burden me with this petty stuff." Devin pondered for a moment. "I'll bet there are two or three suggestions for what she wants to be buried in. She surely wouldn't want to leave that to my last-minute grab for something." She paused. "Knowing Aunt Aggie, it's probably bagged and tagged in the back of the closet."

"Do you know where her funeral plans are?"

"In the closet where we keep all the suitcases, inside one of the big ones in the back. All the books and papers and stuff she didn't want in the house anymore when she found Lisè had all the books pulled out, laying all over the library. She figured Lisè was looking for a will, given the kinds of questions she'd been asking."

"But you said yourself your aunt had nothing of value."

"Nope. She learned the look and sound of money and how to get it on a budget when she was working. When she left all that to take care of me, I recall telling my uncle, as eloquently as any nine-year-old could, he had to make sure she had enough money so she could keep looking pretty." She fell silent for several minutes. "Obviously, she was really good at keeping up the act."

They rode in silence until Ria reached the first fencepost on Hightower property. Devin sighed. "The first thing I have to do now is call Uncle Zack."

"Do you think the police found anything?"

Devin looked out the window to see where they were. "We'll know soon."

A police car was parked just off the road, and Ria was stopped as soon as she turned into the drive. She was allowed to proceed as soon as the policeman recognized who she was, and that Devin was with her.

She glanced over at Devin. "I guess they finally realized that we were having a problem after all. If you're okay, I'm going to go."

As Ria drove away, two policemen carried equipment out the back door to waiting vehicles. Two more followed, with more equipment.

Devin approached one man. "Is Officer McChesney still here?"

"He left a little while ago. We're done inside. We went through the entire house, from the attic down, took fingerprints and pictures. Checked every lock, every door, every closet, and looked at absolutely every nook, corner and cranny of that house, and there's no one hiding anywhere in there." He shook his head. "Stan just called, though. Said he has questions about your monitoring service, and expect him back here in a little while."

"My—what?"

"The alarm system. That's all he said. We're putting someone here in the house and at your house in town tonight, just for insurance, till that can be investigated. Right now, I'm going to take a run down by the barn and see that all's well there."

After Devin locked the door behind the policeman, she went to Aggie's bedroom and stood in the door, looking around. A room right out of a Martha Stewart layout, with everything in place, just so. She opened the closet door to total organization: all fronts of clothing and all hangers facing the same direction, blouses in one section, skirts in another, slacks in another, dresses in another. Everything hung from lightest color to black. Flat shoes on one shelf, light to black. Heeled shoes on another, one row for low heels, light to black, another for higher heels, organized by heel height and color, in the same fashion. A slotted cube for handbags. A drawer for sweaters, a drawer for scarves, a drawer for belts and jewelry.

Devin pulled out the jewelry drawer and touched each of the costume pieces there. Nothing was missing. "If they had found this, I wonder if they would have known none of these were worth anything." She signed and looked around the closet. "Then ripped everything apart in search of the real stuff." She slid the slim drawer shut.

She flipped through the dresses to the bagged ones in the back: Lovely grey beaded crepe that she'd worn to Devin's graduation from MIT. Sophisticated cobalt blue two piece she'd worn to a Boston Pops concert with Bella and Doris last summer. Mint green cutwork frock she'd taken with her on their Caribbean cruise last spring. Burgundy crepe two piece, with beadwork and cutwork, kelly green silk, royal blue suit, mauve lace–Devin knew which shoes and which bag was to go with each outfit. But none was marked "for my funeral."

"That's not like you, Auntie," she remarked, closing the door. *Maybe she described it in her funeral plans.* She sighed. She'd have to find and read those papers later, once she went home.

Home, where Officer McChesney said something might be wrong with her alarm system.

Devin carefully locked the back door behind her when she left the house. She took her riding boots from her trunk and pulled them on and drove to the barn, parking in the middle of the lane between the house and the old barn's site. She wanted the car in plain view while she was exercising her horses in the field across from the paddock.

All three were antsy from being cooped up in their stalls for two days. She closed the open gate with a piece of portable fence before letting Shaman and Chief out into the paddock, then saddled Apollo right outside the barn door. Even with a uniformed policeman standing by, she locked that before leading Apollo to the gate.

The stallion must have sensed her uneasiness, snapping at her and shying away as she put the reins over his head and tried to mount. "Yeah, I know, Pal. Everything's different right now, and you don't like it." She settled herself into the saddle, pulled the reins tight, and reached down and tightened the girth one more notch. She patted his neck. "Sorry you have to go through this nightmare with me."

The field had a low stone fence on two sides, a row of hedges on a third near the lawn, and, closest to the paddock, several fence posts that had once been strung with wire. "Okay, Pal, let's watch out for holes. Nice and easy the first time around."

Walk, trot, controlled canter, just like the warm-up exercises she put the horses through at the shows. She reversed direction and repeated the exercise. There would be no jumps today, just the gaits over the flat to keep him limber.

Apollo bucked and tossed his head more than usual during the workout. "That's okay, Pal. That's about how I feel too." She reined him in to a walk to cool him down before going back to the paddock, to repeat the procedure with Shaman.

Shaman proved to be more skittish than Apollo had been. He reared, bucked, kicked and pawed as she tried to convince him to enter the small field. She looked around, trying to locate the distraction, but saw nothing. "Oh, yeah, Sammy, that really settles my nerves," she told him, pulling his head to face the lane where her car was parked. "Let's just go up there a ways, then come back. Maybe you'll be willing to go into the field then."

She allowed him to trot about halfway to the burnt-out barn then turned back towards Aggie's house. He broke into a very slow, showy exaggerated trot that he did when he seemed exceptionally pleased with himself.

"What's this act for, you big show-off? No crowds today, just you, me, Pal, the kid and the cop. And I don't think he's impressed. Let's just go into that field and do some figure-eights and hack around a little."

She reined him into the field between two fence posts and kept him aimed at the middle of the field. Shaman apparently no longer noticed whatever had distracted him before, but Devin caught herself glancing around, holding her breath.

The horse took advantage of her diverted attention, side-stepping, shying, bucking. He'd back up when she wanted him to turn, do a sideways trot when she wanted him to canter. She finally pulled him to a stop, again in the middle of the field, stroking his neck. "You're going to keep up with that fancy footwork, and find yourself a dressage horse where you have to act refined and proper."

Shaman tossed his head, up and down, for all the world looking as if he was agreeing with her.

"Well, dressage it is. We'll start at the end of the show jumping season. How's that grab you?" She dismounted as he vigorously shook his head. "Too bad. You already made your decision."

Chief wasn't as animated as Shaman had been, or as irritated as Apollo. He simply wanted to run. "Walk" and "trot" weren't on his agenda for the workout. Pulling hard on Chief's mouth, Devin kept him within a series of tight figure-eights and ess-turns, working on lead changes as he persisted with cantering the entire time.

She felt totally wrung-out when he finally settled down to a walk after their battle of wills. When they reached the far side of the field during the second lap of the field, as she cooled down the colt, she saw a police car drive up behind her Thunderbird.

McChesney climbed out of the car as she turned Chief through the center of the field, toward the opening between two of the fence posts. She unsaddled Chief and let him into the paddock with the other two horses before turning her attention to the policemen.

"Is everything okay?" she asked, noting McChesney was more tired-looking and drawn than she'd ever seen him before.

He gave his head a slight shake. "Let's walk. Matt'll keep an eye on them." He looked at the patrolman standing nearby, and cocked his head in the direction of the paddock. "Won't you, Matt?"

He didn't wait for a response, but walked past the Thunderbird, clearly expecting Devin to follow. She tossed Chief's saddle on top of the metal gate, draped the bridle across it and trotted up to the policeman.

"What's up?"

"I've had some very unexpected visitors, heard some very unsettling information since I left here this morning. You won't be staying in your house tonight, or in this one. You're going to pack these horses up and get them out of here. Don't worry, they're going to a place where Ian can't bother them."

"Where?"

"You'll drive to the Florian Police Station parking lot. You'll get directions there."

"What's going on?"

The policeman looked over the bucolic green acreage around him, turned his head to watch a brilliant red cardinal fly into the row of pines near the road. "Mark followed someone from your house this morning and found where the person lived. There's substantial, frightening evidence, "he looked directly at her, "in a diary I think I'm going to have bad dreams about. You, Ria and Mark have been stalked by at least one person for quite a while. Mark took pictures, followed someone to a building where he saw the nameplate of the company that allegedly performs monitoring on your security system."

When Devin opened her mouth to comment, he held up a hand to stop her. "The company happens to belong to the missing owner of the missing Crown Victoria. A building maintenance person said he hasn't seen anyone there for two weeks, but some of the equipment's been removed."

"Okay, but–"

"Wait, there's more. A landlady let Mark into the person's apartment. According to her neighbor, the woman came over with her cat in a carrier and seemed to be in a big hurry, explaining that she and her husband needed to go out of town for a few days on family business, then left. Another neighbor said the landlady left about forty-five minutes after Mark did–he was probably talking to me at the time. Both neighbors called us when they heard what they said sounded like furniture being thrown against the wall in the landlady's flat. The home was totally trashed."

Devin stared at him, hugging her arms around herself. "You said Ian–"

"I'm getting to Ian." He exhaled, shook his head. "Mark gave us the address of a garage where he saw a woman put the beat-up Toyota. The Toyota wasn't there but the Crown Victoria and what's left of Mark's stolen Firebird were."

"What's left of it?"

"The rest is in an evidence locker in Boston. Ria came in and looked at the pictures we received of the missing home-care nurse, and said she was pretty sure it was the same person she saw in some pictures she said you were sent in the mail."

"They're in my car."

"Ria said this person was in a couple classes with her at Boston College a couple years ago. She said you had said the same thing about-"He shook his head. "Someone."

He opened his ever-present notebook and displayed a sketch of a short-haired woman with a thin face, angular nose and deep-set eyes.

Devin studied the drawing and nodded. "She looks like the woman in the pictures I have. Some were from this year's Tampa Invitational, and the other ones–the other ones somebody sent me, all of them of her and Mark."

He tapped the picture. "A member of one victim's family made the sketch. That's the missing nurse."

He set another photo in front of the first one. "Who is this?"

Devin gave her head a slight shake. "Jesse, Ian's girlfriend!"

He nodded. "Ian came in while I was talking with Ria. Said he overheard Jesse on the phone at his mother's house, telling someone Mark had pictures and they were in trouble. He asked her who she was talking to, and she allegedly said if he was smart, he wouldn't ask any more questions and he'd keep his mouth shut. Then she got into his truck and left. He unplugged the phone and brought it and a glass she drank from to us. Jesse and the missing nurse appear to be the same person."

He looked at the peaceful landscape around him. "She called herself Jessica Hamilton when she clerked for us for several months last fall, doing data entry and filing." He gave his head a slight shake. "Now, put that Thunderbird of yours into the barn where it'll be safe, and pack up your horses."

# CHAPTER THIRTEEN

Devin stopped the truck at the end of the driveway to pick up her aunt's mail. As she walked across the road, she leafed through Aunt Aggie's delivery of magazines and junk mail. There also was a small parcel wrapped in brown grocery-bag paper criss-crossed with packing tape. It had no return address and its postmark was smudged.

Curious, she carefully opened the package's back flap. A slip of paper, stuck onto the packing tape, pulled out of the item inside. "Aggie, this is what I was telling you about. I can do this to you. Watch me." She pulled a battered paperback book from the wrapper.

"*The Godfather* by Mario Puzo?" She flipped through the pages, watching for underlining or a flash of neon highlighting, but saw none. "Maybe the note was the marker?" She carefully slipped it back into the wrapper, wondering about its significance. And its sender.

She opened the truck door, dropped the mail onto the seat, and walked up the driveway to take one last look at the barn. "Okay, Officer McChesney, you said there's a place for the horses where Ian won't be welcome. We're on our way." She squared her shoulders as she walked back to the truck. She paused to look over the house, then climbed into the cab and slammed the door. One of the horses kicked the back gate in response.

"Yeah, I hear you, Sammy. Let's get going."

Two police cars, their lights flashing, waited on the road to escort the truck, one in front, one behind.

"I hope you're watching, Ian, Jesse, Lisè, or whoever else you may be. You haven't beaten me yet."

She drummed her fingers on the steering wheel, her mind whirling. Ian had gone to the police. *A guilty conscience about helping Jesse, or had he truly stumbled onto something he'd known nothing about? And what had Mark found, wherever he'd been earlier in the day?* Obviously enough for one more innocent person to be attacked.

*McChesney said something about the company that was 'allegedly' monitoring my system? Does that mean those big checks I've been writing for months have been paying for no security at all?*

"Huh." She slumped against the seat, feeling the hair on her arms standing up as a sick feeling settled in her stomach.

As the parade turned into the police department parking lot, Devin saw Wendy, Officer McChesney, and a weather-beaten woman she instantly recognized as Susan Holt, the owner of Sleeping Giant Stable, the riding stable that had left Hightower the previous year. No, Ian wouldn't dare show his face at *that* woman's establishment! Devin let out a small sigh of relief as she climbed down from the truck cab.

Wendy met her, jumping up and down. "You said you needed to find a place where Ian couldn't go, Miss D, so I called Sleeping Giant. Mrs. Holt said they'd be very happy to help you out!"

The woman stepped forward, extending her hand. As Devin clasped it, Mrs. Holt said, "Nobody gets on my property if they haven't paid for the privilege to be there."

"I appreciate you taking us in on such short notice."

She put an arm around Wendy. "I'd love to hire this child away from you, but since that's not possible, I'm more than happy to help you out till you're able to make your barn safe. We have quarters on site for her, so she'll be under our protective wing too."

As Wendy giggled at the praise, McChesney motioned to Devin, wearing the same stony face he'd put on when he ordered her to move the horses. "We've inspected the barns and the security system, and, in my opinion, given the day's problems, Wendy found a good temporary solution. Mrs. Holt will take your truck, and we'll escort it to her farm. Wendy will go with her."

Devin asked, "You're good with this plan?"

"Given what I know, yes. Mrs. Holt's not kidding when she says you don't get in if you don't belong there."

"But you don't know—" She stopped, not sure how to finish her question.

"Where Jesse is, or who she really is? We wouldn't be having this conversation if I knew." As the truck's engine rumbled to life, the cop added, "Now, are you going with them, or have you made other arrangements?"

"Wait, there's something in the truck you need to see."

The cop waved to Mrs. Holt as the truck started to roll.

The older woman handed the package and Aggie's mail down to Devin, then drove on. Devin watched the truck till it turned a corner out of sight, instantly regretting turning care of her prized horses over to someone else, even with Wendy going with them. She turned back to the policeman waiting nearby.

He looked at the package in her hand. "What's that?"

"This was in my aunt's mail today. *The Godfather* by Mario Puzo. And a note saying something about doing something to her."

McChesney gave his head a slight jerk. "I take it you never read the book or saw the movie."

"No." She shook her head, confused. "Neither. Why?"

"The Godfather, head of a Mafia family, orders gruesome murders with a wave of a hand when someone crosses him or a member of his family. Hollywood producer has a prized race horse, displeases the Godfather. The producer wakes up with the horse's head in his bed."

As Devin stood by, a hand over her mouth, he continued, "A copy went to your house, too. Ria opened it and called us, probably just before she received the news about your aunt. I found that out about the same time I heard about the security system you may never have had at your house and your aunt's. That's why I told you to get the horses out of there."

Devin studied the pavement at her feet.

"The owner of that security outfit - when he disappeared, he was developing pet tracking equipment, tiny computer chips that are normally inserted under the animals' skin. He was the owner of the Crown Victoria your fake cop drove."

"I've heard of those chips. I recently talked with my vet about getting them for my horses."

"All the tracking equipment and all the chips are gone. They're probably all over you now and in a good share of your clothing and personal items."

"Is that why they always know where I am?"

McChesney nodded. "Ria also found a bottle of your aunt's medicine in the bathroom, with some of the capsules broken open on the sink. She found it after she came back from taking you to the hospital to see your aunt. She insisted it wasn't there when you left for the farm this morning, or after the cleaning lady left."

"How'd someone get into the house? Again."

The cop shook his head. "Miss St. Amont was very upset when she found it. She said she might have forgotten to lock the back door when she left."

"You said some of the pills were broken open on the sink. You also said all those missing people had had home-care nurses. Whoever messed with my aunt's medicine had to know she had an arrhythmia."

"We've already checked the contents of the capsules. Two of them in your bathroom had cocaine in them, as did one in Miss Hall's purse."

She drew in a ragged breath. "My mother died, doing cocaine at a party." She put her hand over her mouth. "My mother's autopsy report was one of the papers Auntie found Lisè reading a few months ago." She took a few steps away from the policeman. "And now my aunt is dead, since she may have taken a pill filled with cocaine that some wack job put into her medicine bottle." She bent over, hands on her knees, sobbing.

The cop stood nearby until she composed herself. "One more thing, then I know you have to deal with your aunt's arrangements." He paused, keeping his eyes on her face. "And you're not staying at your house or here tonight."

"No, I already have reservations at the Hampton Inn, but I have to go to my house tonight to find Auntie's written requests about everything."

McChesney nodded. "Remember that I told you the fingerprints we found at your house belonged to an AWOL soldier who allegedly died two years ago?"

Devin nodded as he was speaking, but kept her eyes on the pavement at her feet.

"A man's body was discovered in a cell after a fire at a small county jail. The body was burned beyond recognition, no fingerprints left, teeth all knocked out, so it couldn't be identified. At the time it was assumed he had died in the fire. But the fingerprints in your house and your aunt's belonged to that person, who was some sort of electronics specialist, cameras, sound, wiring, who'd been arrested and was awaiting transfer back to his unit.

"But–?" Devin asked, looking up at McChesney.

"His fingerprints were in the Crown Victoria. We're waiting for pictures and other information."

Devin shook her head without responding.

"You mentioned getting Caller ID, and all your prank calls came from Cambridge. One of the products the soldier had been working on when he went AWOL was equipment to mask phone numbers, so what was coming up on your Caller ID wasn't the actual number. Those calls may have been coming from that apartment in West Haven."

She was unlocking the front door of her beach house when Mark drove up. "I'm sorry to hear about your aunt." He paused. "No, 'I'm sorry' doesn't begin to cover how I feel. She was a gracious, kind lady. The whole world's poorer tonight."

"Thank you."

"I'm surprised you're here alone."

Devin looked toward the street. "Blue Toyota in front of the next house. He called himself Jack the cop when he showed me his badge."

"Find out from Jack the cop if it's all right if I take you to supper, without his presence."

"Mark, I just want to pick up some instructions Aunt Aggie wrote for her funeral, then check into some hotel, order up room service and sink into a hot bath. The horses and Wendy are somewhere safe, so I don't even have to worry about them tonight."

"How safe?"

"Sleeping Giant Stable is out near the park, on the grounds of what used to be a chi-chi girls' boarding school. That stable is what I realize Hightower has to become—totally fenced, with electronic gates and key cards like hotels are starting to use."

He touched her hair, almost smiling. "It must be hard for you to have let them go."

She rolled her eyes and nodded. "But when I saw who would be taking them in, I knew they'd be fine."

"Good. I have something to show you. I promise I'll deliver you to that hotel and hot bath in a couple hours. Right now, go wash your face, pack a bag, and I'll talk to Jack."

"But—"

"No buts. Officer McChesney knows about this. Go."

As Mark drove under the traffic light near the mall, he commented, "I understand you heard about some of my morning escapades." He reached inside his jacket and pulled out the bundle of letters from Lisè's apartment and handed it to Devin.

As she looked at them—and realized what they were—she said, "Officer McChesney told me about the apartment."

"It was beyond creepy."

She looked through the envelopes again. "Where were these?"

Mark didn't reply immediately, turning a corner, then waiting for a light. "In a drawer in the kitchen."

Devin shuffled through the envelopes he had given her, studying the postmark on each one to put them into chronological order.

"He said she's been stalking you a little longer than she's been stalking Ria and me."

She glanced at Mark and quickly averted her eyes. She didn't want him to see her eyes, bloodshot from crying, rimmed by puffy lids.

"I couldn't say when I became aware of her, since there are always people just hanging around on campus, and the dorm where I was living last fall always had a party going on somewhere."

"How'd she get the picture of you in the shower?" She fidgeted with her watchband and a gold bracelet.

"How do you know about that?"

"A bunch of pictures came in the mail over the weekend." She picked at her nails until he covered her cold hands with one of his warm ones.

"I keep a very predictable schedule. I go for a run every morning at six, then come back and take a shower. Some mornings there were as many women in the dorm shower rooms as there were men. One Saturday morning, this woman pushed into the stall right after I turned the water on. She dropped her raincoat and said she had bet someone she could get a picture of the two of us together naked. I told her she lost the bet and shoved her out of the stall. She had some guy with a camera with her, so I obviously wasn't fast enough."

Devin turned her face to the window, glancing at the county line marker as it flashed past.

"That's all that happened. She's nothing to me except someone hanging around wherever I went."

Silence filled the car for several miles. Mark turned from one country road to a smaller one, lined on either side by fences built of loose stone. On his side of the road, a rail fence ran behind the stone, with horses grazing in the pasture beyond.

"She was at the show Saturday night during Chief's class, and then Sunday afternoon. Does Jules Walter mean anything to you?"

She shook her head.

"She had on a white or light-colored top, but I couldn't say if it was a UMass sweatshirt." After a few more moments of silence, Mark ventured, "What about Zannie Annie?"

She looked at him for a fleeting instant, then past his face, out the driver's window. "It's a nickname Ria's father gave her. Her given name is Zandria."

He caressed her cheek. "'Zannie Annie' was sewn in the lining of a coat."

"Was the coat denim and brown leather?"

He nodded.

"It's Ria's."

"It's in shreds, nailed to the wall in a bedroom full of assorted things this person or these people have stolen. It was like a trophy room. I described it to the police, and gave them the address."

"Officer McChesney said they found what's left of your Firebird."

"I got that call. It had been in your barn. That trim piece I picked up the other night was from the front nameplate." Mark seemed angry when he continued, "I understand I might have endangered the landlady, and nothing is admissible in court, because technically, what I did was breaking and entering."

Devin stared out the window for a few more miles. "How'd you meet the people you were with at the show?"

"Your uncle introduced us."

She gave her head a slight shake. "Uncle Zack? Where'd they meet him?"

"They think very highly of him." There was an edge in Mark's voice. "I didn't ask the details of how they met. Probably at one of your horse shows, since this particular couple have horses and money. Since I advise people how to invest their money, it's been advantageous for all of us."

Devin turned back to the window.

The narrow road wound through lush fields and woods blanketed with violets. Mark slowed the car to allow a trio of wild turkeys to amble across the road. A few car lengths beyond the turkeys he turned onto a driveway flanked on both sides by overgrown rosebushes. The deeply rutted drive had a tired-looking shed and a rusty tractor on one side and a rail fence covered with vines on the other.

He continued up the lane past a farmhouse with blistered, peeling white paint, weathered woodwork around the windows and broken steps on the front porch. "No one's home today. The owners—the friends I mentioned—offered use of their farm until your problems end. They made me promise I'd bring you over to look around."

In silence Devin gave the house and farmyard a sweeping glance. Mark stopped in front of a faded red barn with rail fencing stretching as far as one could see on either side of it. The expanses of fence were punctuated with bright new rails replacing old damaged ones. "It isn't Farm Beautiful like Hightower, but it's safe."

"Until three days ago, I thought Hightower was."

When Devin reached for the door handle, Mark said, "Wait a minute. I have something else for you."

He pulled a large parcel wrapped in a crumpled grocery bag from behind Devin's seat, and held it out to her. "Sorry. I didn't have time to find silver paper and gold ribbon. This will have to do."

Keeping her eyes on his, she took the package from him, a confused look on her face.

"I'm finding out that angels don't always have long flowing golden hair and wings. They can be ladies with rollers in their hair, smoking cigars, wearing faded house coats and blue eye shadow. The one I met found that in the trash and figured I might be coming around and want it."

Devin hesitantly loosened the tape holding one end of the bag, then pulled open the folded end and peeked inside. "Oh! I thought I'd never see it again!" She quickly tore the paper off the picture inside, touching the broken glass that covered a rubbing of her father's name as it appeared on the Viet Nam Memorial Wall. "Thank God she found it!"

"I don't know if she knew it belonged to you, but she hurried inside to get it after she showed me the apartment. Everything's still there." After a pause, he added, "Given how smashed up it is, I was *surprised* everything was still there."

She studied the picture of her father, holding her. "I don't even remember him," she mused. She looked up at Mark. "She has no idea how much this means to me!"

"I think she did. She must have had an idea she was risking a lot to let me into that apartment. Mrs. Smith is the one you need to thank."

"Officer McChesney said her neighbors saw her leave in a hurry and apartment was trashed. But I need to meet her and thank her."

"There was something else in that apartment–I just got a glimpse of it before Mrs. Smith took me to see where the letters were, and insisted we get out of there. After I left, I kept trying to remember what it was."

"Did you remember?"

"Did you ever watch *Saturday Night Live*?"

She shrugged. "I've spent a lot of time in motel rooms watching bad TV. I'm sure I have."

"They had a sketch about two Austrian weightlifters with Arnold Schwarzenegger accents. The comedians wore body suits padded and painted to resemble muscles."

"Hans and Franz. I remember."

"You said Wendy told McChesney her assailant was big and strong, but his arm felt squishy."

"Something like that."

"When McChesney called me about my car, he told me about finding a padded suit like they used in those Saturday Night Live sketches. And the person I took pictures of this morning at your house had something under his clothes."

He pointed to the car door. "There's more to see."

She climbed out of the car and walked to the fence.

He joined her by the gate. "This is a weekend retreat. My friends run a rehab facility for racehorses in New York."

Devin leaned on the fence, looking out over the pasture, thinking how serene and peaceful Hightower had seemed to her just that morning.

"Come with me." Mark tugged at her arm. He opened a side door and led her into the barn, past a row of feed bins and a stack of water buckets.

"No one's home and the barn's unlocked? How can it be safe?"

He touched a finger to her lips. "Right now, you don't worry about security or people stalking you or what's safe."

When he kissed her, she melted against him. She wanted to feel sheltered, protected, and for a few moments, in his arms, she did. But she pulled back.

"What?"

"I shouldn't have come here. I should be home if the police have any more questions. And Aunt Aggie–I have phone calls and arrangements to make."

"This won't take long." He sounded tired, resigned. "Come with me." Mark walked through the barn, with stalls on either side of the walkway, to the half-door that opened to the pasture. He held it open for Devin, and motioned for her to go outside.

He whistled, a two-note signal. Four horses grazing in the shade of a clump of maples lifted their heads. A horse in the back of the group picked its way around the others and crossed the meadow at an easy canter. Its long black mane and tail rippled like banners in the wind and its hide shone like patent leather.

Devin gasped. "He looks just like Chief!" She stood beside Mark, smiling, watching the colt's long fluid strides.

Mark put his arm around her shoulders and pulled her close. "He should. Chief is his sire."

She shook her head. "No, he was too young when we were asked about stud service from him. That must have been two years ago."

The young horse stopped twenty yards away, snorting and pawing the patchy grass. Devin never took her eyes from him. "This is the horse rescued from the fire, isn't it?"

"I was going to give him to you that night. The woman I talked to on the phone said you'd be so surprised. A stall would be ready for him right by the tack room. At the horse show, I got nervous when I saw the woman who had been bugging me, Ria walking the ring with you, and some stranger taking care of your horses. And then I saw the policeman. I almost left then to move him."

Devin said nothing, watching the colt paw and snort.

"His name is LJ's Chief, and he's yours."

"Chief's colt?" She looked up at Mark. "How? We refused the request."

"Someone who worked for you at the time needed a favor. I helped him and he procured what I needed." He whistled again. "I had the opportunity to create the perfect horse for you."

"The perfect horse?" She laughed, skeptical.

"A few years ago, you leased a horse named Lady Jane."

"She was the only mare I ever had, and one of the best horses I've ever ridden in competition. I was disappointed when the owners didn't renew the lease."

"She developed arthritis, could barely walk much less jump, and her owners dumped her on my friends, then skipped out on the bill. When we were able to verify it was the same horse, nothing was going to stop me."

Devin looked from the wary black horse to Mark, who was smiling as he watched the animal's deliberate approach.

"Come here, son, this is the nice lady I told you about."

The youngster ventured up, sniffing noisily.

"Come here, baby," Devin said, in that voice people reserve for animals and small children. "I won't hurt you." She walked slowly towards the colt, but he jumped back and whirled around, galloping across the meadow to rejoin the other horses under the trees.

When Mark came up behind her and folded his arms around her, she pulled away. "Who else knows about this farm and the colt?"

"Jules or Jesse or whoever she is doesn't know where he is. I thought someone was following me a couple of times, but there are a lot of back roads and lanes to shortcut and backtrack on, and I usually pull my car inside and close the door when I'm here."

She looked down, silent, studying the sparse grass at her feet.

"They want you to give up."

She turned away, toward the barn. "I already feel like I failed. Ria left, Aunt Aggie—Aunt Aggie went to a friend's house, but that didn't protect her or save her. Wendy found the place for the horses. I'll be in a hotel tonight." She stopped at the barn door. "They won."

As Mark latched the paddock gate, Devin looked into the tack room then went inside for a closer look at something propped atop a row of coat hooks on the back wall.

She carefully took down the mangled weathervane she'd pulled from the barn wreckage the morning after the fire. "When I realized I'd left it in your car I wondered what you'd done with it."

"One of my friends knows someone who knows someone who knows an old coppersmith in New Hampshire who might be able to fix or reproduce it."

She turned it over and over, pretending to study what was left of the horse and hound and the lumps that formerly were bold directional letters. When her tears began splashing down onto it, Mark gently tried to take it out of her hands.

She held it tightly. "No, I'm taking it back with me."

"Then put it by the door."

When she turned toward the door, she noticed a faded blue sweatshirt hanging on its inside knob. "You've stayed here, haven't you?"

He took the shirt from her, folded it, covered the top of a feed bin, and carefully placed the weathervane across it. Then he put his arms around her. "No one's ever followed me all the way here. I told you it was safe."

She didn't pull away. "I'm not sure anywhere is safe anymore."

"Believe me, she never found her way here." He gave her a long lingering kiss. "But right now, it's only you and me, remember?"

She slipped from his arms and went to the door, latched it, and pushed a tack trunk in front of it. She pulled off her sweater. "Show me then."

It was late afternoon when the sound of a car engine turning over jarred Devin from a nap. Mark's arms were around her. *Is this a dream?* She kept her eyes closed, trying to remember. She felt the weight of his arm across her upper torso, his body warm against her.

She opened her eyes, wondering where she was. A barn. He had brought her here to show her this barn and a horse. And this cramped bed.

"Did I hear a car starting up outside?"

"It was the neighbor. I heard him talking to the horses when he brought them in and fed them. You were asleep and I didn't want to disturb you by getting up."

She closed her eyes for a few minutes, trying to decide whether to believe him. "He didn't knock on the door?"

"I heard the car door open and close. He probably saw it was mine, figured I was asleep in here, took care of the horses and left." He propped himself up on one elbow and stroked her breasts and stomach. "Where were we, when you decided to take a nap?"

She turned to him. "We were doing something like this." She pressed her body against him, biting his neck, pulling him onto her. If this was a dream, she'd make it one she'd enjoy recalling.

He ran his fingers through her long hair. "I won't want to leave you to go back to class on Monday."

"You said it was only for three more weeks. And you said we weren't talking about that stuff while we were here."

He kissed her, moving down her body. He said he wanted to go slow, take his time, but she was impatient to have him on her, in her again. No one else had loved her the way he did, cared whether she enjoyed it or not. And she wanted him to go back to Cambridge and wonder how soon he'd be able to come back to her.

Afterward, she could feel his sweat trickling down her sides as she stroked his hair.

Mark slowly sat up. "We have to get back."

She watched him get dressed. "You told me I needed a change of scenery. I didn't think it would be like this."

He sat beside her to put on his sneakers. "There haven't been many days in the last year and a half I didn't think of that night I spent making love with you. I couldn't believe you didn't care anymore. After I talked to Ria the other day, all I could think about was–" He looked away. "She told me how Ian wouldn't leave you alone."

"He thinks I'm jealous of him and Jesse. Huh!" Devin stood before him, still naked. "Couldn't be *further* from the truth. I didn't appreciate his concerned act the other night. I–"

He pulled her down onto the bunk on top of him, nuzzling her breasts. "You better get dressed or we aren't going to leave anytime soon."

Devin considered teasing him a little more to see if he meant it. But the tack room was filled with shadows. She climbed off the bunk and looked for her panties.

Mark swatted her behind as he passed her. "I'm going to say good night to the colt."

She still couldn't put him and a horse together. She hurried to finish dressing to see how he'd treat his baby. The animal whinnied when Mark opened the tack room door.

Mark handed her an apple when she came to the stall. "I told him the two of you need to get acquainted. He didn't seem too impressed. Feed him, though, and you'll have a friend for life."

The colt hesitantly sniffed Devin's offering. The way he carefully lifted it out of her fingers was exactly the same as his sire. He cocked his head and sniffed at her pockets, just as Chief did. She ran a hand down his neck, along his back and down one leg. He shifted his weight and allowed her to lift that hoof.

She looked up to find Mark watching her. "You taught him that? Who taught you?"

"I had help. Taking care of him kept me sane, knowing one day I'd turn him over to you and I'd see that look on your face."

"What look?"

He smiled. "Your face lit up, like Christmas morning when you open the present you wanted the most but didn't think you were going to get. I was twelve years old again, at that street fair, sitting down in front of the most beautiful girl in the world, madly in love."

Someone followed Mark almost all the way to the highway, but turned in the opposite direction. They had been on the main road several minutes when Devin asked, "Is that car still behind you?"

He glanced at the rearview mirror. "It was the neighbor who fed the horses. He left a note on the door." He smiled. "You kept me awake, talking in your sleep today."

"Did I say anything interesting?"

"You were mumbling and thrashing around."

"I thought I'd been sound asleep. It was nice to wake up with you."

"I didn't mind watching over you."

As he waited at the light at the Boston Post Road, the car's turn signal blinking to turn toward the hotel, she said softly, "Can you take me to the cottage first, so I can get my things?"

"No problem."

As Mark turned onto Devin's street, he said, "Geez, what now?" Two police cars and an ambulance blocked the road in front of her house, with the vehicles' headlights trained on a car parked on the sand.

"Mark!" Devin grabbed his arm, digging her nails into his skin. "There's the Toyota, on the sand bar!" She leaped from the car, not taking time to close the door.

As she ran to the steps down to the beach, a woman crossed the street and called her name. "The police have been knocking on your door since they took a look in that car."

"Why?" Devin glanced up at Mark as he caught up to her and took her hand. A policeman approached.

"It's pretty gruesome. Blood all over," the bystander told them. "I heard there's a body in the car."

Another onlooker chimed in. "I heard it's body *parts*."

# CHAPTER FOURTEEN

Devin scanned the faces of the curious spectators as the Toyota was winched up onto a flatbed truck and hauled away. Jack, the cop assigned to watch her house, asked if any of them might be her assailant. She shook her head. "Just my neighbors. Nobody I don't recognize."

Bella Paige, her aunt's friend, appeared at the fringe of the crowd.

"My goodness, *what* is going on?" Mrs. Paige demanded when Devin reached her. Stretching tall and craning her neck to see over heads, she continued, "When I saw all the police lights, I was afraid something had happened to you!"

"There was a car on the beach." Devin took her arm, steering her away from the group. Mark and Jack moved with them, remaining a few feet away, scanning the thinning crowd of onlookers like a pair of Secret Service men. Devin stopped under a streetlight and turned to Mrs. Paige. "What brings you out so late at night?"

"I really need to talk to you about your aunt. I left several phone messages. I guess you were out." She fanned as a bug flitted around her face, and glanced around the street. "I'd rather not talk here."

Devin nodded. "I'm here to pick up some things, then I'm going to a hotel for the night. We can step inside for a bit of privacy."

Bella frowned. "Well, all right." She waved a hand. "Oh, I have Aggie's suitcase in my car. Let me get it."

Devin watched her bustle down the street to retrieve the suitcase.

"Isn't that one of your aunt's friends?" Mark asked.

"She said she called and left messages, and needs to talk." She sighed. "I so just want to sink into a bubble bath!"

He reached for the suitcase as the older lady walked up, and gave her his most charming smile. "Here, let me take that. Devin needs to gather up a bag for the night. Would you like some tea?"

As she fished in her jacket pocket for her house keys, Devin saw him give a quick nod to the hovering policeman. She hurried ahead of Mark and Mrs. Paige to unlock the door and hold it open for them. Mrs. Paige followed her to the kitchen, shadowing Devin as she filled the tea pot and set it onto a burner.

Mrs. Paige perched on a kitchen stool. "Who do the police think this car belongs to?" She kept glancing across the room at Mark, who stood at the door to the hall.

"We've seen it in front of the house." She wasn't sure how much information she should share with this lady.

The tea pot whistled, and Devin jumped, surprised by the noise. She heard Mark say, "I'm getting Jack. Maybe he should hear what Mrs. Paige has to say." She busied herself assembling mugs, tea bags, cream and sugar, then poured water into each mug with exaggerated care.

"I heard that woman tell you there was a body in the car."

Devin set a plate of cookies out on the counter and urged Mrs. Paige to fix her tea.

"This body," Mrs. Paige rapped a finger on the counter top, "do you think it might be one of the people bothering you and your aunt?"

Mark returned with the patrolman before Devin has decided how to respond. Smiling at Mrs. Paige, Jack asked, "Can you tell us about Miss Hall?"

She spoke hesitantly. "Aggie called me at three in the afternoon and said she thought someone was upstairs."

"Did she say who, or where they were?"

"She just said upstairs. I told her I'd come out and pick her up, but she should call the police. I got there as fast as I could. She was standing out by the road, terrified, absolutely white, when I arrived."

Devin gave an involuntary shudder, wondering how long her aunt had to wait, possibly in danger. "Did you call the police?"

"She wouldn't let me." Mrs. Paige punctuated each word with dramatic hand motions and jangling bracelets. "Aggie jumped into my car and said, 'Get me away from here!' She sat there, wringing her hands and saying nothing. I asked her where we should go, and she answered, 'Anywhere. Just go.'"

"She left a note for me saying you were going to a movie and dinner—"

"She was shaking so! We stopped for coffee, but she didn't touch hers."

"I'm glad she had you to come help her." As Devin watched the lady nibble a cookie and sip her tea, she wondered what magic words would get Mrs. Paige to fast-forward to the point in her story where Aunt Aggie told her what had happened.

"We went to the outlet shops and walked around for a while. She finally started talking about an hour after I picked her up. She said Lisè was doing some sort of painting in the powder room, and other people were in the house."

"Yes, I saw Lisè's painting."

"But there was another woman who asked Aggie where the rest of the books were, but Aggie didn't know what she meant. That's when she called your house and left a message for you, with the woman beside her the whole time threatening to kill her if she told you anything or called the police."

"Did Aunt Aggie say anything about her?"

Mrs. Paige shrugged. "She said the woman was tall, with brown hair and had a husky voice. Aggie said she was creepy—no, that wasn't the word she used. 'Eerie'. She couldn't explain what she meant, but this woman really frightened her."

"Did you call the police then?"

"She wouldn't hear of it, even when I told her to stay with me. She sat there, rocking in her seat for the longest time before she said anything else."

"Did the woman do anything to my aunt—hit her, twist her arm, push her around?"

Mrs. Paige shook her head. "If she'd done anything to Aggie, Aggie didn't mention it. But she did say someone else was with the woman—she knew this person, and I got the distinct impression she didn't like him."

Devin gave Mrs. Paige her full attention. "A man?"

"Someone you know, an associate, maybe a boyfriend—" She shot a dark look in Mark's direction, as he began shaking his head.

Devin leaned over the kitchen island toward the white-haired lady. "Did she say who he was?"

"She was so upset!" Putting a hand to her forehead and closing her eyes, Mrs. Paige rattled on. "I wasn't sure what she meant. She gave me the impression he knew her, but yesterday he didn't treat her the way he usually did."

Devin glanced from Mark to the policeman before clearing her throat. She put a hand on the older lady's hand. "Mrs. Paige, this is very important. Think really hard about what she said about this person."

Nodding, Mrs. Paige fingered her gold necklace. "She said he grabbed the chain on her neck, and told her to give him the key or he'd rip it off. The woman told him to let it go because she already had one." She pulled her hand away from Devin and opened her purse. As Mrs. Paige pulled a tissue from its depths, Devin could see a tear on her cheek.

Devin sighed, shaking her head. "That key doesn't open anything. It was a gift from some friend."

"Aggie said he laughed then and twisted the chain a little." She struggled to get the words out. "He said he just wanted to scare her."

"Like she wasn't already terrified." Devin closed her eyes and swallowed hard. "Did she describe him in *any* way, except that he was someone I knew?"

Mrs. Paige seemed to ponder the question for several seconds before shaking her head. "She sat there, clutching her little bag, shaking her head, saying over and over, 'I never did like that little weasel.'"

Devin gave Mrs. Paige a surprised look. "What did she call him?"

"I'm sure she said 'that little weasel.'"

"Did she say anything else?"

"She said the woman told him to leave Aggie alone, they didn't need her. He twisted the chain again and she said he gave her a real–" She paused for a moment, staring off into space, as if she might be trying to remember Aggie's words. "Something about his smile. Ugly or cruel or–sinister. I think that's what she said."

Devin nodded. "Had they left by the time you got there?"

"Aggie said they had just driven away."

"Did she happen to say what kind of car they had?"

Mrs. Paige reached over and patted Devin's hand. "My dear, as upset as your aunt was, I'm sure they could have left on a flying carpet and she wouldn't have noticed."

Devin nodded, realizing Mrs. Paige was probably right. "Yesterday morning I found her sitting room open, something she never does when she goes out. She'd left her journal and her camera on a kitchen counter. They were both destroyed when I went in this morning."

"Maybe they thought she had taken pictures of them."

"She could have written something in the journal too." Devin straightened up and forced a smile. "Did my aunt say anything else about these people?"

Mrs. Paige closed her eyes and gave her head a slow, exaggerated shake. She flipped her hand to accentuate her words. "She wouldn't say another thing. We were driving past the mall, and she must have looked at the movie marquee, because she all of a sudden said, 'Let's go see that *Titanic* movie again.' So that's what we did, and she called you to go with her to pick up her things once it was over."

Jack the cop asked Mrs. Paige for her phone number, "in case we need to talk to you again." He wrote it in his notebook and asked the white-haired woman if she'd like a police escort home.

Mrs. Paige giggled like a schoolgirl. "Oh, my goodness, no, I'll be fine!" As she spoke, Mrs. Paige patted the young man's arm. "I just wanted Devin to know what happened." She stood up, pushed in the stool and threw her arms around Devin. "My dear, you look exhausted! I'm going to run along so you can get some rest. Be sure to call me right away if you need anything."

Devin let out a sigh after closing the door behind Mrs. Paige. She looked from the policeman to Mark and back to the cop. "My aunt always referred to Ian as 'the little weasel' after Susan Holt packed up her riding school and left last fall. She gave me a long rambling lecture about my business dealings with him, and told me to distance myself from him before he had a chance to 'screw me over.'"

She paused. "That term coming from my aunt's mouth was like hearing anyone else say the f-word."

She woke with a start, wondering where she was, surprised to find herself fully dressed, curled up on a strange bed that hadn't been turned down. The lighted digital numbers on the bedside clock displayed a red 2:00 in the blackness of the hotel room. Her pounding head reminded her of all that had gone wrong the previous day. She shuffled into the bathroom for a glass of water and some aspirin. She had clearly heard Mrs. Paige's voice saying, "They asked Aggie where the rest of the books were."

*Ian threatened and terrified my aunt for some books? What would he know about the books that might have been in the house?*

Devin padded back to the bed and turned on the light. She opened the suitcase she'd put on the second bed, and carefully lifted out a thick softbound Hale family genealogy, a brittle, oversized family Bible, a photo album, and a pair of ledger books that were part scrapbook, part journal. The previous fall, Aggie had found the collection lying on the floor in the library. As she tucked a fat envelope into the front of the Bible, she instructed Devin to "take them somewhere for safekeeping."

Devin hoped whoever had been studying them in November had left something behind to answer the endless stream of questions bombarding her in the past days. Any kind of clue, something to explain who Jesse or Jules was to her, and how she had wronged or angered the woman. Or why.

She paged through the ledger books she had read many times, chronicles of her father's parents' lives, stopping to study a picture here, a notation there. Her paternal grandfather had been a diplomat, stationed mainly in the Middle East, and he and his wife had traveled the world. The pictures and notes in the ledgers traced their far-flung adventures, which had included their tiny granddaughter as often as possible.

She felt a familiar coldness when she turned the page and confronted the newspaper headlines and clippings of the hijacked airliner that had been blown up in a Saudi desert, the airplane taking her grandparents back to Syria after the Christmas holidays following her seventh birthday. The pages following held their pictures, obituaries, funeral programs, and cards and letters of condolence, in several languages, from all corners of the world.

Devin riffled the last empty pages of the second book and set it aside before picking up the genealogy. As she flipped the pages, a sheet of notebook paper slid out. Taped to the lined page was a photocopy of her maternal grandmother's obituary. Catherine Suffolk's maiden name, Hall, was misspelled "Hale" in the clipping. A penciled notation read "Who is this? No DOB listed for a Catherine Hale after 1881." Her sister was listed in the obituary as "Ardith G. 'Aggie' Hale."

She leaned against the headboard. *Had Lisè found this and told her accomplice that Aggie was sitting on some huge fortune, easy pickings like the other victims Officer McChesney had described?*

She opened the Bible for Aunt Aggie's packet, where she found half a dozen sheets of paper: Her mother's yellowed coroner's report and death certificate. Her father's death certificate and Medal of Honor citation. The deed to Hightower Farm, listing the Hale mansion, the caretaker's house—where Ian and his family lived—and "all barns and outbuildings," and indicating Devin as sole owner. And the passports a flight attendant on the doomed airliner had begged the hijackers to let her keep to someday deliver "to that little girl in the picture for souvenirs of her grandparents."

And a piece of parchment stationery, written in Aggie's flowery hand, listing her wishes for her "last big party." Three hymns, four Bible verses, several gentlemen she knew from her social circle to be pall bearers, a menu for the after-service luncheon, and a request to be buried in the grey dress she'd worn to Devin's graduation.

"I can do all of that for you, Auntie, every bit of it." Tears slid down her cheeks. She closed her eyes, satisfied she'd found that piece of paper, ready to carry out Aggie's last wishes, first thing in the fast-approaching morning.

Someone pounded on her door at 6:30, calling out, "Room service!"

"I didn't order room service," she mumbled, half asleep, stumbling to the door to squint through the peephole. The person was turned away from the door, standing behind a cart with a huge domed dish atop it. The server wore the black pants, black satin vest and white shirt she'd seen on employees in the lobby the evening before.

The person banged on the door again. "Room service!"

Immediately wide awake, Devin jumped to find and dump her purse, to find her cell phone. "She's here," she told the 911 operator, after she stumbled over her name and room number at the Hampton Inn. "Whoever she is. Pretending she's room service, only I didn't order room service."

"Someone will be there in a couple minutes. Keep your door locked."

The pseudo room server disappeared, but before a single policeman arrived, a curious hotel guest lifted the domed lid on the serving cart. A piercing scream instantly opened doors all up and down the floor, and brought uniformed policemen running from either end of the hall.

Devin opened her door as far as the safety latch would allow when she heard the ruckus—a gunshot, the sound of running feet and screaming. A human head stared up at her from the table in front of her door. She slammed her door and leaned against it. She closed her eyes but the image of the head wouldn't go away. She pressed her fingertips into her eyes until she saw an explosion of neon colors, but the disturbing sight remained.

Someone knocked on the door. "Florian Police, Miss Marques. You called us. Are you all right?"

She peered through the peephole and saw about a dozen people outside her door. One of the policemen who had been at Aggie's house the previous morning was right in the middle, telling someone to "cover it up and take it out of public view." Then he rapped on her door again and repeated his announcement, holding his badge in front of the peephole.

She called through the door, "Did you catch her?"

Peering through the peephole she saw the cop shake his head. "She stabbed one of the patrolmen in the stairwell, and he thinks he shot her as she ran away. I've been instructed to stay at your door until you're ready to leave, then take you wherever you might need to go."

As she dressed—her last day, Officer McChesney had assured her, wearing clothes filled with tracking tags in the expectation of luring Jules into police custody—Devin called Sleeping Giant to check on Wendy and the horses, and retrieve any messages left on her automated voice mail.

A Mr. Gosnell from the Gosnell Funeral Home would meet her at the hospital that morning, at her convenience, of course. Her uncle would be arriving at noon at Sikorsky Airport in Bridgeport. Ria called to make sure she *wasn't* home. Twice someone had called and hung up. The last message she replayed for the policeman: "The old lady's the only safe one, because she's dead. Don't get too comfortable up there in that hotel room."

When her police escort asked, "Where to first?" Devin needed only a split second to decide.

"I have to go out to my aunt's house to pick up the dress she wants to be buried in." *I'll be much happier after that dress is safe in hand*, Devin repeatedly told herself all the way to the farm, staring out the police cruiser window but seeing nothing.

She was relieved to see the grounds seemed no different than the previous day, but held her breath as she entered the back porch.

"Is everything all right?" the policeman queried.

Devin looked around at the mess that had been left the day before, when Ria had taken her to the hospital to see Aggie. "It's no worse than it was yesterday, so I guess that's a plus. Ask me again when I get further in."

She felt her heart pounding harder and harder as she went up the back stairs and moved closer to her aunt's bedroom. She paused when she saw the defaced door.

The policeman stopped beside her. "Are you all right?"

"Give me a second." She stared at the black footprints for a few moments. "I don't remember whether I left the door open or closed." The cop fidgeted as she wrested the door open.

"I'll take a look around." He went in a few steps and peered inside. "It looks fine."

"Just let that dress be in there." She cautiously walked to the closet. She reached out to the door knob, afraid to touch it. Afraid if even after new locks and police searches, someone somehow had managed to enter and desecrate her aunt's things.

She pulled back the door to the same display-perfect closet she'd browsed before. Devin grabbed the chosen grey dress and the silver crepe shoes she knew Aggie had worn with it. She looked at her guardian. "I don't know if they want shoes or not, but I'll give them some." She looked on a shelf for a bag of some sort and carefully nestled the shoes inside, closed the closet and rummaged in a dresser for underwear. "I never had to bury anyone before," she confessed when she noticed his half-smile. "What do they need?"

He shrugged. "I never had to do it either. Is there anything else?"

"I just want out of here. "She left Aggie's bedroom and hurried down the hall to the back stairs. She clattered to the first floor, not waiting for the policeman.

She waited by the outside the door, keys in hand, nervously looking around until he joined her.

"I need to put on the deadbolt." *Not that I know if it's really going to keep anyone out, not that it matters anymore.* She turned the key in a lock, then another key in another lock. *As much as I love this house, will I ever want to enter it again?*

"Okay, where now? Funeral home?"

"The hospital. I have to sign some papers there so the funeral home can pick up–pick up my aunt's–my aunt's–" She swallowed hard. "My aunt's body. The funeral-home person is supposed to meet me there this morning."

They rode to the hospital in silence. Devin alternately stared out the window and closely inspected the dress her aunt had chosen, afraid she'd find some sort of damage or one of the dreaded cut-and-paste notes.

McChesney met them at the hospital entrance, and told Devin's escort to go to the stable temporarily housing her horses. Before she had a chance to ask why he said, "That's his assignment today." He held up a hand as if to stop a reply from her. "Our information is that everybody there is fine this morning, and you need to be here to care for your aunt." He motioned to the hospital entrance. "I've already spoken with the gentleman from the funeral home, who's here waiting for you."

The route to the morgue from the hospital's main entrance seemed even longer than it had the previous day. A policeman stood between its door and one just beyond it. Devin waited at the morgue entrance as McChesney approached the guard. They spoke quietly, but she clearly heard the guard say, "They just brought it in."

He returned to her side. "You don't have to go back in there if you don't want to. The gentleman waiting to see you is in the medical examiner's office."

"I need to see Aunt Aggie again."

He looked around the hall. "I understand."

They stared at one another before Devin whispered, "I have to tell her that everything's going to be the way she planned it."

She swallowed hard, remembering what the officer had told her about the relevance of the paperback book in Aunt Aggie's mail. "Somebody pretending to be Room Service delivered a human head this morning. I guess getting it that way might be better than waking up beside it. It was put outside my hotel room door for a reason."

"Shock value when you opened the door and lifted the lid. She probably thought you were the person who screamed as she was running away." He glanced away momentarily.

"Do you know yet how much Ian had to do with all this?"

McChesney shook his head. "All I will say is that we've already talked to Ian and he confessed that he was at your aunt's house with your multi-named assailant, and he did threaten your aunt. But he insists he had nothing to do with killing her. And I can't say any more than that."

Devin was surprised by his sharp tone and blunt answer. She took a backward step. "Did you arrest him?" As the cop shook his head, she whispered, "Please let me see my aunt."

McChesney opened the morgue door, and again Devin was surprised at the room's brightness, not the dim atmospheric lighting of late-night TV cop show reruns.

Someone entered the morgue behind them. Devin turned to see the medical examiner she'd met the previous afternoon and a gentleman in a three-piece suit. She recognized him from newspaper ads as the owner of Florian's largest funeral home. She held out the dress and bag containing her aunt's shoes and undergarments. "Hold this, please. I'll be with you in just a moment."

A table near the middle of the room held a black body bag. "Is that it?" she asked, pointing to the bag.

McChesney said nothing as he took her arm and steered her away from the table to the wall of body drawers. A drawer was rolled open, a sheet pulled back, to reveal the older lady's body.

"I have your dress, Auntie, and the shoes you wore with it. And I'll make sure they get someone from Samantha's shop to do your hair so it's just right." Her tears fell on the small still figure. "I have all the papers here, so everything will be just like you wanted. They're going to take you and get you ready now." She leaned down and kissed Aggie's forehead, then stroked her cheek. "I'll see you later."

A few moments later, in the medical examiner's office, after Devin had signed the necessary release forms, she took a deep breath and stood up very straight. Looking the funeral home director straight in the eye, she asked, "Mr. Gosnell, will there be—will you take extra care to make sure my aunt's body is protected and no one harms her any further?"

"I can understand your concern, Miss Marques. I've already discussed extra precautions with my staff so as few people as possible have access to the preparation area during her time there." He paused. "This area is well away from any visitors and guests of grieving families. Someone coming in off the street can't simply walk in."

She didn't like his smile or condescending air, but gave him a short nod of her head. She tried to smile. "I'm counting on your people to make her look good for what she calls her last party." She bit her lip. "I need to find the ladies' room."

Gesturing toward the door, Mr. Gosnell gave her another of the smiles she disliked. "Across the hall, my dear."

She leaned over a sink and splashed water on her face, looking in the mirror as she patted her face dry to see red-rimmed eyes and dark circles that make up didn't cover.

She entered a stall, latched the door and sat, fully clothed, on the toilet, trying to compose herself. Someone came in and used the next stall. That toilet flushed, water was run in the sink, towels taken from the dispenser and rustled as they were used. The restroom door opened and closed as the other person exited.

Devin knew she shouldn't keep Officer McChesney waiting any longer. She should already be on her way to Sleeping Giant to see for herself that Wendy and her horses had a safe night. She stood up and opened the stall door.

Taped to the mirror was a note written in bold black marker: "So you think you and the cop have it all figured out. We'll see about that."

# CHAPTER FIFTEEN

She screamed. McChesney flung the door open with such force that a tile fell off the wall when the doorknob hit it.

"Who was in here?" she demanded, pointing at the mirror.

Giving his head a jerk toward the emergency room, he barked, "Get that woman from housekeeping that just came out of here!"

The housekeeper had stringy dirty-blonde hair pulled back into a ponytail, and seven or eight earrings in each ear. Her complexion was marred by acne. Loudly chewing her gum, she looked from Officer McChesney to the policeman who had escorted her back to the morgue, then to Devin. When the cop asked where the note had come from, she moved the gum from one side of her mouth to the other. "He said it was a joke."

"Who?" McChesney demanded.

"The hottie who tol' me to do it." She glanced at each person again. "He gave me a hundred bucks to put it on the mirror."

"Who was he?" he demanded.

"I don' know! Came in right around eight–shift change, y'know? Wanted me to put it on some old lady's body in the morgue, but I couldn't–too weird. "She shuddered. "He woulda give me five hundred for that."

"What did he look like?" McChesney sounded impatient.

She rolled her eyes and smiled. "Like a rock star! Black hair, brown eyes, whatta bod!" She gave her hips a sensuous shake, waving her arms and snapping her fingers. "Woo-ooooh! Lay it on me, baby, y'know?" She shrugged. "He said it was just a joke. I needed the money, so I said sure."

Devin glanced at McChesney, who raised an eyebrow and asked, "Ian?"

Even though she heard him, Devin fixed her attention on the housekeeper. "Do I look like I'm laughing? That 'old lady in the morgue' is my aunt."

Giving her gum a couple thoughtful chews, the woman looked Devin over. "Do I look like I care? I needed the money," she replied, slowly pronouncing every word. "I gotta get back to work." The woman snapped her gum. "He's in the main lobby hitting on the receptionist if you're looking for him."

Devin sprinted down the hall towards the information desk and found Ian leaning on it, oozing charm and sweetness, smiling down at the woman on duty.

"So, Ian, the note was just a joke," she called out in a loud voice. He jumped and looked her way. "Did I find it funny?" She moved closer. "Was it worth the hundred bucks for the cleaning lady to plant it in the bathroom? Or five hundred to have her put it on my aunt's body in the morgue?"

"I don't know what you're talking about."

The receptionist stood up. "Ma'am, I'll have to call security if you don't quiet down."

"Honey, security is right behind me," Devin watched the receptionist shrink down into her chair as two policemen stepped into the lobby from the hall, and another came through the front door.

"You think I'm scared of you and a couple of cops?" Ian sneered.

"No, and I'm not scared of you either. Hiding behind a woman to get your dirty work done? I thought you were more of a man than that."

He let out a snort. "You wouldn't know a man if you fell over one."

"If you believe that, I gave you way more credit than you deserve," she snapped, hoping she sounded stronger than she felt. She couldn't allow herself to cry in front of him. "Why, Ian?" She willed herself to keep her voice steady. "Why did my aunt deserve to die?"

"Collateral damage." His lip curled. "She got in the way."

"You threatened and terrorized her in her own home!"

"It's Jesse's home too. She's your half-sister."

"And you believe that?"

"She said she can prove your uncle in Florida is her father, even though he doesn't claim her."

She shook her head. "No, Ian, even if Uncle Zack was her father, which he isn't, she'd be my cousin, not my half-sister. But the Hale house and Hightower *still* wouldn't be anything to her. It all belonged to my father's family, not my mother's."

As he stepped closer to her, he scowled then snarled, "You gave Jesse's job to that little freak."

"Freak? I wouldn't care if Wendy had dropped out of a spaceship so long as she could handle the horses."

"You said you needed a groom, and I told you I knew someone who wanted the job."

"And I told you I had to see how she got along with the horses before I could hire her."

"That was Jesse's job."

"I need the person the horses liked, not the person you want, just because you want her. I never saw Apollo go after anyone the way he tried to attack Jesse the minute she walked near him at the Expo stalls. Shaman still lays back his ears and bares his teeth like a dog at her. When Wendy wandered in at that show, they nuzzled and cuddled up to her right away, like a couple of huge puppies."

He stepped back, jabbing a finger in her face with every word as he loudly repeated, "That was supposed to be Jesse's job!"

"Why? What did she promise you if she got the job? How would you benefit?"

"Don't you get it? We were going to have everything."

She shook her head. "'We'? How?"

"All I had to do was give her information, and you were always so easy with it. Your keys, your phone numbers, where you'd be. Your aunt was away all the time. Jesse could get what she needed to prove her story, and we'd be set for life."

"And you were stupid enough to believe her."

"Yeah. You and your screwed-up family – I figured she had to be onto something." His composure seemed to crumble a little. "But yeah I was stupid. She woke me up at three this morning, standing over my bed. She already knew I'd gone to the police–she'd put bugs in my clothes, just like you have in almost everything you own. That's how she always knew where you were. She took the tracking equipment from someone she said she'd killed. My phone was tapped, just like yours are."

"After you threatened my aunt and terrorized her in her own home–"

He took another step back. "How do you know about that?"

She bit her lip before asking, "What did Auntie always call you?"

He made an ugly face. "A little weasel."

"I never would have known you were there, except her best friend said she made that comment about someone in the house the other night. And if the horses hadn't been whinnying when you were running around the barn after the fire -"

Ian's eyes narrowed. "Lisè and I were told we had to be there." He rolled his eyes. "Show our loyalty."

"Why were you in maroon, when the others wore black?"

"That's what we were told to wear. Lisè was terrified she'd be killed because she knew you had a gun, and you'd shoot her when you opened the barn door." He let out a humorless laugh. "Jules laughed in her face because she knew you already got rid of the gun. Told her she better give an Oscar-worthy performance at what was left of the barn the next morning."

"Before or after she beat her up?" Devin didn't wait for a response but stared him in the eye, demanding, "Why?"

"What?" Ian looked as if he was ready to cry. "She showed me Lisè's head, said I was still alive only because she still needed my help."

"To put a note on my aunt's body, here at the morgue."

"She went wild when she found your aunt had no money–"

258

"How many times did I tell you that? Auntie gave up her career for me when she and Uncle Zack found out your mother was spending maintenance money intended to take care of me to dress you and your brother at The Gap and Old Navy and stores like that while everything of mine came from yard sales and thrift stores. Auntie took care of me, so I swore as soon as I was old enough to inherit my father's estate, she'd have anything she wanted."

His chin quivered. "The old lady had nothing."

"Right. You helped get a little old lady killed for *nothing*."

He gave his shoulders a little twitch. "Jules said the old lady had a bad heart and was on borrowed time, and was going to die anyhow. This way she didn't suffer."

Devin turned away, repulsed by the cold emotionless way Ian delivered the sentence. She whipped around to get right up in his face. "Auntie wasn't suffering! And you and that woman didn't have a right to decide anything about my aunt's health."

He backed away from her. "Devin, please—"

"Please what?" she demanded. "My aunt is dead because of you. Does that even matter to you?" She looked from Ian to the policeman as he reached for the receptionist's telephone and dialed a number.

Devin strained to hear McChesney's conversation, but he hung up after a terse string of "yes," "no," "now," "do it."

He looked at Ian. "If you know what Jesse or Jules or whoever she is, is planning to do, you better talk fast."

Ian shook his head, the bravado totally gone. "She said she knew Devin would be here at the morgue first thing, so I had to make sure the note was either on the body or someplace she'd be sure to see it. She tossed my truck keys in the air and caught them, and smiled this evil smile. She said she didn't–" his voice broke and he looked at the lobby ceiling. "She said she didn't need me anymore, and she left with the head. That's all I know."

McChesney gestured to the other cops. "You know what to do."

A policeman handcuffed Ian and recited the Miranda statement.

McChesney looked at the two policemen. "Take him away."

Cowering by the door, Devin had never ridden in a police car, much less one with the siren was screaming and the lights were flashing, with cars plunging to the shoulder of the road to get out of the way. She wasn't sure she liked the experience, especially since McChesney wore a stony expression and said absolutely nothing until they were on the turnpike.

"Ian's been somewhat cooperative."

"Could he have prevented my aunt's death?"

"Probably not. When he came to us yesterday afternoon about overhearing Jesse's phone call, he'd already discovered all of his bank accounts had been cleaned out, and he didn't know where his truck was. By then we had impounded the cars in the garage at the address Mark had given us. We found information about a second garage in one of those cars."

"And–?"

McChesney took the exit for Sleeping Giant State Park and went through the traffic light at the end of the ramp before continuing. "I think Ian knew he had outlived his usefulness to this woman. I'm pretty sure figured he was lucky to still be alive, and maybe he was afraid he'd be next if he didn't come to us to for protection by getting himself arrested."

"But you said you didn't arrest him."

Silence.

Huddled by the door, Devin stared out the car window. "What about Lisè? Was that her body in the car? Had she become expendable too?"

"Probably. And I would guess Jules or Jesse thought she knew too much." He turned off the siren. "Silent mode. We aren't even using any radio communication today." When Devin didn't respond, he added, "The second garage contained part of the tracking and scanning equipment missing from the security alarm place. She probably has the rest in Ian's truck. The bugs Ian was talking about in your clothes are thin plastic chips less than a half inch long. It's pet ID equipment–"

Devin nodded. "That's what you said yesterday. I can see myself throwing away my entire wardrobe just to make this nightmare end."

He shook his head. "We'll come out and scan your house and clothes, find the chips and remove them." He slowed at an intersection, looking right and left before proceeding through it. "We also found the police shield and uniform you saw the other night. That shield belonged to a New Haven policeman named Walt Schuler, who didn't get a promotion he thought he deserved. He was drunk the night he took an unsuspecting family of five with him over the side of the Tappan Zee Bridge. His family insisted upon keeping his shield. They were deeply in debt, and his wife had to give up the dream home they'd just built. There was an eighteen-year-old girl named Jamie. Till Walt died, she was an honor student and standout track star, in line for several scholarships to just about anywhere she wanted to go." He paused for a moment. "I compared her yearbook picture to the ones I showed you yesterday."

Devin straightened up in her seat. "Same person, and I have everything she feels cheated of?"

"Maybe the same person, in a different lifetime. Something like that, I suppose."

"Jamie Schuler. She was in my English Lit class, my first semester at MIT. She'd go for coffee with the rest of the group I hung with."

"The person you said you remember from college?"

Nodding, Devin explained, "We were studying *Canterbury Tales.* She was very knowledgeable about the time period, and I really enjoyed our discussions about Chaucer. I recall being sad to hear she had dropped out after Thanksgiving break."

"That's when her father died."

"She wanted to be an architect. She loved everything Art Deco."

"She might be surprised you remember her."

She made a face and shrugged her shoulders. "Didn't you say Ria told you Jesse was in some classes with her at Boston College?"

"The following semester." He was quiet for a few moments. "She's been your shadow for at least six months. Not only did this woman enter your home, but according to a diary she's been keeping, she'd stand over your bed while you were sleeping at night."

Devin shuddered. "That really creeps me out."

He drove in silence a good five minutes before continuing. "She became a nurses' aide, and was very good at it. So good that she had no trouble being hired by hospice for home care to dying victims. Then, about a year and a half or so ago, Jamie Schuler just disappeared, and a very skilled woman named Jules Walter was hired in her place. Patients started dying, and the families discovered things missing, but could never positively link the nurse to either the deaths or the thefts. When several well-to-do but terminally ill patients disappeared, so did Jules Walter."

Devin glanced over to see him shaking his head. "I remember Susan Holt saying her mother died while she had hospice care. The care nurse supposedly quit because she came in one evening to a burglary in progress and was afraid to go back."

"Was anything taken?"

"Some money and jewelry. Nobody was ever arrested."

"Hmpf." He rearranged himself in the driver's seat. "I didn't sleep much last night after reading that diary. She worked for us, calling herself Jessica Hamilton." He pounded a fist on the steering wheel. "She worked for us, looked at your file, and said, 'Oh, this poor woman. How frightened she must be.'"

"Why did she quit?"

McChesney shook his head. "She just stopped coming to work."

Devin bobbed her head. "After making sure my complaints and problems disappeared."

"We've found bits and pieces. Some in a file for Armond Rist, some in a file marked Justin Hall, and a third marked Anne Eldridge."

"Huh. She did her research." She stared at the passing scenery a few moments.

"Something like that."

No response.

"What about that guard at my house, the one you said you made a mistake about. What about him?"

McChesney shrugged. "Like the young lady at the hospital said, he needed money. From some of the records we saw at the alarm system place, Jesse had access to lots of it to pay people to do her dirty work."

He sighed, then continued, "Miss Wendy's sweatshirt was in that apartment, too. But I'll make sure she gets a new one. It was beyond disgusting what had been done to it since the last time you saw it."

"What?" Devin jerked around in her seat to stare at him.

"It had more than grease on it, Devin. I'll leave it at that." He paused and glanced around. "And we may have found the person who belonged to the fingerprints in your house."

"The AWOL soldier who supposedly died two years ago but knew all about surveillance equipment and wired up my house and Auntie's?"

"That's the one. He apparently had outlived his usefulness too, as his body was in one of the cars in one of the garages. Getting the information on his specialties in the Army is one of the reasons we did not want you staying in your house or your aunt's. I shudder to think what sort of camera and listening equipment will be pulled out of those two houses."

Devin stared out the window in silence for several minutes till she caught sight of the fence that ran the perimeter of the riding stable's land. She kept her eyes on the black wrought iron as she replied, "I just want to know why she did what she did."

"So far, it's all come down to money, Devin. You have it, she wanted more of it than you've already given her. She had a knack for finding people who will believe whatever story she's told them. Ian apparently had enough anger at you to believe her story about you trying to bilk Jesse out of her inheritance." He gave the farm a sweeping glance. "Looks pretty quiet from here. In case you're wondering, the colt was brought here from Mark's friends' farm right after the two of you left last night. And, yes, at his request, there will be extra patrols around there to make sure all's well." He slowed the car as it neared Sleeping Giant Farm's driveway.

Devin expected to see the farm's front gate ripped out of its brick and concrete standards and tire tracks across the front lawn. But the cop had to press a code into the keypad for the gate to open, and it slammed shut right behind the car. Several horses grazed in a pasture on one side of the driveway; at least a half-dozen chickens foraged on the lawn on the other.

Four trucks were parked near the barn, normal for that time of the morning. Devin knew there were stalls to muck, tack to clean, horses to exercise.

But no sign of Ian's big black truck.

Apollo and Shaman were in the paddock closest to the barn, sniffing and pawing. She opened the cruiser door just as Wendy and Chief emerged from the barn.

Chief was pulling on his lead the way he always did, impatient for Wendy to remove his halter and be turned loose. After Wendy slipped off the halter, Chief cantered to the middle of the pasture and began his ritual of nosing the ground, pawing and rolling.

*Everything's okay.* Devin whispered, "Thanks, God."

"I'll be right back," McChesney said. "I'm going to take a quick drive to the back gate and make sure all's quiet on that front."

"Okay. We seem to be fine here."

"Let's hope it stays that way."

As he drove away, Devin pasted on a smile for Wendy and headed for the door into the barn from the parking lot. She paused in the entry way, then stepped into an eight-foot-wide walkway with a row of stalls on either side.

The barn wasn't a massive, ancient edifice like the one that had burned at Hightower, but relatively new with light aluminum sliding doors and foam-insulated panel walls. This section of the building contained about twenty large box stalls, adjoined an indoor riding ring.

According to Wendy's report after the truck arrived the previous night, the first three stalls on each side had been empty. Their usual occupants were off to the New York show that had been on Devin's schedule before the week's nightmare had begun. Chief had been given the fourth stall on the left, with Apollo and Shaman in the fourth and fifth stalls on the right.

"Morning, Miss D!" Wendy chirped, headed into Shaman's stall, armed with a wheelbarrow and pitchfork.

At the sound of squealing tires outside, followed by a *WHUMP!* they both turned toward the entry door. Seconds later, a chrome truck grille bashed through the door Devin had just closed. The driver gunned the engine, and the huge Ford F250 lunged its entire length into the barn, demolishing the first four stalls and trapping Wendy inside the one she had just started to clean.

Devin was on the clay floor, momentarily stunned when a stall support knocked the wind out of her. She heard Wendy's screams and pushed the pole away. The truck was backing up, aimed directly at the damaged stall.

Devin leaped up and swung the pole, bringing it down as hard as she could on the hood of the truck. She yanked the driver's door open and grabbed the woman behind the wheel.

Jules stepped on the gas pedal as Devin jerked the steering wheel to the left, keeping a death grip on it as the truck lurched forward. Jules pulled Devin's hair with one hand and tried to steer the truck back toward the stall with the other.

Devin scrambled to get her feet under her on the truck's running board, clutching the wheel. She elbowed Jules and heaved herself into the cab, between the other woman and the steering wheel. Devin grabbed the truck keys, turned off the ignition and threw the keys out the truck's open door.

Jules wrapped an arm around her neck. "I'm going to kill you."

Devin jabbed both elbows back into Jules' ribs and banged her head into her face. "No, you're not."

As Jules loosened her grip, Devin raised the adjustable steering wheel and jumped from under it. Her foot slid off the running board, but she was able to grab Jules' arm as she fell. They tumbled together, out onto the floor, Devin on the bottom.

She had a split second to grab a handful of Jules' short hair, and she yanked with all her might as Jules twisted around and snaked a hand toward her throat.

Tensing her body, letting out a grunt, Devin rammed Jules' forehead into the side of the truck, the only solid thing she could see. As Jules went limp, Devin pushed her away and slowly struggled to her feet. She could hear Wendy crying.

"Where's Wendy? Someone find Wendy!" McChesney called from the other side of the truck. He looked Devin up and down. "You're a lot meaner than I ever imagined."

She put on a weak smile. "Self-defense classes, and wrestling horses for a living."

Jules moaned and slowly sat up. Blood ran down her face and from her nose. She swung at the policeman trying to help her up, and hauled herself up onto the truck running board. "You think you're tough, don't you?" she growled at Devin.

"Yeah. When I have to be. And I think you're pathetic. I remember when you were Jamie Schuler and you were going to set the world on its ear, the designer of beautiful cities and homes."

"Shut up, bitch." Jules coughed, then let out a short moan. "You don't know anything about me."

"No, I don't." Devin's stare never wavered from Jules' face. "But Jamie had dreams and talent that could have taken her anywhere."

"She didn't have money, bitch. Money's all that gets you anywhere in this world."

McChesney walked up with Wendy.

"How bad are you hurt?" Devin asked the girl.

Wendy burst into tears, and she screamed as Devin put an arm around her shoulders. "It hurts! It hurts! My arm, my shoulder."

"My arm, my shoulder," Jules mimicked, then the throaty growl returned. "She's lucky she's still alive. I wanted to let her burn in the fire."

A tall paramedic appeared, bending down to Wendy's height, asking, "Where does it hurt, child?"

An ambulance backed into the door from the pasture, and the medic walked Wendy to it, explaining in a soft voice, "I'm going to wrap your arm against your body so it won't move while we take you to the hospital."

Satisfied Wendy was being cared for, Devin turned her attention back to Jules, who was looking in Wendy's direction.

"I should have killed her when I had the chance."

"Your fight's with me, not her."

"You gave her my job," Jules snarled, through clenched teeth.

"You didn't want to be a groom–"

Jules cut her off. "It would get me where I wanted, and what I wanted." She smiled what would have been a sexy, sultry look if not for the blood all over her face, then added, in the little-girl voice Devin was accustomed to hearing Jesse use, "It got me Ian." The smile disappeared, and Jules continued in her true voice, "All he ever saw, all he ever wanted was you, and you ignored him like you ignored me."

Devin shrugged. "I didn't know I was supposed to be noticing you." She stared at Jules a moment. "You went to a lot of trouble to find out everything you could about me."

Replying in Jesse's voice, Jules cooed, "Oh, you're so wonderful." She smiled a coquettish smile and clapped her hands, patty-cake fashion, fingers held out and only the palms tapping together. "Oooh! Everyone told me about all the good little things you did for them."

The voice changed. "They volunteered more than I ever needed to know."

"And Ian gave you whatever you asked."

"Ian was a ticket to ride, so jealous of Mark he could hardly think straight," Jules growled.

"He talked about marrying you."

She wiped some of the blood off her face. "Fool. He thought he'd make you want him if he slept with someone else."

Devin let out a humorless laugh. "You weren't there when he told me I wasn't sexy enough for him because I made it crystal clear I couldn't stand the thought of him touching me. Lucky Ian. He found you."

"I get what I want, and he gave me a door–no, a red carpet–into your life."

"What about Lisè? What did she want?"

"Lisè was nothing. Nothing but a place to crash and someone to get me close to the old lady. Then she screwed up." She struggled to her feet, holding onto the door for support. Her voice turned cold. "I couldn't stand it when she was flirting with Mark the morning after the fire–"

"Mark said he saw Lisè pick you up after she left the farm."

Devin saw Jules wince as she screwed her face into an ugly scowl. "She was flirting with him, and he was mine." She gave Devin a smirk. "Huh. Too bad I missed Mark at the apartment. We could have had some fun." She looked around the barn. "Lisè told me you'd never believe he was involved, and you didn't till he just happened to show up at all the wrong times."

Devin recalled the bruises on Lisè's face the previous afternoon. "Did you beat her up after she picked you up or later?"

"I had to punish Lisè when she didn't listen." Jules paused. "And I heard all of your little conversation yesterday. All about her beautiful voice and artistic talent. She said she was done with me; she was on her way to bigger and better things. She couldn't believe I killed the old lady, because the old lady never hurt anybody. Lisè was on the bed, crying her eyes out. I got tired of hearing her."

Jules looked up, narrowing her eyes. "Nobody leaves me. Not till I'm done with them.

"Like the dead guy in the car? The one who supposedly died two years ago, but knew all about surveillance equipment? Was he the one who followed me around the mall? Was he the fake cop you had my phones rewired to call instead of Florian's?"

She let out a humorless laugh. "So you know all my little tricks now. Goodie for you."

McChesney brushed past Devin and grabbed Jules' arm. He pulled first one arm then the other behind her back. As he handcuffed her, he said, "'You have a right to remain silent'–c'mon, sing along! You learned all the words when you worked for us for six months, losing all of Devin's complaints and erasing computer files. 'You have a right to remain silent. If you give up that right–'"

Susan Holt entered the barn, her leathery face with its deeply etched lines set into a sad mask.

Jules struggled and snapped, "Skip the Miranda. I know my rights, and I'm not worried about being arrested or going to jail. You'll never make any of this stick."

"It'll stick this time," Susan growled. She planted herself in front of Jules. "I saw you lining that truck up to run into that stall and kill Wendy."

"Old lady, you don't know what's in my mind."

"Before today, I only saw evil once in my life, and that's when you were my mother's hospice worker, and her life was slipping away. You were standing over her bed with that smirk on your face, and you looked at me and said, 'It won't be long now.' The next day, I came home and Mama's room was torn apart and you'd left a note that you wouldn't be back because the robbery was too much. I never saw you again until right now. I wish I could prove that you stole the money and jewelry that disappeared from her lingerie drawer."

Jules gave Susan a cruel smile, intensified by the blood on her lips. "You wish." She glanced from Susan to Devin. "I take what I want. Anything that was special to you–that's what I was taking."

"You had no right to take my aunt."

"Tsk, tsk, tsk," Jules taunted, shaking her head. In Jesse's voice, she continued, "All your little pretties, your lingerie, your shoes, your pictures."

She laughed, fixing her eyes on Devin's face and continuing in her own voice, "Even the horse Mark wanted to give you. That was a bonus!"

Devin smiled. "You screwed up."

Jules shook her head. "I don't screw up." The cold voice sounded as if it came from the ugliest, darkest corner of her soul.

"The colt's still alive."

"You're lying."

"No, I saw him yesterday."

"I was the only one who knew he was in the barn when I was setting the fire. I thought my time-delayed ignition device worked pretty well."

Devin shrugged. "Mark must have left the polo grounds with his friends while you were cutting up my truck tires and taking the engine apart to delay my getting back to the farm till the barn couldn't be saved. He got to the farm not long before I did and brought the colt out just as the roof collapsed."

"No." Jules gave her head a vigorous shake, then froze, staring somewhere behind Devin.

# CHAPTER SIXTEEN

Pain shot through Devin's body when she was bumped from behind. She looked down and saw a black nose nuzzling her jacket pocket. The horse wore a halter, so she knew it wasn't one of Wendy's regular charges. When she realized who it was, she asked, "Hey, baby, are we friends today?" She rubbed the velvety black muzzle, and he nibbled at her fingers.

"Here's Mark's colt, Jamie–"

"Don't call me that!" Jules shouted.

The colt jumped away at the noise, almost knocking Devin off her feet, into Susan. As Susan steadied her, Devin yelped in pain.

"You're bleeding!" Susan sounded surprised when she pulled her hand away from Devin's back.

"It can't be more serious than brush burns," Devin replied, looking around for the colt.

Jules kicked Devin in the leg as Officer McChesney walked her to a police car that had backed into the barn through the pasture entrance. The ensuing pain sent a wave of nausea through her body, and she doubled over, retching, hand clamped over her mouth.

The police car drove away, and another ambulance backed in. McChesney appeared with one of its squad members. "You are the grand prize winner of transportation to deluxe accommodations at a local spa we call the Yale-New Haven Medical Center. While you're there, they'll check you out and patch up whatever might need patching up."

Devin opened her mouth to protest.

He held up his hand. "Humor me. Get on the bus, take the ride, make sure nothing's broken. There's a tow truck waiting to haul that, "he nodded toward Ian's battered truck, "out of here as soon as we're done with it."

"Your horses will be fine," Susan added. "Last night Wendy introduced them to all the other boarders and their owners, so there are plenty of folks here to take care of them."

"The barn—"

Susan cut Devin off. "Right now, you get yourself taken care of. Then you bury your aunt. You can worry about the barn later."

Ria was waiting at the Medical Center emergency-room entrance when Devin was wheeled in. Ria reached for her hand and walked along. "I already saw Wendy. She said you were pretty banged up."

"She was hurt—"

"A separated shoulder and cracked collarbone, I heard. And they're keeping her for observation because she was complaining that her back hurt too."

Devin winced as her gurney bounced on an uneven spot in the floor. "I think the grating between the stalls fell in on her."

"She said you saved her life by jumping into the truck and driving it away."

Devin nodded. "I managed to turn it away from the stall she was in." She smiled. "I thought of your dad yelling at the TV set during some car-chase scene in some movie 'Turn off the ignition, you idiot!' So that's what I did. I threw the keys out the window, opened the door and pulled Jules out."

"That must have been who I saw when I first got here, shackled to the gurney, all bloody, screaming and thrashing around. They wheeled her out a few minutes ago."

Devin studied the ceiling as she was rolled down the hall to an examining room. "I can get on the bed myself," she told the nurse there, who placed a paper examining gown on the foot of the bed.

"I can help her get into that," Ria offered.

"Okay, then. I hear you're the lady who stopped a truck. And you look a little the worse for wear for it. One side is all scraped up. Does anything else hurt?"

"I had a support beam fall on me, and I pulled the driver out on top of me, and then she kicked me. But other than that, I think I'll be fine once I get a cup of real good coffee and a bagel."

The nurse looked confused. "A doctor will be here shortly." She pulled the curtains around the cubicle and hustled away.

"I guess she didn't know if you were being serious or sarcastic," Ria said as she looked at the swaying curtains.

"I'm serious, Ria! I don't think I had any breakfast this morning."

"Well, here, let's get this paper thingy on you, and I'll go see if I can find that good coffee and a bagel." She gently pulled Devin's sweatshirt up and gasped. "Oh, maaan! Your skinny ribs look like hamburger here, girl! No wonder you hurt!"

"I guess I did that when I fell out of the truck. I don't remember."

"I'll get you something clean to wear home too. New stuff, I promise. No tracking devices."

They both looked up as a female doctor and an intern entered the cubicle. "I hear you're the last person involved in the brawl at the farm," the white coated woman remarked.

"I'd like to see my groom as soon as possible."

The doctor pulled on a pair of examination gloves. "Let's take a look at you first, then go from there."

Three cracked ribs and a painful wound cleaning later, Devin was roused from a fitful nap by something bumping her bed, and the scent of coffee. Ria stood on one side with coffee and a small bag from one of their favorite delis, and Mark stood on the other.

"C'mon, girl," Ria urged, pushing a bedside table closer, "wake up and smell the coffee!" She set the food on the table. "Where's the control thing that raises the bed?"

Mark leaned down and gave her a kiss. "Hey, you're the talk of the ER, something along the lines of the big fight at the OK Corral!"

She winced as the bed moved. "I doubt we're quite that notorious."

"The woman at the information desk said they rarely get three banged-up women involved in the same incident, when drugs, alcohol and/or men aren't involved," he explained, smiling.

"I was surprised when I saw your baby nosing around my pockets," Devin replied, sipping her coffee.

He smiled again. "I heard Jules was even more surprised."

Devin nodded. "I saw her face. And I called her 'Jamie'; she screamed at me and spooked him." She set her coffee down. "I need to see Wendy."

"Her boyfriend said she's probably going to be here overnight," Ria answered. "She was asleep when I looked in on her."

"I still need to go see her."

"Are they letting you leave?" Mark asked.

"It may be against medical advice, but I'm outta here. Nothing's broken, just banged up real good."

"Let's get you dressed then."

Wendy's boyfriend Tony met them at the door to her room. "You can't come in here!" he snapped. "She's not coming back to work for you, not this time!"

"Is that what she wants?" Devin asked.

"You let them in here!" Wendy's feeble little voice sounded far away.

"No. I told you–"

"No, I'm telling you," she squeaked, "You can't make me quit my job."

"You coulda been killed."

"So could Miss D, but she saved my life." Wendy struggled to sit up. "If she wants me back, I'm back, and you don't need to stay in this picture if you don't like it."

"Whoa, bravo, girl!" Ria exclaimed, clapping.

"You're gonna get yourself killed," Tony insisted.

"You don't choose what I do." Wendy's voice had a hard edge Devin had never heard before, even the morning after the fire when she had complained about the guard stationed outside her room.

"I don't want you working there anymore."

"Then there's the door. And don't come back."

Devin and Ria gave each other a quick look at Wendy's stern albeit squeaky pronouncement, then stepped away from the door as Tony stalked out.

Wendy struggled to sit up as they approached her bed. "You don't need to worry about my sweatshirt anymore. I don't need that one anymore."

"You'll need to talk to Officer McChesney then, as he said he'd make sure you got a new one."

"You will let me come back, won't you?" she whispered.

"You'll be back when you're healed up, not before," Devin assured her. "Till then, Mrs. Holt's crew is taking care of the guys."

"When will you move them back to Hightower?"

She sighed. "I don't know, Wendy, but not this week." She looked around the room for a clock. "My uncle's flight! What time is it?"

Mark glanced at his watch. "Quarter of twelve."

"Uncle Zack said he'd be getting in at noon."

Mark nodded. "I'll make a phone call and see that someone meets him."

Devin glanced out the door to Wendy's room as a white-haired woman passed by. She covered her face with her hands. "I can't believe Auntie's gone!"

At nine the next morning, Devin was in sweats, wearing no make up, her hair in a ponytail, when the phone in her hotel suite rang. "I don't want to talk to anyone this morning," she mumbled, reaching for the phone.

Officer McChesney asked her to meet him in the hotel restaurant, and greeted her with a big smile. "I would bet you haven't had breakfast yet."

"My uncle bet the same thing, and brought some pastries and coffee when he stopped by a little while ago. He's taking care of some of my aunt's arrangements this morning."

Smiling, he asked, "Did you finally get a decent night's sleep?"

"I think I slept, once I gave up finding a comfortable spot on the bed and piled pillows and blankets in one of the chairs."

"Good. You needed that." Nodding, he smiled again. Then the smile disappeared. "Devin, it's over. Jules committed suicide this morning."

"Why am I not surprised? All the death and destruction she caused–" She shook her head. "Coward's way out."

She turned away from the policeman. "I checked my voice mail at the cottage earlier. A neighbor near the farm said he saw a U-Haul truck being loaded at the caretaker's house yesterday afternoon. Ian's mother brought the keys over to him just before it drove away. She supposedly told him I could dispose of whatever they left, however I wanted."

"Have you been out there yet?"

"Last night. My uncle took me out to the mansion to get my car out of the barn. We walked through the caretaker's house–they left some furniture, clothing, stuff like that. Put holes in some walls, and cement in a couple of the toilets. No note, no forwarding address." She lifted an eyebrow. "One more mess to clean up."

Devin then made a face. "But Uncle Zack said my stepfather, who's an architect, contacted him about designing a new barn for me, and they'll be meeting over lunch today. Supposedly, bigger and better for tomorrow's Hightower, and using whatever might be salvageable of the old barn." She rolled her eyes. "With the best security money can buy."

"I hear that." McChesney sighed. "We're still cataloging stolen property and wondering how Jules did what she did and got away with it as long as she did. We've been to two garages and a storage locker, found four stolen cars and three safe deposit boxes that contained almost a dozen coin collections, seven or eight bags of jewelry, pawn tickets for more jewelry–"

"If you find any pearl necklaces, I'd like to see them. Lisè borrowed and never returned one that had been my grandmother's. Auntie was surprised and touched when my grandfather gave it to her after Grammy died." She shook her head, almost smiling. "They never got along."

"Well, I just happen to have something for you." Smiling, he lifted a small bag. "No notebook today, just a bag." He looked into the bag, then lifted out a small box covered in gray silk moiré fabric, with an engraved sterling plate on its top. He turned the box so the writing faced Devin. "Is this someone you know?"

Devin read the plate, Catherine Merritt Hall, in elegant script. "That's my grandmother!"

He opened the box to reveal a strand of perfectly matched pearls. "I told the guys in Evidence that this was going to its rightful owner the minute I could deliver it."

She fingered the pearls. "Pappy gave them to Grammy on their wedding day. My mother wore them at her wedding, and so did my uncle's wife. I thought they were gone forever." She hugged him. "This means so much to me."

"I'm just trying to change your image of Florian's cops. We do care." He paused. "And something for you to think about: In July I'll be attending a seminar that will address stalking and some proposed laws up for preliminary discussion and deliberation regarding victim rights and how to best protect them. Would you be interested in attending and giving a victim's story?"

"You can count on it!"

Devin wasn't surprised to learn Officer McChesney was the policeman sent to escort Aunt Aggie's funeral procession from the venerable First Congregational Church in Milford to the family cemetery at Hightower. "I think my aunt would be happy to know you're with her on her final trip home," she remarked, trying to smile.

"I was honored when the Milford police asked if I'd care to participate. Miss Hall was a good soul," he replied, nodding.

Devin couldn't answer. She dabbed her eyes and looked out over the serene lake across from the church.

He cocked his head toward the church. "I think they're waiting for you."

She watched flower arrangements being placed on the back of the hearse, but looked away as the silver casket was lifted inside, Mark and her uncle on either side at the head of it. "This is a bad dream. This isn't happening." She covered her face with her hands as Ria's mother, a tall regal woman in an impeccable black suit and veiled black pillbox hat, came up and folded Devin into her arms as she wept.

"It's time, my love," Mrs. St. Amont whispered, gently turning her to the waiting limousine.

The Hale family cemetery was tucked among tall pines and maples, a lush green park bounded by a manicured hedge, dotted with ornate headstones. Aggie would be laid to rest between Ashley, Devin's mother, and Uncle Zack's wife, who had died with their baby during childbirth.

Devin stared at the canopied gravesite for several minutes, looking away as the casket was carried to it and placed on the frame that would lower it into the earth. The limousine driver opened the door by Devin and held his hand out to her. She shook her head. "Not yet, please. I'm not ready."

"Child, it doesn't get easier," Mrs. St. Amont whispered.

Mark approached the car, and Mrs. St. Amont gave Devin a little push.

Mark stepped in front of the driver and offered Devin his hand. As she climbed out, she looked around at the few assembled mourners: Bella Paige was all but holding Doris Baker up as she loudly sobbed. Wendy, her arm in a sling, standing off by herself and looking forlorn and lost, gave a little wave. A handyman Devin frequently called to work at the farm seemed uncomfortable in his blue suit. Ria hurried over to Wendy and put an arm around her shoulders, and the pair moved closer to Ria's parents. Devin could see they were talking, with Wendy smiling a little and nodding her head. She looked beyond Ria and Wendy and was surprised to see her stepfather and his latest wife.

Mark led her to the grave, beside her uncle, who held a small cage. Zack Suffolk looked down and smiled.

He put his arm around her and pulled her close. "How are you holding up, sweetie?"

"I–I don't know."

"We'll get past today, and start putting the pieces back together."

"What's left of them."

Zack opened his mouth to reply, but the pastor stepped up and asked Devin if she was ready for the final ceremony. She gave a slight nod in reply, and felt tears well up again.

The pastor could have been saying nothing but "blah blah blah" as he spoke the prayer her aunt had written and final blessing. Devin didn't comprehend his words, only that her aunt was gone forever. She was handed a rose from one of the bouquets and instructed to place it on the casket. She stared at the flower for a moment, then mechanically did as she'd been told.

Zack tugged at her arm and held up the cage. "Very old family custom," he reminded her, carefully removing a bird from the cage. "We always release a white dove, the bird of peace. You were too small to remember your mother's funeral."

"I remember Grammy's. Pappy wouldn't let me near the cage."

"Your grandfather–my father, stubborn old man that he is–didn't feel up to the trip, but he insisted we remember this." He gently placed the bird in her hands.

She felt its heart beating wildly under her fingers. She stroked its feathers as she ducked out from under the canopy and carefully walked around her mother's grave to a spot she knew wasn't an ancestor's resting place. She kissed the top of its head. "Find your way home, little bird. Lift Auntie's spirit to heaven on your way." She raised it high up over her head and opened her hands. Tears rolled down her cheeks as she watched it flutter away, above the trees.

Mark came up close behind her and put his hands on her shoulders. "She'll always be near, watching over you."

"I know. But it won't be the same."

"No, it won't." He turned her around and wiped her face.

"I never got to tell her I'll be riding in the Hampton Classic."

"Ah, you know she wouldn't miss it for the world. Just picture her at the in gate, wearing that big straw hat of hers, with a Long

Island Iced Tea in one hand, a big smile on her face, pointing as you ride past and telling everybody you're her niece, and you're going to sweep the field."

Devin had to smile. "That's Auntie." She nodded her head. "I can hear her now."

www.ingramcontent.com/pod-product-compliance
Lightning Source LLC
Chambersburg PA
CBHW020401110726
47899CB00006B/1804